John Gerard, G. R. Kingdon

During the Persecution

Autobiography of Father John Gerard of the Society of Jesus

John Gerard, G. R. Kingdon

During the Persecution
Autobiography of Father John Gerard of the Society of Jesus

ISBN/EAN: 9783741177934

Manufactured in Europe, USA, Canada, Australia, Japa

Cover: Foto ©Raphael Reischuk / pixelio.de

Manufactured and distributed by brebook publishing software
(www.brebook.com)

John Gerard, G. R. Kingdon

During the Persecution

DURING THE PERSECUTION

AUTOBIOGRAPHY

OF

FATHER JOHN GERARD

OF THE SOCIETY OF JESUS

TRANSLATED FROM THE ORIGINAL LATIN

BY

G. R. KINGDON

PRIEST OF THE SOCIETY OF JESUS

LONDON

BURNS AND OATES

GRANVILLE MANSIONS W

1886

✠

JUSTUM ET TENACEM PROPOSITI VIRUM,

NON CIVIUM ARDOR PRAVA JUBENTIUM,

NON VULTUS INSTANTIS TYRANNI,

MENTE QUATIT SOLIDA.

PREFACE.

THE Latin manuscript, of which the following pages contain a translation, is preserved at the College of Stonyhurst, in Lancashire. It was copied from the original, which was then in Sant' Andrea, the noviciate of the Society at Rome; and is entitled *Narratio Patris Johannis Gerardi de rebus a se in Anglia gestis.* It is written continuously, without any divisions. I thought it best to break it up into chapters, as the English reader naturally looks for some such resting-places in a long narrative. The style of the translation is intentionally antique, as harmonizing better with the tone and manner of the original; though there is no pretence of imitating the English of the time.

It was first printed privately some twenty years ago. Then, in 1871, it was published by Father Morris, S. J., as an introduction to Father Gerard's

"Narrative of the Gunpowder Plot."[1]   In 1881,
it was published again, but separately, by the
same Father, with many illustrative and confir-
matory documents gathered by him from the
Public Record Office.   These added immensely to
the value of the book, especially for historical
students.   But the tale that Father Gerard tells
in this his autobiography is of such transcendent
and romantic interest, that it was thought a
reprint of the narrative by itself would meet with
a good reception in a more extended circle of
readers.   In fact this account of his frequent
hair-breadth escapes from the constant pursuit of
the priest-hunters, his ultimate capture, his torture
in the Tower thrice repeated, and his extraordinary
escape from prison, are episodes more startling to
our modern sense, than anything to be found in
the most sensational novels.

Father Morris in his researches was particularly successful in identifying most of the persons
mentioned by Father Gerard.   In his narrative
names are usually omitted, out of extreme caution
lest any one should be brought into trouble by

---

[1] The principal title of Father Morris' book was, *The condition
of Catholics under James I.*   It was published by Longmans.

such mention. Where he does use names, it is always in the case of those who were beyond the reach of persecution, either from having been already martyred, or from living in safety on the Continent. Father Morris has been able to discover the names thus omitted, in all the most important instances; and he has allowed me to make use of his results. I have therefore mentioned these names in the foot-notes, adding the letter M to indicate the source of the information.

The narrative of Father Gerard has been known to historians through Bartoli, who used it extensively in his "Inghilterra." Lingard indeed quotes from Bartoli the passage in which Father Gerard describes his feelings when under torture. The autobiography seems to have been written at Louvain in Belgium in the latter part of the year 1609, three years after Father Gerard left England for good. He wrote it at the order of his Superiors, who doubtless wished to have from so competent a witness, authentic materials for future history. His language is full of Scripture phrases, and at times he does not spare hard words for the persecutors. For the last I think

he will be readily forgiven by the reader; for if
anything has been brought out with startling
clearness by late historical researches, it is the
contemptible characters· of the principal agents·
of the persecution.

The reader will of course remember that this·
is no pretended autobiography, no sham Diary,
dressed up by a modern writer to give a fancy
picture of past times. It is the written experience of an actual participator in the events described. In reading it we look three hundred years
back through a time-telescope, and become actual
witnesses of the sufferings of the Catholic priests
and gentry under Elizabeth and James. We witness the successful zeal, the unremitting labours,
the daily and nightly perils of those missionary
priests who returned to their country with their
lives in their hand, to preserve the Catholic Faith
in· England. And in witnessing these things our
hearts cannot fail to swell with gratitude to those
who thus sacrificed themselves for our salvation,
and to long for the time when we may pay them
that public honour which the Church will sanction
by their canonization.

It remains only to say a word of Father

Gerard's family, which I can best do by quoting from Father Morris.

"John Gerard was the second son of Sir Thomas Gerard of Bryn in Lancashire, knight, and Elizabeth, daughter and coheiress of Sir John Port of Etwall in Derbyshire, knight. When, in his Narrative of the Gunpowder Plot, Father John Gerard had occasion to speak of his elder brother Thomas, who received knighthood from James I. on his accession, he says, 'That was to him no advancement, whose ancestors had been so for sixteen or seventeen descents together.' This Sir Thomas was made a baronet at the first creation of that dignity in 1611, and from him the present Lord Gerard of Bryn, the first baron, and thirteenth baronet, is lineally descended."

I must now let Father Gerard speak for himself.

G. R. KINGDON, S.J.

St. Stanislaus' College, Beaumont.
June, 1886.

CONTENTS.

CHAPTER I.

I was born[1] of Catholic parents, who never concealed their profession, for which they suffered many inflictions from our heretic rulers : so much so, that when a child of five years of age I was forced, together with my brother who was also a child, to dwell among heretics under the roof of a stranger, for that my father, with two other gentlemen, had been cast into the Tower of London, for having conspired to restore the Scottish Queen to liberty and to her kingdom. She was at that time confined in the County of Derby,[2] at two miles distance from our house. Three years afterwards, my father, having obtained his release by the payment of a large sum, brought us home, free however from any taint of heresy, as he had maintained a Catholic tutor over us.

At the age of fifteen, I was sent to Exeter College, Oxford, where my tutor was a certain Mr. Leutner, a good and learned man, and a Catholic in mind and heart. There however I did not stay more than a twelvemonth, as at Easter the heretics

---

[1] On the 4th of October, 1564. M.

[2] Father Gerard is slightly mistaken here. Tutbury, where Mary was then confined, is in Staffordshire, though close to the borders of Derbyshire. Etwall, his father's house was in Derbyshire, but as he says not far off. M.

sought to force us to attend their worship, and to
partake of their counterfeit sacrament. I returned
then with my brother to my father's house, whither
Mr. Leutner himself soon followed us, being resolved
to live as a Catholic in very deed, and not merely in
desire. While there, he superintended our Latin
studies for the next two years, but afterwards going
to Belgium, he lived and died there most holily.
As for Greek, we were at the same time placed
under the tuition of a good and pious priest,
William Sutton by name, to whom this occupation ＇
served as an occasion for dwelling in our house
unmolested. He afterwards entered the Society,
and was drowned on the coast of Spain whither
Superiors had called him.

At the age of nineteen I passed over to France,
by permission, with the object of learning the
French tongue, and resided for three years at
Rhemes. While there, though yet a lad, and far
from being solidly grounded in my Humanities, I
applied myself to the study of Sacred Scripture,
consulting the commentators for the sense of the
more difficult passages, and writing down with my
own hand the explanations given publicly to the
theological students. Being my own master, I did
not, as I ought to have done, lay a sufficiently solid
foundation. My own taste guided my choice of
authors, and I sedulously read the works of St. Ber-
nard and St. Bonaventure, and such other spiritual
writers. About this time, I made, by God's providence, the acquaintance of a saintly young man,
who had been admitted into the Society at Rome,
but having for reasons of health been sent out for a
time, was then living at Rhemes. He gave me the
details of his past life; he told me (may the Lord

reward him) how he had been educated in the household of God; he taught me how good and wholesome it was for a man to have borne the yoke from his youth. He taught me the method of mental prayer; for which exercise we were wont to meet together at stated hours, as we were not living in the College but in different lodgings in the town. It was there that, when about twenty years of age, I heard the call of God's infinite mercy and loving-kindness inviting me from the crooked ways of the world to the straight path, to the perfect following of Christ in His holy Society.

After my three years' residence at Rhemes, I went to Clermont College, at Paris, to see more closely the manner of the Society's life, and to be more solidly grounded in Humanities and Philosophy. I had not been there one year, when I fell dangerously ill. After my recovery, I accompanied Father Thomas Darbisher to Rouen, in order to see Father Persons, who had arrived thither from England, and was staying incognito in that city, to superintend the publication of his *Christian Directory*, a most useful and happy work, which in my opinion has converted to God more souls than it contains pages. The heretics themselves have known how to appreciate it, as appears from a recent edition thereof published by one of their ministers who sought to claim the glory of so important a work. To Father Persons then did I communicate my vocation, and my desire of joining the Society. But as I was not yet strong, nor fit to continue my studies, and moreover, as I had some property to dispose of, and arrangements to make in England, he advised me to return thither, so as to recruit my health by breathing my native air, and at the same time to free myself from every obstacle which might prevent or delay me in my pursuit of perfection and the religious life. I accordingly went home, and after settling my affairs, set out on my return, in about a year; this time however without having asked for a license, for I had no hope of obtaining it, as I did not venture to communicate my plans to my parents.

I embarked then with some other Catholics, and after having been kept five days at sea by contrary winds, we were forced to put in at the port of Dover. On arriving thither, we were all seized by the Custom-House officers, and forwarded to London in custody. My companions were imprisoned, on a warrant of the Queen's Privy Council. For my own part, though I declared myself a Catholic, and refused to attend their worship, I escaped imprisonment at that time, as there were some of the Council that were friendly to my family, and had procured me the license to travel abroad on the former occasion. They entertained, it would seem, some hopes of perverting me in course of time, so I was sent to my maternal uncle's, a Protestant, to be kept in his custody, and if possible, to be perverted. He, after three months, sought to obtain my full liberty both by bribes and begging; but being asked whether I had *gone to church*, as they call it, he was obliged to acknowledge that he could never bring me to do so. Thereupon the Council sent me with a letter to the pseudo-bishop of London, who having read it asked whether I would allow him to confer with me on religious matters. I replied, that as I doubted of nothing, I had rather decline. "You must in that case," answered he, "remain here in custody." I replied that in this I was obliged to acquiesce, through force and the command of the Government. He treated me with kindness, with a view perhaps of thus drawing me over. But he ordered his chaplain's bed to be brought into my chamber. At first I repeatedly declared my determination not to enter into any dispute with this man on matters of faith, as to which my mind was settled, nor to receive religious instruction from him ; but as he ceased not pouring forth abuse and blasphemy against the saints in Heaven, and against our Holy Mother the Church, I was forced to defend the truth, and then almost the whole night was spent in disputing. I soon discovered that in him at least God's truth had no very formidable adversary. After two days, as they saw my case was hopeless, they sent me back to the Council with letters of recommendation forsooth, for the so-called bishop told me that he had greatly striven in my favour, and that he had great hopes of my being set at large. It was however a Uriah's letter that I carried, for no sooner had the Council read it, than they ordered me to be imprisoned until I had learnt to be a loyal subject. For they hold him a bad subject who will not subject himself to their heresies and their sacrilegious worship.

Being committed to the Marshalsea prison, I found there numbers of Catholics and many priests awaiting judgment of death with the greatest joy. In this school of Christ I was detained from the beginning of one Lent to the end of the following, not without abundant consolation of mind, and good opportunity for study.

We were twice during this interval dragged before the Courts, not to be tried for our lives, but to be fined according to the law against recusants. I

was condemned to pay 2000 florins (200*l.*). Once on
my return from the Court which was in the country,
some six miles out of London, I got leave to go and
visit some friends, having pledged my word to return
to the Marshalsea that night. I went then to visit
a prisoner detained in that horrible dungeon called
Bridewell, as I had heard that he was sick. His
story deserves notice. He had formerly lived in
Father Campian's service, and on account of some
words he had let fall in praise of Father Campian,
he was arrested and detained a long time in the
Marshalsea. On my arrival there I saw him laden
with heavy fetters on his legs, besides which he
wore a very rough hair-shirt. He was most lowly
and meek, and full of charity. I happened one day
to see a turnkey strike him repeatedly without the
servant of God uttering a single word. He was at
length taken with three others to the filthy Bridewell. One of their number died of starvation a
few days after their transfer. When I visited this
poor man, he was lying ill, being worn out with
want of food, and labour on the tread-wheel. It
was a shocking sight. He was reduced to skin and
bone, and covered with lice that swarmed upon him
like ants on a mole-hill; so that I never remember
to have seen the like.

At times our cells were visited, and a strict search
made for church-stuff, Agnus Dei's, and relics.
Once we were betrayed by a false brother, who had
feigned to be a Catholic, and disclosed our hidden
stores to the authorities. On this occasion were
seized quantities of Catholic books and sacred objects, enough to fill a cart. In my cell were found
nearly all the requisites for saying Mass: for my
next-door neighbour was a good priest, and we dis-

covered a secret way of opening the door between us so that we had Mass very early every morning. We afterwards repaired our losses, nor could the malice of the devil again deprive us of so great a consolation in our bonds.

In the course of the following year, my liberty was obtained by the importunities of my friends, who however were bound as sureties, to the extent of a heavy sum of money, for my remaining in the kingdom. I was moreover to present myself at the prison, at the three months' end. And these sureties had to be renewed three or four times before I was able to resume my project. At length the long-wished-for opportunity presented itself. A very dear friend of mine offered himself as bail to meet whatever demand might be made, if I was discovered to be missing after the appointed time. After my departure, he forfeited not indeed his money but his life : for he was one of the most conspicuous of those fourteen gentlemen who suffered in connection with the captive Queen of Scots, and whose execution, as events soon showed, was but a prelude to taking off the Queen herself.[8]

Being at length free I went to Paris; and finding Father William Holt, who had just arrived from Scotland, ready to start for Rome with the Provincial of France, I joined myself to their company. At Rome I was advised to pursue my studies in the English College, and to take priest's orders before I entered the Society. I followed this advice, despite my ardent desire of entering religion, which I communicated to Father Persons, and to Father

[8] Babington, to whose plot Father Gerard here alludes, was executed with his associates on September 20th, 1586; and Mary Queen of Scots on the 8th of February following. M.

Holt, the then Rector of the English College. But as the Roman climate was not suited to my constitution, and I had an extreme desire of going to England, it seemed good to the Fathers to put me at the beginning of the year to casuistry and controversies; I went therefore through a complete course of positive theology. Towards its close, when the Spanish Armada was nearing the coasts of England, Cardinal Allen thought fit to send me to England for various matters connected with Catholic interests, but as I still wanted several months of the lawful age of taking priest's orders, a Papal dispensation was obtained. I was most unwilling to depart unless I was first admitted into the Society, so Father Persons, out of his singular charity towards me, obtained my admission to the novitiate, which I was to finish in England. There were at that time in the English College some others who had the like vocation, and we used to strive to conform ourselves as much as possible to the novices at St. Andrea's, serving in the kitchen and visiting hospitals. On the Feast of the Assumption of the Most Blessed Virgin Mary, A.D. 1588, our Very Rev. Father General Aquaviva received Father Oldcorne of blessed memory and my unworthy self into the Society of Jesus, and gave us his blessing for the English mission.

CHAPTER II.

MY ARRIVAL IN ENGLAND AS A PRIEST.

I STARTED then on my homeward journey, in company with Father Oldcorne and two other priests who had been students at the English College. On our way through Switzerland, after having passed a night at Basle, we were curious to see the vestiges of the ancient faith, which the Lutherans usually allow to remain, and the Calvinists generally destroy. As we were going round the church, we were joined by a certain person, who offered to show us all the curiosities of the place. We were somewhat astonished at this ready civility on the part of a Lutheran towards Catholic priests (for we travelled in clerical habit), and, as our new friend spoke French, I began by inquiring of what country he was. I found out that he was from Lorraine. On inquiring his reasons for thus forsaking the land and the faith of his fathers, he replied that he found the laws of the Catholic Church too stringent. I asked which laws, as the Catholic Church imposes none other yoke than that of the Gospel, which, as Christ bears witness, is sweet, and the burden thereof light. At length I discovered that the unhappy man was a priest, an apostate, who had taken refuge at Basle, and lived there with a woman he called his wife, in the very same house at which we had put up, supporting himself and her

by usury. I dealt very earnestly with him to leave
this path of damnation, and to return to the way of
heaven ; to leave a share of his money to the
woman, and to lend no more at unlawful interest ;
but to seek his future gains by labour or some
lawful traffic. He promised at last to take my
advice, and gave me a letter for his Bishop, asking
for reconciliation. I sent it as I passed through
Lorraine, and I hope that the poor man persevered
in his good purpose.

As we passed through Rhemes, where there was
an English Seminary, and through Paris, we kept
the strictest incognito. At length we came to Eu,
where a College for English youths had been established, which was afterwards abandoned on account
of the wars, and another more extensive establish-
ment erected at St. Omer's. Our Fathers at Eu,
after conferring with those who had the management of the College in that town, all strongly
opposed our venturing into England, as circumstances then were, for that the Spanish attempt
had exasperated the public mind against Catholics,
and most rigid searches for priests and domiciliary
visits had been set on foot : that guards were posted
in every village along the roads and streets : that
the Earl of Leicester, then at the height of his
favour, had sworn not to leave a single Catholic
alive at the close of the year : but this man of blood
did not live out half his days, for he was cut off in
that very same year. We were compelled then to
stay there for a time, until fresh instructions were
sent us by Father Persons in the name of Father
General. They were to this effect, that the state
of affairs had indeed much changed since our departure from Rome, but that as it was the Lord's

business that we had to do, he left us free either
to await the return of greater calm, or to pursue
the course we had entered upon. On receiving this
desirable message, we did not long deliberate, but
immediately hired a ship, to land us in the Northern
part of England, which seemed to be less disturbed.
Two priests from Rhemes joined us, as our former
companions preferred to take time before they faced
the dangers which awaited them on the opposite
shores.

The ship then set sail with four priests on board ;
a goodly cargo indeed, had not my unworthiness
deprived me of the crown, for all those other three
suffered martyrdom for the faith. The two priests
were soon taken, and being in a short space made
perfect, they fulfilled a long time. Their names were
Christopher Bales and George Beesley,[1] but my
companion, the Blessed Father Oldcorne, after
having spent eighteen years of toil and labour in
the Lord's vineyard, watered it at length with his
blood.

After crossing the Channel, as we were sailing
along the English coast on the third day, my companion and I seeing a convenient spot in which
the ship's boat might easily set us on shore, and
considering that it were dangerous if we were to
land all together, recommended the matter to God
and took counsel with our companions. We then
ordered the ship to anchor off that point until dark ;
and in the first watch we were put ashore in the
boat and left there, whereupon the ship immediately
set sail and departed. We remained there awhile
commending ourselves in prayer to God's Provi-

[1] Christopher Bales is commemorated in Challoner on March
4th, 1590 ; and George Beesley on July 2nd, 1591.

dence, then we sought out some path which might lead us further inland, at a greater distance from the sea, before the day should dawn. But the night being dark and cloudy we could not strike out any path that would lead us to the open country, but every way we tried always brought us to some dwelling as we were made aware by the barking of the dogs. As this happened some two or three times, we began to fear lest we might rouse some of the inhabitants, and be seized upon as thieves or burglars. We therefore turned into a neighbouring wood, where we proposed to rest during the night. But the rain and the cold (for it was about the end of October)[2] rendered sleep impossible, nor did we dare to speak aloud to one another, as the wood was in the neighbourhood of a house, but we deliberated in whispers whether to set out together for London, or to part company, so that if one were taken, the other might escape. Having pondered the reasons on both sides, we determined to set forth each by himself, and to take different routes.

At day-dawn then we cast lots who should first leave the wood, and the lot fell on the good Father who was also the first to leave this world for heaven. We then made an equal division of what money we had, and after embracing and receiving one from the other a blessing, the future martyr went along the sea-shore to a neighbouring town, where he fell in with some sailors who were thinking of going to London. Being prudent and cautious, he strove by cheerfulness to accommodate himself to their humours in indifferent things. But twice

[2] Father Morris, in his *Life of Father John Gerard*, shows that it must have been the middle of November. Writing so long after, Father Gerard's slight inaccuracy may be excused.

or thrice he could not withhold from reproving their
coarse and filthy language, though he imperilled
himself by so doing, as he afterwards told me.
And indeed his zeal in this matter was very great,
as is proved by many accounts which I have often
heard related. One instance may serve for· all.
Father Oldcorne while in London visited a certain
Catholic gentleman who was greatly attached to
him. On the window of his room was painted a
picture of Mars and Venus; and although the
house was not the property of his friend, but rented
by him, the Father could not endure such an object,
so he struck his fist through the pane, and told his
host how unbecoming it was to allow such things
to remain. Such was this good Father's zeal for
God's honour, and his love of truth. Joining himself then to the aforesaid sailors, he knew how to
combine the prudence of the serpent with the
simplicity of the dove, and behaved himself in such
sort that though he did not conceal that the evil he
saw in them was displeasing to him, yet evil as
they were he won their esteem, and by their means,
and the protection they unwittingly afforded, he was
enabled to reach London without molestation; for
the watchers, who were in almost every town
through which he passed, taking him to be one of
the party, cared not to annoy those whose appearance and carriage distinguished them so completely
from those for whom they were keeping watch.

When my companion had departed, I too set out,
but by a different road. I had not gone far before
I saw some country folks coming towards me. I
went up to them, and inquired about a stray falcon,
whether they had heard the tinkling of his bells.
For I wanted them to think that I had lost a falcon,

and was going through the country in search of it, as is usual with those who have sustained such a loss, so that they might not wonder why I was strange to the country, and had to ask my way. They of course had neither seen nor heard any such thing of late, and seemed sorry that they could not direct my search. I then went with a disappointed air to examine the neighbouring trees and hedges, as if to look for my bird. Thus I was able, without awakening suspicion, to keep clear of the highway, and to get further and further from the sea shore, by going across country. Whenever I saw any one in a field I went up to him and put the same series of questions about the falcon, concealing thereby my anxiety to keep out of the public roads and villages, where I knew sentinels were posted with power to examine every stranger. I thus managed to expend the best part of that day, walking some eight or ten miles, not in a straight line, but by doubling and returning frequently on my steps. At length being quite soaked with rain, and exhausted with hunger and fatigue, for I had scarcely been able to take any food or rest on board ship for the tossing of the waves, I turned into a village inn which lay in my road; for those who go to the inns are less liable to be questioned.

There I refreshed myself well, and found mine host very agreeable, especially as I wanted to buy a pony he had in his stable. I concluded the bargain at a reasonable price, for the owner was not very rich; but I took it as a means of safer and more speedy transit, for foot-passengers are frequently looked upon as vagrants, and even in quiet times are liable to arrest.

Next morning, I mounted my pony and turned

towards Norwich, the capital of that county. I had
scarce rid two miles when I fell in with the watchers
at the entrance of a village, who bade me halt and
began to ask me who I was and whence I came. I
told them that I was the servant of a certain lord
who lived in a neighbouring county (with whom I
was well acquainted, though he was unknown to
them), that my falcon had flown away, and that I
had come to this part of the country to recover him
if he should have been found. They found no flaw
in my story, yet they would not let me go, but said
I must be brought before the Constable and the
Beadle,[8] who were both in church at the time, at
their profane heretical service. I saw that I could
neither fly nor resist, nor could I prevail with these
men; so yielding to necessity, I went with them as
far as the churchyard. One of the party entered
the church and brought word that the Beadle
wished me to come into the church and that he
would see me when Service was over. I replied
that I would wait for him where I was. "No, no,"
said the messenger, "you must go into church."
"I shall stop here," I returned, "I don't want to
lose sight of my horse." "What!" said the man,
"you won't dismount to go and hear the word of
God! I can only warn you that you will make no
very favourable impression; as to your horse, I
myself will engage to get you a better one, if you
are so anxious about him." "Go and tell him,"
said I, "that if he wants me, either he must come
at once, or I will wait here." As soon as my

---

[8] "Ad subcuratorem pacis, et ad censorem."—*MS.* The above
are conjectural renderings. These seem to have been only village
officials. In the times of persecution the parish-beadle not un-
frequently had duties of this kind to perform.

message was taken to him, the Beadle came out with some others, to examine me. I could easily see he was not best pleased. He began by demanding whence I came. I answered by naming certain places which I had learnt were not far off; to his questions as to my name, condition, dwelling, and business, I made the same answers as above. He then asked whether I had any letters with me ; on which I offered to allow him to search my person. This he did not do, but said he should be obliged to take me before the Justice of the Peace.[4] I professed my readiness to go should he deem it needful, but that I was in a hurry to get back to my master after my long absence, so that if it could be managed I should be better pleased to be allowed to go on. At first he stood to his resolution ; and I saw nothing for it but to go before the Justice and to be committed to jail, as doubtless would have been the case. But suddenly looking at me with a calmer countenance he said, " You look like an honest man : go on in God's name, I don't want to trouble you any more."

Nor did God's Providence abandon me in my further journey. As I rode onward towards the town, I saw a young man on horseback with a pack riding on before me. I wanted to come up with him, so as to get information about the state of the town, and ask the fittest inn for me to put up at, and he looked like one of whom I could make such inquiries without exciting suspicion ; but his horse being better than mine I could not gain upon him, urge my pony how I would. After following him at a distance for two or three miles, it chanced by

---

4 " Irenarchâ aut curatore pacis."—*MS.*

God's will that he dropped his pack, and was obliged to dismount in order to pick it up and strap it on. As I came up I found he was an unpolished youth, well fitted for my purpose. From him I acquired information that would have been very useful had any danger befallen, but, as it was, by his means the Lord so guided me, that I escaped all danger. For I inquired about a good inn near the city gate, that I might not weary my horse in going from street to street in search of one. He told me there was such an inn on the other side of the city; but that if I wanted to put up there I must go round the town. Having learnt the way thereto and the sign of the house, I thanked my informant, and left him to pursue his road which led straight through the town, the same way I should have followed had I not met with such a guide, and in that case I should have run into certain danger, nor would any of those things have befallen which afterwards came to pass for God's greater glory and the salvation of many souls.

Following then the advice of the young man, I went round the skirts of the city to the gate he had described, and as soon as I entered I saw my inn. I had rested me but a little while there, when a man who seemed to be an acquaintance of the people of the house came in. After greeting me civilly, he sat down in the chimney corner, and dropped some words about some Catholic gentlemen who were kept in jail there; and he mentioned one whose relative had been a companion of mine in the Marshalsea some seven years since. I silently noted his words, and when he had gone out, I asked who he might be. They answered that he was a very honest fellow in other points, but a Papist. I

c

enquired how they came to know that. They replied that it was a well-known fact, as he had been many years imprisoned in the Castle there (which was but a stone's throw from the place where I was); that many Catholic gentlemen were confined there, and that he had been but lately let out. I asked whether he had abandoned the faith in order to be at large. " No, indeed," said they, "nor is he likely to, for he is a most obstinate man. But he has been set free under an engagement to come back to prison, when called for. He has some business with a nobleman in the prison, and he comes here pretty often, on that account." I held my tongue, and awaited his return.

As soon as he came back, and we were alone, I told him I should wish to speak with him apart, that I had heard that he was a Catholic, and for that reason I trusted him, as I also was a Catholic : that I had come there by a sort of chance, but wanted to get on to London : that it would be a good deed worthy of a Catholic, were he to do me the favour of introducing me to some parties who might be going the same road, and who were well known, so that I might be allowed to pass on by favour of their company : that being able to pay my expenses, I should be no burden to my companions. He replied that he knew not of any one who was then going to London. I hereon enquired if he could hire a person who would accompany me for a set price. He said he would look out some such one, but that he knew of a gentleman then in the town, who might be able to forward my business. He went to find him, and soon returning desired me to accompany him. He took me into a shop, as if he were going to make some purchase. The gentleman he had mentioned was there, having appointed the place that he might see me before he made himself known. At length he joined us, and told my companion in a whisper that he believed I was a priest. He led us therefore to the cathedral, and having put me many questions, he at last urged me to say whether or no I was a priest, promising that he would assist me,—at that time a most acceptable offer. On my side, I inquired from my previous acquaintance the name and condition of this third party; and on learning it, as I saw God's Providence in so ready an assistance, I told him I was a priest of the Society, who had come from Rome. He performed his promise, and procured for me a change of clothes, and made me mount a good horse, and took me without delay into the country to the house of a personal friend, leaving one of his servants to bring on my little pony. The next day we arrived at his house, where he and his family resided, together with a brother of his who was a heretic. They had with them a widowed sister, also a heretic, who kept house for them [5]; so that I was obliged to be careful not to give any ground for them to suspect my calling. The heretic brother at my first coming was very suspicious, seeing me arrive in his Catholic brother's company unknown as I was, and perceiving no reason why the latter should make so much of me. But after a day or so, he quite abandoned all mistrust, as I spoke of hunting and falconry with all the details that none but a practised person could command.

[5] Dr. Jessopp, in a note printed by Father Morris, makes it clear that the brothers were Edward and Charles Yelverton, and their sister (or rather half-sister) Jane, widow of Edward Lumner of Mannington.

For many make sad blunders in attempting this, as
Father Southwell, who was afterwards my companion in many journeys, was wont to complain.
He frequently got me to instruct him in the techni-
cal terms of sport, and used to regret his bad
memory for such things, for on many occasions
when he fell in with Protestant gentlemen, he found
it necessary to speak of these matters, which are
the sole topics of their conversation, save when
they talk obscenity, or break out into blasphemies
and abuse of the Saints or of the Catholic Faith.
In these cases it is of course desirable to turn the
conversation to other subjects, and to speak of
horses, of hounds, and such like. Thus it often
happens that trifling covers truth,[6] as it did with
me on this occasion. After a short sojourn of a
few days, I proposed to my newly found friend the
Catholic brother, my intention of going to London,
to meet my Superior. He therefore provided me
with a horse, and sent a servant along with me ;
begging me at the same time to obtain leave to
return to that county, and to make his house my
home, for he assured me that I should bring over
many to the faith, were I to converse with them
publicly as he had seen me do. I pledged myself
to lay his offer before Father Garnet, and said that
I would willingly return if he should approve of it.
So I departed, and arrived in London without
accident, having met with no obstacle on the road.
I have gone into these particulars, to show how
God's providence guarded me on my first landing in
England ; for without knowing a single soul in that
county, where until then I had never set foot, as it
was far distant from my native place, on the very

[6] Ut vanitas veritatem occultet.—*MS.*

first day I found a friend who not only saved me from present peril, but who afterwards, by introducing me to the principal families in the county, furnished an opportunity for many conversions; and from the acquaintance I then made, and the knowledge the Catholics in those parts had of me in consequence, all that God chose hereafter to do by my weakness took its origin, as will appear by the sequel.

CHAPTER III.

MY RESIDENCE IN THE COUNTY OF NORFOLK.

ON my arrival in London, by the help of certain Catholics I discovered Father Garnet, who was then Superior. Besides him, the only others of our Society then in England were Father Edmund Weston, confined at Wisbech (who, had he been at large, would have been Superior), Father Robert Southwell, and we two new-comers.

My companion Father Oldcorne had already arrived, so the Superior was rather anxious on my account, as nothing had been heard of me; but yet for that very reason hopes were entertained of my safety. It was with exceeding joy on both sides that we met at last: I stayed some time with the Fathers, and we held frequent councils as to our future proceedings. The good Superior gave us excellent instructions as to the method of helping and gaining souls, as did also our dear Father Southwell, who much excelled in that art, being at once prudent, pious, meek, and exceedingly winning. As Christmas was nigh at hand, it was necessary to separate, both for the consolation of the faithful, and because the dangers are always greater in the great solemnities.

I returned then to my friend in the county where I was first set ashore. This time the Superior provided me with clothes and other necessaries, that I might not be a burden to my charitable host at the outset. But afterwards, throughout the whole period of my missionary labours, the fatherly providence of God supplied both for me and for some others. My dress was of the same fashion as that of gentlemen of moderate means. The necessity of this was shown by reason and subsequent events; for, from my former position, I was more at ease in this costume, and could maintain a less embarrassed bearing, than if I had assumed a character to which I was unaccustomed. Then too, I had to appear in public and meet many Protestant gentlemen, with whom I could not have held communication with a view to lead them on to a love of the Faith and a desire of virtue, had I not adopted this garb. I found it helped me, not only to speak more freely and with greater authority, but to remain with greater safety, and for a longer interval of time, in any place or family to which my host introduced me as his friend and acquaintance.

Thus it happened that I remained for six or eight months, with some profit to souls, in the family of my first friend and host; during which time, he took me with him to nearly every gentleman's house in the county. Before the eight months were passed, I gained over and converted many to the Church: among whom were one of the brothers of my host, his two sisters, and later on his brother-in-law. One of these two sisters, as I have before mentioned,

was my friend's housekeeper, and had been all along
a red-hot Calvinist. A very remarkable thing had
happened to her some time previously. Being very
anxious as to the state of her soul, she went to a
certain doctor of the University of Cambridge of
the name of Perne,[1] who she knew had changed
his religion some three or four times under different
Sovereigns, but yet was in high repute for learning.
Going to this Doctor Perne then, who was an
intimate friend of her family, she conjured him to
tell her honestly and undisguisedly what was the
sound orthodox Faith whereby she might obtain
heaven. The doctor finding himself thus earnestly
appealed to by a woman of discretion and good
sense, replied, " I entreat you never to disclose to
another what I am going to say. Since then you
have pressed me to answer, as if I had to give
account of your soul, I will tell you, that you can,
if you please, *live* in the religion now professed by
the Queen and her whole kingdom, for so you will
live more at ease, and be exempt from all the vexa-
tions the Catholics have to undergo. But by no
means *die* out of the faith and communion of the
Catholic Church, if you would save your soul."
Such was the answer of this poor man, but such was
not his practice ; for putting off his conversion from
day to day, it fell out that, when he least expected, on
his return home from dining with the pseudo-arch-
bishop of Canterbury, he dropped down dead as he
was entering his own apartment, without the least
sign of repentance, or of Christian hope of that
eternal bliss which he had too easily promised to

[1] Dr. Andrew Perne, Master of Peterhouse, Cambridge, and
Dean of Ely, changed his religion four times, to suit the different
Sovereigns under whom he lived.

himself and to others after a life of a contrary
tendency. She to whom he gave the above-mentioned advice was more fortunate than he, and
though she at first by no means accepted his estimate of the Catholic Faith, yet later on, having
frequently heard from me that the Catholic Faith
alone was true and holy, she began to have doubts,
and in consequence brought me an heretical work
which had served to confirm her in her heresy, and
showed me the various arguments it contained.
I, on the other hand, pointed out to her the quibbles,
the dishonest quotations from Scripture and the
Fathers, and the mis-statement of facts which the
book contained. And so, by God's grace, from the
scorpion itself was drawn the remedy against the
scorpion's sting, and she has lived ever since constant in her profession of the Catholic Faith to
which she then returned.

I must not omit mentioning an instance of the
wonderful efficacy of the Sacraments as shown in
the case of the married sister of my host. She had
married a man of high rank, and, being favourably
inclined to the Church, she had been so well prepared by her brother, that it cost me but little labour
to make her a child of the Catholic Church. After
her conversion she endured much from her husband when he found that she refused to join in
heretical worship, but her patience withstood and
overcame all. It happened on one occasion that
she was so exhausted after a difficult and dangerous
labour, that her life was despaired of. A clever
physician was at once brought from Cambridge,
who on seeing her said that he could indeed give
her medicine, but that he could give no hopes of
her recovery; and having prescribed some remedies,

he left. I was at that time on a visit to the house, having come, as was my wont, in company with her brother. The master of the house was glad to see us, although he well knew we were Catholics, and used in fact to dispute with me on religious subjects. I had nearly convinced his understanding and judgment, but the will was rooted to the earth, "for he had great possessions." But being anxious for his wife whom he dearly loved, he allowed his brother to persuade him, as there was no longer any hope for her present life, to allow her all freedom to prepare for the one to come. With his permission then we promised to bring in an old priest on the following night; for those priests who were ordained before Elizabeth's reign were not exposed to such dangers and penalties as the others. We therefore made use of his ministry, in order that this lady might receive all the rites of the Church. Having made her confession and been anointed, she received the Holy Viaticum; and, behold, in half an hour's time she so far recovered, as to be wholly out of danger; the disease and its cause had vanished, and she had only to recover her strength. The husband seeing his wife thus snatched from the jaws of death, wished to know the reason. We told him that it was one of the effects of the holy Sacrament of Extreme Unction, that it restored bodily health when Divine Wisdom foresaw that it was expedient for the good of the soul. This was the cause of his conversion; for admiring the power and efficacy of the Sacraments of the true Church, he allowed himself to be persuaded to seek in that Church the health of his own soul. I, being eager to strike the iron while it was hot, began without delay to prepare him for confession ; but not wishing just then that he should know me for a priest, I said that I would instruct him as I had been instructed by priests in my time. He prepared himself, and awaited the priest's arrival. His brother-in-law told him that this must be at night time. So, having , sent away the servants who used to attend him to his chamber, he went into the library, where I left him praying, telling him that I would return directly with the priest. I went down stairs and put on my cassock, and returned so changed in appearance, that he, never dreaming of any such thing, was speechless with amazement. My friend and I showed him that our conduct was necessary, not so much in order to avoid danger, but in order to cheat the devil and to snatch souls from his clutches. He well knew, I said, that I could in no other way have conversed with him and his equals, and without conversation it was impossible to bring round those who were so ill-disposed. The same considerations served to dispel all anxieties as to the consequences of my sojourn under his roof. I appealed to his own experience, and reminded him, that though I had been in continual contact with him, he had not once suspected my priestly character. He thus became a Catholic; and his lady, grateful to God for this twofold blessing, perseveres still in the Faith, and has endured much since that time from the hands of heretics.

Besides these, I reconciled to the Church, during the period of my appearance in public, more than twenty fathers and mothers of families, equal, and some even superior, in station to the above mentioned. For prudence' sake I omit their names. As for poor persons and servants, I received a great many, the exact number I do not remember. It was my good fortune moreover, to confirm many weak and pusillanimous souls. I also received numbers of general confessions. Many too received at that time the inspiration to a more perfect life : among whom I may mention the present Father Edward Walpole, professed of three vows, who was then living a good and pious life, and had to endure much for conscience' sake, and not from strangers only, "for his enemies were those of his own household." He was heir to a large estate, but his father was a Calvinist, and the rest of his family were also heretics. His father at his death disinherited him, and divided his estate between his younger brother and his mother, who was to hold one half during her life-time, so that his only share was a yearly revenue of four hundred florins (40*l.*), on which he was then living. His father's house was less a home than a prison, he lived there without seeing or speaking to any one save at meals ; the rest of the day he spent in his room, and he diligently read the Fathers and Doctors, as he had already studied Humanities and Philosophy at Cambridge. At that time he began to visit me, and to frequent the Sacraments. He thus obtained that vocation which he followed a year after, when he went to Rome and entered the Society. He persuaded his cousin Michael Walpole, who is now professed of the four vows, to accompany him. At this period of my story the latter was my assistant, and used to go with me as my confidential servant, to the houses of those gentlemen with whom it was necessary for me to maintain such a position. The two cousins are now zealous labourers in the Lord's vineyard, and by their great abilities have made up for what my neglect or mediocrity has marred or left undone.

After some six or seven months, I received a visit from a Catholic gentleman of another county, a relative of one of my spiritual children, who was very desirous to make acquaintance with a Jesuit. He was a devout young man, and heir to a pretty considerable estate, one half of which came into his possession by his brother's death, the other portion being held for life by his mother, who was a good Catholic widow lady. Her son lived with her, and they kept a priest in the house. He had then sold a portion of his estate, and devoted the proceeds to pious uses, for he was fervent and full of charity. After the lapse of a few days, as I saw his aspirations to a higher life and his desires of perfection wax stronger, I told him that there were certain spiritual exercises, by means of which a well-disposed person could discover a short road to perfection, and be best prepared to make choice of a state of life. He most earnestly begged to be allowed to make them. I acceded to his request, and he made great spiritual profit thereby, not only in that he made the best choice, which was that he would enter the Society of Jesus as soon as possible, but also because he made the best and most proper arrangements to carry his purpose into execution, and to preserve meanwhile his present fervour. After his retreat he expressed the greatest wish that I should come and live with him, and I had no rest until I promised to submit the matter for my Superior's approval. For mine own part, I could not but reflect that my present mode of life, though in the beginning it had its advantages, could not be long continued, because the more people I knew and the more I was known to, the less

became my safety and the greater my distractions.
Hence it was not without acknowledging God's
special Providence that I heard him make me this
invitation. So, after having consulted with my
Superior and obtained his permission to accept the
offer, I bade adieu to my old friends, and stationed
a priest where they might conveniently have recourse
to his ministry. He still remains there, to the great
profit of souls, though in the endurance of many
perils.

CHAPTER IV.

MY NEW RESIDENCE, AND ANOTHER CHANGE.

In my new abode,[1] I was able to live much more
quietly and more to my taste, in as much as nearly
all the members of the household were Catholics;
and thus it was easier for me to conform to the
Rule of the Society, both as regards dress and the
arrangement of my time; and moreover I had
leisure to pursue my studies. In this house, I found
some matters which needed change or improvement.
Among other things, the altar furniture was not
only antique but antiquated, and by no means cal-
culated to excite devotion, but rather to extinguish
it. But I saw that I must be cautious, lest the
chaplain, who had been some time in the house,
should take offence at these changes being introduced by me, especially as he could not but notice
that the master of the house followed my advice in
all things. But, by God's help, all went off admirably. As for the things that required immediate

---

[1] His new host was Henry Drury of Losell in Suffolk.—M.

attention, I took care to get the master of the house himself to propose and carry them through. Then also I showed some church ornaments that had been given to me, the beauty of which quite capti- vated the good widow, and made her set about making as good for herself. But this was not all : the good priest hearing the master of the house extol the Spiritual Exercises, wished to try them himself for once. He went through them with great profit, and frequently declared that until he had made them he knew not what was the duty of a priest. He conceived moreover a great attach- ment to me, as I afterwards experienced by his alms and the charity he showed me when I was imprisoned ; he ever consulted me in his doubts and difficulties ; he gained thrice as many souls as before to God and His Church, and was more esteemed of all. When an Arch-priest was at length elected, he was appointed one of his assis- tants, and remains so still.

While in this residence (and I was there all but two years) I gave much time to my studies. At times I made missionary excursions, and not only did I reconcile many, but I confirmed many Catholic families in the Faith, and placed two priests in stations where they might be useful to souls. At the same time I gave the Spiritual Exercises to some with considerable profit.

First, I had two gentlemen who were related to each other: they both resolved to enter the Society, and after they had settled their affairs they went to France, where, having finished their studies, one of them, Father Thomas Everett, was admitted, and is now a zealous labourer in the English mission ; the second took priest's Orders, but being rather pusillanimous wished first to return to England, and ill came of it.[2] I also gave a Retreat to two fine young men who were brothers,[3] who both came to the resolution of entering the Society. One of them had gone through his course of Humanities and Philosophy at Cambridge, and had been a law-student in London for nine years, and being very talented and indefatigable in his application to study he made such progress, that I have known competent judges to rank an opinion of his as high as that of any of the most celebrated lawyers, whether of past or present times. He was so prudent and grave in his bearing, that Father Southwell said to me, at a time when the young man himself had never dreamt of changing his state, that if he had a vocation to our Body none would be so fit for government as he. By the advice then of my host, who was an intimate friend of theirs, they placed themselves under my direction and went into Retreat. The younger brother met with no obstacle whatever ; but the elder during the first week was in a state of complete dryness. He afterwards found out the reason thereof, and re-moved it. I had counselled him to adopt certain regulations for the treatment of his body, which were comparatively unimportant, and, as he objected on the score of health, I yielded ; but afterwards deeming this reluctance of his, though in a slight matter, a hindrance to God's grace, one day as I visited him to exhort and console him under his desolation, he threw himself at my feet, and, begging pardon, refused to rise until in token of full forgiveness I would allow him to kiss my feet.

[2] The original seems studiously obscure.
[3] Thomas and John Wiseman.

After that he was ever overflowing with consolation, and a light arose in his heart which showed him so clearly the way wherein he should walk, that there was no room left for doubt. Hence, though he had much to do both with his own affairs and the business of others before he could leave England, and had determined to sell his estate, so as to preclude all desire of returning, with such wonderful rapidity did he settle it all, that within five or six weeks he had started with his brother for Rome.

The two brothers, on their arrival in Rome, went to the novitiate of St. Andrea without delay; they completed their training under the names of Starkie and Standish, which they assumed as a remembrance of me, for under these I passed in the first and second county where I took up my residence. The younger of the two died holily (as I heard) at St. Andrea's; the elder, while pursuing his studies in the Roman College, being perhaps somewhat indiscreet in his fervour, fell into consumption, and coming some time after to Belgium, died at St. Omer's, to the great regret but no less to the edification of all who knew him.

The elder of these brothers, before he left England, succeeded in persuading his eldest brother,[4] over whom he had great influence, to make a trial of the Spiritual Exercises. This gentleman was indeed a Catholic, but without the least care for Christian perfection. He had lately come to his estate, on the death of his father, and had made himself a large deer-park in it. There he lived like a king, in ease and independence, surrounded by his children, to whom as well as to

[4] William Wiseman of Braddocks (Broad oaks), in the parish of Wimbish in Essex.

his wife he was tenderly attached. As he kept clear of priests from the Seminaries, he lived unmolested, feeling nothing of the burden and heat of the day; for the persecutors troubled chiefly those who harboured the Seminarists, not caring to enquire after those who kept the old priests, that is, those who had taken orders before the reign of Elizabeth. So now-a-days a great difference is made between seculars and the priests of the Society; the persecution being much fiercer against Ours and our friends, as may be seen from what occurs when they who afford us comfort and shelter are discovered. The cause of this I take to be that seeing our numbers increase, the authorities try to crush first the most uncompromising party, and to deter our friends by terrible examples from shelter- ing and supporting us. But the Israelites increased despite the rage of Pharao who sought their lives.

This good gentleman then, who lived in calm and safety in his house and possessions, and evaded so cautiously the wiles of the persecutor, perceived not and dreaded not enough the wiles of Satan; yet he did not escape the toils of God's grace, but came to them willingly, and once taken wished not to be free. On the third day of the Exercises, after having well pondered the purpose of God in creating him and all other things, feeling the stirring of the waters, he went down into the pool and was healed. He succeeded admirably in each meditation, as the resolutions he made and the lights vouchsafed to him proved. He left nothing within or without which he did not strive to rectify and order unto God's greater glory : he resolved no longer to enjoy, but only to use, all created things, and that sparingly; to govern his household as a charge

D

committed unto him by God; and to get two other
priests, one of whom he insisted should be a Jesuit,
to whom he would commit the direction of himself
and of all belonging to him. He further purposed
to spend his leisure hours in pious reading, or in
the translation of spiritual books. For he was
learned and able, and did afterwards publish many
such translations; among others the life of our
Blessed Father, the *Dialogues* of St. Gregory the
Great, Father Jerome Platus' work on the *Advantages of the Religious State*, and others of the same
kind. He set himself very useful rules of conversation, not only for his personal direction, but in
order to brotherly correction and the encouragement
of virtue in his neighbours.

Such were his resolutions; such too was his
subsequent practice. From the first, he expected
an obstacle, which he could not but foresee. His
servants were heretics for the most part; and he
could not hope that his wife would second his
plans. Again, he had as chaplain one of the old
priests, and these were not often wont to agree
with younger men, especially with those of the
Society, whom they looked upon as troublesome
reformers. He could not then but be anxious. But
having, through God's goodness, conceived a firm
and practical resolution, he determined to dismiss
his servants in a kindly and open-handed way, and
to take good Catholics in their stead; to prevail
over the opposition of his lady and the chaplain,
if possible by reason and affection, but should these
fail, to show that he was master of the family, and
to make use of the authority given him by God.

This being settled, he began to urge me with all
earnestness to come and take up my abode with

him, alleging reasons that I could not fairly meet. Moreover at that time my host (Henry Drury), for whose sake especially I had come to my present abode, was preparing to depart; for Father Garnet had settled that he should come and live with him in London until he should be sent abroad; and the good priest I found there was well able to administer to the spiritual wants of this gentleman's mother. Another advantage of this proposed change was that it brought me nearer to London, and placed me in a family where I could do much more good than in my present abode after the departure of my host. I submitted all these considerations to the judgment of my Superior, with whom I was going to leave my hospitable friend after I had introduced him. As Father Garnet approved my availing myself of this new opportunity, which God's Providence had offered me, I accepted the invitation, and after a couple of months I went to my new dwelling, having taken care, in order to escape odium and jealousy, to get my host to inaugurate his improvements, so far as could be done, before my arrival.

We procured then a staff of good and faithful domestics, whom I had formerly known in other places, and whose characters I had proved. Nor did I find it so difficult as we had feared, to bring the lady of the house and the old priest to consent to the changes. Far from opposing, they furthered my views; the wife especially outshone all the household in her zeal for the decoration of the altar, and the charity she showed to me. This lady was of a rather quick temper, and had great difficulty in observing the rule of patience with her servants and others, yet I never let any such fault pass without either private or (if the nature of the case required it) public notice and reproof. This I never omitted during the whole of my stay with this family, but this notwithstanding, she not only bore with me cheerfully, and tried to subdue her temper, but ever showed me fresh marks of attachment and respect, as will appear in the sequel.

As to the chaplain, when he saw that after my arrival he and all that belonged to him were placed on a better footing, he not only became friendly, but both by word and deed repeatedly showed his satisfaction at my coming. For the increase of piety and devotion in the household had wrought a corresponding increase of reverence for him, and he gained many other advantages which he had not had before.

In this house there was living my host's mother, a most excellent widow lady, happy in her children, but still happier in her private virtues. She had four sons and four daughters. These latter without exception devoted their virginity to God. Two had already joined the holy order of St. Bridget before my arrival, and one of these is even at this day Abbess in Lisbon. I sent the two others to Flanders, where they still serve God in the order of St. Augustine. Her sons were all pious young men; two died in the Society, as was related above; a third chose the army, and was lately slain in a battle with the heretics in Belgium, — he fell fighting when many around him had surrendered; the fourth was the master of that house, who, to his mother's great joy, had given himself up to every good work. Such was this good widow's fervour, that she deemed herself to have attained the summit of her desires in this world.

At my first entrance into this house, she desired her son to bring me up to her chamber; as I came in she fell at my feet, and besought me to allow her to kiss them, saying I was the first ot the Society she had seen; as I refused, she kissed the ground on which I stood, and arose filled with a holy joy, which still abides in her : and now, living apart from her son, she maintaihs with her two Priests of our Society, having in the meanwhile endured a great many tribulations, which shall be related hereafter.

CHAPTER V.

MY EXCURSIONS, AND THEIR FRUIT.

WHEN the house had been thus settled, I found time both for study and for missionary excursions. I took care that all in the house should approach the Sacraments frequently, which none before, save the good widow, used to do oftener than four times a year. Now they came every week. On feast days, and often on Sundays, I preached in the chapel; moreover I showed those who had leisure the way to meditate by themselves, and taught all how to examine their conscience. I also brought in the custom of reading pious books, which we did even at meals, when there were no strangers there ; for at that time we priests sat with the rest, even with our gowns on. I had a cassock besides and a biretta, but the Superior would not have us use these except in the chapel.

In my excursions I almost always gained some to God. There is however a great difference to be observed between these counties where I then was, and other parts of England; for in some places, where many of the common people are Catholics, and almost all lean towards the Catholic faith, it is easy to bring many into the bosom of the Church, and to have many hearers together at a sermon. I myself have seen in Lancashire two hundred together present at Mass and sermon; and as these easily come in, so also they easily scatter when the storm of persecution draws near, and come back again when the alarm has blown over. On the contrary, in those parts where I was now staying there were very few Catholics, but these were of the higher classes; scarcely any of the common people, for they cannot live in peace, surrounded as they are by most violent heretics. The way of managing in such places, is first to gain the gentry, then the servants: for Catholic masters cannot do without Catholic servants.

About this time I gained to God and the Church my hostess' brother,[1] the only son of a certain knight. I ever after found him a most faithful friend in all circumstances. He afterwards took to wife a cousin of the most illustrious Spanish Duke of Feria. This pious pair are so attached to our priests, that now in these terrible times they always keep one in their house, and often two or three.

I now persuaded my host's mother, the good widow, to go to her own house and maintain there a priest whom I recommended, in order that so noble a soul, and one so ready for all good deeds, might be a profit not only to herself but to many,

[1] Henry, son of Sir Edmund Huddlestone, of Sawston in Cambridgeshire.—M.

as in fact she became. Her house was a retreat and no small protection both to Ours and to other priests. She used moreover so to abound with joy when I or others came to her house, that sometimes she could not refrain from clapping her hands or some like sign of gladness; she was indeed *a true widow*, given to all manner of good works, and especially occupied with zeal for souls.

Indeed, besides others of less standing whom she brought me to be reconciled, she had nearly won over a certain great Lady,[2] a neighbour of hers. Though this Lady was the wife of the richest Lord in the whole county, and sister to the Earl of Essex (then most powerful with the Queen), and was wholly given to vanities, nevertheless she brought her so far as to be quite willing to speak with a priest, if only he could come to her without being known. This the good widow told me. I consequently went to her house openly, and addressed her as though I had something to tell her from a certain great lady her kinswoman, for so it had been agreed. I dined openly with her and all the gentry in the house, and spent three hours at least in private talk with her. I first satisfied her in all the doubts which she laid before me about faith; next I set myself to stir up her will, and before my departure I so wrought upon her, that she asked for instructions how to prepare herself for confession, and fixed a day for making it. But the judgments. of God are a deep abyss, and it is a dreadful thing to expose oneself to the occasions of sin. Now there was a nobleman[3] in London, who had loved

[2] Lady Penelope Devereux, wife of Robert, Lord Rich.

[3] This nobleman is by Father Gerard's subsequent description identified with Charles Blount, Baron Mountjoy, created Earl of

her long and deeply; to him she disclosed her
purpose by letter, perchance to bid him farewell;
but she roused a sleeping adder. For he hastened
to her, and began to dissuade her in every kind of
way; and being himself a heretic and not wanting
in learning, he cunningly coaxed her to get him an
answer to certain doubts of his from the same guide
that she herself followed : saying that if he was
satisfied in this, he too would become a Catholic.
He implored her to take no step in the meantime, if
she did not wish for his death. So he filled two
sheets of paper about the Pope, the worship of
Saints, and the like. She sent them with a letter
of her own, begging me to be so good as to answer
them, for it would be a great gain if such a soul
could be won over. He did not however write from
a wish to learn, but rather with the treacherous
design of delaying her conversion. For he got an
answer, a full one I think, to which he made no
reply. But meanwhile he endeavoured to get her
to London, and succeeded in making her first post-
pone, and afterwards altogether neglect her resolution. By all this however he was unwittingly
bringing on his own ruin: for later on, returning
from Ireland laden with glory, on account of his
successful administration, and his victory over the
Spanish forces that had landed there, (on which
occasion he brought over with him the Earl of
Tyrone, who had been the most powerful opponent
of heresy in that country, and most sturdy champion
of the ancient faith,) he was created Earl by His
present Majesty; and though conqueror of others,

Devonshire by James I.   He married Lady Rich, after her
divorce, and in the lifetime of her husband.   He died a few
months after this marriage.

he conquered not himself, but was kept a helpless captive by his love of this lady. This madness of his brought him to commit such extravagancies that, he became quite notorious, and was publicly disgraced. Unable to endure this dishonour, and yet unwilling to renounce the cause of it, he died of grief, invoking, alas! not God, but his *goddess*, as he called her, and leaving her heiress of all his property. Such was his miserable end, dying in bad repute of all men. The lady, though now very rich, often afterwards began to think of her former resolution, and often spoke of me to a certain Catholic maid of honour that she had about her. This latter coming into Belgium about three years back to become a nun, related this to me, and begged me to write to her and fan the yet un-quenched spark into a flame. But when I was setting about the letter, I heard that she had been carried off by a fever, not however before she had been reconciled to the Church by one of Ours. I have set this forth at some length, that the provi-dence of God with regard to her whose conversion was hindered, and His judgment upon him who was the cause of the hinderance, may more clearly appear.

I used also to make other missionary excursions at this time to more distant counties towards the north. On the way I had to pass through my native place, and through the midst of my kindred and acquaintance; but I could not do much good there, though there were many who professed them-selves great friends of mine. I experienced in fact most truly the truth of that saying of Truth Himself, that no prophet is received in his own country; so that I felt little wish at any time to linger among them. It happened once that I went to lodge on one of those journeys with a Catholic kinsman.[4] I found him in hunter's trim, ready to start for a grand hunt, for which many of his friends had met together. He asked me to go with him, and try to gain over a certain gentleman who had married a cousin of his and mine. I answered that some other occasion would be more fit. He disagreed with me however, maintaining that unless I took this chance of going with him, I should not be able to get near the person in question. I went accordingly, and during the hunt joined company with him for whose soul I myself was on the hunt. The hounds being at fault from time to time, and ceasing to give tongue, while we were awaiting the renewal of this hunter's music, I took the opportunity of following my own chase, and gave tongue myself in good earnest. Thus, beginning to speak of the great pains that we took over chasing a poor animal, I brought the conversation to the necessity of seeking an everlasting kingdom, and the proper method of gaining it, to wit by employing all manner of care and industry; as the devil on his part never sleeps, but hunts after our souls as hounds after their prey. We said but little on disputed points of faith, for he was rather a schismatic than a heretic, but to move his will to act required a longer talk. This work was continued that day and the day after; and on the fourth day he was spiritually born and made a Catholic. He still remains one, and often supports priests at home and sends them to other people.

On an occasion of this kind there happened a very wonderful thing. He went once to visit a

---

[4] Probably his elder brother, Sir Thomas Gerard.

friend of his who was sick in bed. As he knew him to be an upright man, and one rather under a delusion than in wilful error, he began to instruct him in the faith, and press him at the same time to look to his soul, as his illness was dangerous. He at last prevailed with him, and was himself prevailed upon by the sick man to seek for a priest to hear his confession. Accordingly, after instructing the invalid how to stir up in himself meanwhile sorrow for his sins and make ready his confession, the other went away. Not happening to have a priest at home at the time, he had some difficulty in finding one. In the meantime the sick man died, but evidently with a great desire of confession; for he had repeatedly asked whether that friend of his was coming who had promised to bring a physician with him, under which name priests often visit the sick. What followed seemed to show that his desires had stood him in good stead. Every night after his death there appeared to his wife in her chamber a sort of light, flickering through the air and sometimes entering within the curtains. She was frightened, and ordered her maids to bring their beds into the room and stay with her; they however saw nothing, their mistress alone saw the appearance every night and was troubled at it. At last she sent for that Catholic friend of her husband, disclosed to him the whole cause of her fear, and asked him to consult some learned man. He asked a priest's advice, who answered that very probably this light meant that she should come to the light of faith. He returned with the answer, and won her over. The widow on becoming a Catholic had Mass said in the same room for a long time, but still the same light appeared every night. This increased her trouble, so that the priest consulted other priests, and brought back an answer to the widow, that probably her husband's soul was on the way to heaven by reason of his true conversion of heart and contrition accompanied with a desire of the Sacrament, but still he stood in need of prayers to free him from his debts to God's justice. He bade her therefore have Mass said for him for thirty days, according to the old custom of the country. She took the advice, and herself communicated several times for the same intention. The night after the last Mass had been celebrated in the room, she saw three lights instead of one as before. Two of them seemed to hold and support the third between them. All three entered within the bed-curtains, and after staying there a little while, mounted up towards heaven through the top of the bed, leaving the lady in great consolation. She saw nothing of the sort again; from which all gathered that the soul had then been freed from its pains, and carried by the Angels to heaven. This took place in the county of Stafford.

CHAPTER VI.

MY FIRST HIDING-PLACE.

My journeys northwards were undertaken for the
purpose of visiting, and strengthening in the faith,
certain persons who there afforded no small aid to
the common cause. Among them were two sisters
of high nobility, daughters of an Earl of very old
family who had laid down his life for the Catholic
faith.[1] They lived together, and manifested a great
desire to have me not merely visit them sometimes,
but rather stay altogether with them. Though this
could not be, they gave themselves up entirely to
my direction, that I might lead them to God. The
elder, who had a family, became a pillar of support
to that portion of our afflicted Church. She kept
two priests with her at home, and received all who
came to her with great charity. There are numbers
of priests in that part of the country, and many
Catholics, mostly of the poorer sort. Indeed I was
hardly ever there without our counting before my
departure six or seven priests together in her house.
Thus she gave great help to religion in the whole
district during her abode there, which lasted till I
was seized and thrown into prison ; whereupon she

---

[1] Thomas Percy, Earl of Northumberland, was beheaded at
York in 1572 ; this is the nobleman alluded to by Father Gerard.
His eldest daughter, Lady Elizabeth was married to Mr. Richard
Woodroff ; the other sister here mentioned was Lady Mary Percy.

was constrained by her husband to change her abode and go to London, a proceeding which did neither of them any good, and deprived the poor Catholics of many advantages. Her sister was chosen by God for Himself. I found her unmarried, humble and modest. Gradually she was fitted for something higher. She learnt the practice of meditation; and profited so well thereby, that the world soon grew vile in her eyes, and heaven seemed the only thing worthy of her love. I afterwards sent her to Father Holt in Belgium. He wrote to me on one occasion about her in these terms: " Never has there come into these parts a country-woman of ours that has given such good example, or done such honour to our nation." She had the chief hand in the foundation of the present convent of English Benedictine Nuns at Brussels, where she still lives, and has arrived to a great pitch of virtue and self-denial. She yearns for a more retired life, and has often proposed to her Director to allow her to live as a recluse, but gives in to his reasons to the contrary.

At first I used to carry with me on these journeys my altar furniture, which was meagre but decent, and so contrived that it could be easily carried, along with several other necessary articles, by him who acted as my servant. In this way I used to say Mass in the morning in every place where I lodged, not however before I had looked into every corner around, that there might be no one peeping in through the chinks. I brought my own things mainly on account of certain Catholics my entertainers not having yet what was necessary for the Holy Sacrifice. But after some years this cause was removed; for in nearly every place that I came

to they had got ready the sacred vestments beforehand. Moreover I had so many friends to visit on
the way, and these at such distances from one
another, that it was hardly ever necessary for me
to lodge at an inn on a journey of one hundred
and fifty miles; and at last I hardly slept at an
inn once in two years.

I used to visit my Superior several times a year,
when I wished to consult him on matters of importance. Not only I, but all of us, used to resort
to him twice a year to give our half-yearly account
of conscience and renew the offering of our vows
to our Lord Jesus. I always remarked that the
others drew great profit from this holy custom of
our Society. As for myself, to speak my mind
frankly, I never found anything do me more good,
or stir up my courage more to fulfil all the duties
which belong to our institute, and are required of
the workmen who till the Lord's vineyard in that
country. Besides experiencing great spiritual joy
from the renewal itself, I found my interior strength
recruited, and a new zeal kindled within me afterwards in consequence; so that if I have not done
any good, it must have come from my carelessness
and thanklessness, and not from any fault of the
Society, which afforded me such means and helps
to perfection;—means peculiar to itself and not
shared by any other Religious Order.

On one occasion we were all met together in the
Superior's house while he yet resided in the country,
and were employed in the renovation of spirit. We
had had several conferences, and the Superior had
given each of us some advice in private, when the
question was started what we should do if the
priest-hunters suddenly came upon us, seeing that

there were so many of us, and there were nothing like enough hiding-places for all. We numbered then, I think, nine or ten of Ours, besides other priests and friends, and some Catholics who were forced to seek concealment. The Blessed Father Garnet[2] answered, " True, we ought not all to meet together now that our number is daily increasing: however, as we are here assembled for the greater glory of God, I will be answerable for all till the renovation is over, but beyond that I will not promise." Accordingly, on the very day of the renovation, though he had been quite unconcerned before, he earnestly warned everyone to look to himself, and not to tarry without necessity, adding, " I do not guarantee your safety any longer." Some, hearing this, mounted their horses after dinner and rode off. Five of Ours and two secular priests stayed behind.

Next morning about five o'clock, when Father Southwell was beginning Mass, and the others and myself were at meditation, I heard a bustle at the house door. Directly after I heard cries and oaths poured forth against the servant, for refusing admittance. The fact was that four priest-hunters, or pursuivants as they are called, with drawn swords were trying to break down the door and force an entrance. The faithful servant withstood them, otherwise we should have been all made prisoners. But by this time Father Southwell had heard the uproar, and guessing what it meant, had at once taken off his vestments and stripped the altar;

[2] As the Church has not yet beatified any of the English martyrs of the Reformation, the epithet " blessed " must be understood only to express Father Gerard's estimate of his Superior's sanctity.

while we strove to seek out everything belonging to us, so that there might be nothing found to betray the lurking of a priest. We did not even wish to leave boots and swords lying about, which would serve to show there had been many guests though none of them appeared. Hence many of us were anxious about our beds, which were still warm, and only covered according to custom previous to being made. Some therefore went and turned their beds over, so that the colder part might deceive any body who put his hand in to feel. Thus while the enemy was shouting and bawling outside, and our servants were keeping the door, saying that the mistress of the house, a widow, had not yet got up, but that she was coming directly and would give them an answer, we profited by the delay to stow away ourselves and all our baggage in a cleverly contrived hiding-place.

At last these leopards were let in. They raged about the house, looking everywhere, and prying into the darkest corners with candles. They took four hours over the business; but failed in their search, and only brought out the forbearance of the Catholics in suffering, and their own spite and obstinacy in seeking. At last they took themselves off, after getting paid, forsooth, for their trouble. So pitiful is the lot of the Catholics, that those who come with a warrant to annoy them in this or in other way, have to be paid for so doing by the suffering party instead of by the authorities who send them, as though it were not enough to endure wrong, but they must also pay for their endurance of it. When they were gone, and were now some way off, so that there was no fear of their returning, as they sometimes do, a lady came and summoned out of the den not one but many Daniels. The hiding-place was under ground, covered with water at the bottom, so that I was standing with my feet in water all the time. We had there Fathers Garnet, Southwell, and Oldcorne (three future martyrs), Father Stanny and myself, two secular priests, and two or three lay gentlemen. Having thus escaped that day's danger, Father Southwell and I set off the next day together, as we had come : Father Oldcorne stayed, his dwelling or residence being not far off.

CHAPTER VII.

SOME ACCOUNT OF FATHER OLDCORNE.

SINCE I have mentioned Father Oldcorne's residence, I will set forth in short how he came to take up his abode there. When he first arrived in England he tarried some time with the Superior, as he had no place of his own to go to. At a little distance from the Superior's residence in the country, there was a fine house [1] belonging to a Catholic gentleman, a prisoner in the Tower of London for

[1] This is Henlip House near Worcester. "The name," says Burke, in his Visitation of Seats, "is variously written, Hindelep, Hinlip, Hendlip, and Henlip. It signifies in Saxon, *the Hind's leap*. It was sold in the fifth year of Elizabeth, to John Habington or Abingdon, cofferer to the Queen. His son Thomas, who married a sister of Lord Monteagle, succeeded to his father's estate, but was a staunch partisan of Mary, Queen of Scots, and for his assisting in the attempt to release her, he suffered six years' imprisonment in the Tower." Father Oldcorne, Dr. Oliver tells us, resided at this house sixteen years. It was here that he and Father Garnet were discovered and captured, at the time of the Gunpowder Plot, after a search of eight days.

the Faith. He had a sister, a heretic, who had been brought up at the Queen's court. There she had drunk so deep of the poison of heresy, that no physician could be found to cure her, though many had tried. She readily spoke with them about religion, but she did so all for the sake of argument, and not for the sake of learning. Thus no profit was made of an excellent Catholic's house, of which she had the charge while her brother was away. The house was one which surpassed all in the county for beauty, pleasant situation, and the many advantages it offered to Catholics.

After many attempts had been made on the lady without effect, Father Garnet wished Father Old-corne to go and try his hand for once. He went, and found her very obstinate; plied her with arguments from Scripture, reason, and authority, but all in vain. The woman's obstinacy however did not foil the man's perseverance. He turned to God, and strove to cast out the deaf devil by prayer and fasting. She, seeing the Father eating nothing for the first and second day, began to wonder at his way of going on. Led on notwithstanding by obstinacy or curiosity, she said to herself, "Perhaps he is not a man but an angel; so I will see whether he subsists on angels' food; and if he does not, he shall not convert me." Accordingly the good Father kept up his fast for four days without tasting anything. By this steadfastness he discomfited the devil, and the woman was cured from that hour. He had truly obtained for her ears to hear, for from being very obstinate and headstrong, she became henceforth very obedient and humble. Father Oldcorne lived for sixteen years together in this residence and by his fruitful labours in this and the neighbouring counties, he won many to the faith, strengthened the wavering, and restored the fallen, besides stationing priests in divers places.

This it was that made several apply to him what St. Jerome writes of St. John, that he founded and governed all the churches in those parts; and in good sooth all looked up to him as to their father. Such was his prudence, that he fully satisfied all; such his diligence and endurance of toil, that he never failed any one in the hour of need; and his alms supplied the wants of many poor Catholics. In fact his house might have been one of our residences in a Catholic country, such was the number of Catholics flocking there to the Sacraments, to hear his sermons, and to take advice in their doubts. His helpmate was Father Thomas Lister, a man of distinguished learning.

While thus serving others, Father Oldcorne treated his own body with great harshness. Not satisfied with the labours I have set forth, and his "care for all the churches" in those parts, which really in great measure seemed to depend on him for everything, he had many ways of macerating his flesh. He applied hard to study while at home. Of his fasts I have already spoken. He made use of the hair-shirt, and still more of the discipline, with great fervour. By all this put together, while he thought only of chastising his enemy and bringing it under subjection, he nearly made himself an unprofitable servant. First he broke a blood-vessel, which caused him to vomit blood in quantities. He managed to get over this, but almost every year he fell into such a weakness that his strength could hardly be restored. From this infirmity there came a cancer in his mouth, which increased to such a degree as to be incurable. The doctors said, as he told me afterwards, that some bones which seemed decayed would have to be taken out. The good Father fearing thereby to be hindered from preaching, in which he was gifted by God with a marvellous talent, resolved first to go on a pilgrimage to St. Winifred's well, a famous place and a sort of standing miracle.

St. Winifred was a holy maiden in North Wales, comely of face, and comelier still for her faith and love of chastity. A son of one of the Welsh chieftains loved her and sought her hand. She rejected him, as well on account of his being a heathen, as because she had already vowed her virginity to God at the hands of the Bishop of the place, and was unwilling to yield it to man. The enraged chieftain's love turned into fury, and he cut off the maiden's head with a stroke of his sword. As this happened on the slope of a hill, the head rolled down to the bottom, where instantly burst forth a powerful spring of water. Ever since, the glen, which before got its name from its dryness, has had in it a copious stream of water, which takes its rise at that spring and flows on to the sea. Such a volume of water gushes out of the spring every minute, that it suffices to turn a mill at fifty paces distance. There are very large stones in the well, all red, as if covered with fresh blood. The people of the place are very loth to allow pieces to be cut off. Such pieces are also red, and the place of the cut changes from white to red in time. In the stream are also found many stones either covered or sprinkled with blood. The Catholics gather these, and treasure them up as objects of devotion, as they do the sweet-smelling moss that sticks to the stones. The water is very cold; but drinking it or bathing in it out of devotion has never done any one any harm. I myself have taken several draughts together fasting without hurt. On the feast of St. Winifred (the third of November), the water rises a foot higher than usual. It turns red on that day, and on the morrow is clearer than before. I visited it once on that day to witness the change, and found the water troubled and of a reddish hue, whereas it is generally so clear that you can see a pin at the bottom. It was winter, and freezing so hard at the time, that, though the ice had been broken the night before by the people crossing the stream, I had hard work to ford it on horseback the first thing next morning. Notwithstanding this severe frost, I went into the well, as all pilgrims do, and lay down and prayed there for a quarter of an hour. On coming out my shirt was of course dripping wet, but I did not change. I put on my clothes over it, and took no harm whatever.

These are wonderful facts, but in addition to them very signal miracles are often wrought there. A heretic visitor seeing the Catholics bathe out of devotion, said scoffingly, "What makes these fellows bathe in this water?—I'll wash my boots in it." He jumped in as he was with his boots on, and sword in hand. No sooner had he done so than he felt the supernatural power of the water, which before he had refused to believe. He was at once palsied and lost the use of his limbs, and his sword could hardly be got out of his hand. For several years he was drawn about in a little cart, a cripple, to punish his own unbelief and to strengthen the belief of others. I myself have spoken to several persons who saw the lame man, and heard the story vouched for both by the man himself and by all who knew him. I learnt from them that the cripple afterwards repented, and recovered his soundness in the same well where he had lost it. There are many other stories of the same sort.

Such was the place where the blessed Father Oldcorne determined to go, but St. Winifred was beforehand with him. He chanced on his way to reach the house of two maiden sisters, poor indeed in their way of life, but rich in the fear of God. They lived together in His service, keeping a priest in their house, whom they supported and honoured as a father. This good priest had a stone taken out of the stream that flows from the well, sprinkled with blood as I described before. He used to place it on the altar with the other relics. When Father Oldcorne saw it, he took it and kissed it with great reverence. Then going apart he fell on his knees and began to lick the stone, praying inwardly as he held part of it in his mouth. In half an hour all pain was gone, and the disease was cured. He travelled on to the well however, rather to return thanks than to ask any further favour. There he recovered also from the weakness of body which was thought to have brought on the cancer, and returned home as strong and hale as he had been for many a year. These are the words in which Father Oldcorne himself told me the story. The priest also in whose abode he found the stone, lately vouched for the facts when I met him at St. Omer's. He gave me an account of other marvels that happened at the death of Father Oldcorne, of which hereafter. So much then for Father Oldcorne, I return now to my own poor self.

CHAPTER VIII.

DURING my stay in this third residence, I gave the Spiritual Exercises to several persons. Among them were two men of high rank, who still stand to the good purposes which they then made. They are our staunchest friends in the districts where they live. One of them, Mr. John Lee, lately defended philosophy at Rome: he is always ready to entertain Ours and furnish them with money. The other has shown himself worthy of trust in many matters of moment. After five or six years each of them made another retreat with the most consoling result.

I sent also some young men abroad to study, with a view of entering on a more perfect state. One died at Douay, after great advancement in his studies, and with a wide-spread reputation for holiness. He had been the comrade of the blessed martyr Father Francis Page, S.J. They were both in an office in London. It was through his means that the blessed Father was first brought to me, to his no small profit, as I shall show hereafter. Some are now Fathers of the Society; for instance, Father Silvester and Father Clare, now living I think at the seminary of Valladolid. Others of my sending are now serving God in divers places and

divers conditions: among whom is Father John
Bolt. Great talent for music had won him the
warmest love of a very powerful man. He spurned
this love however, and all worldly hopes with it, to
attach himself to me; and lent his ear to the
counsels of Christ in the Spiritual Exercises.

At this time I had given me some very fine relics,
which my friends set for me very richly. Among
them was an entire thorn of the holy Crown of our
Lord, which the Queen of Scots had brought with
her from France (where the whole Crown is kept),
and had given to the Earl of Northumberland, who
was afterwards martyred. He always used to carry
it in a golden cross about his neck as long as he
lived, and at his death made it over to his daughter,
who gave it to me. It was enclosed in a golden
case set with pearls :[1] it is now in the hands of my
Superior, along with three other cases made of
silver with glass in front. Two of them are old
relics, rescued from the pillage of a monastery.
They came to me from a source that I could trust.
The third contains the forefinger of the martyr,
Father Thomas Sutton, brother of him whom I
mentioned in the first chapter. By a wonderful
providence of God, this finger, along with the
thumb, was kept from decay, though the whole arm
had been set up to be eaten by the birds of heaven.

[1] This precious relic is now at Stonyhurst. It was formerly at
our College at St. Omer's, and afterwards at Bruges. It was
however plundered at the suppression of the Society, but was
recovered some few years later by Mr. Weld of Lulworth, the
grandfather of the present proprietor, and by him restored to the
Society. The setting corresponds with Father Gerard's description.
The Holy Thorn is almost enveloped in several spiral strings of
pearls, and is enclosed in a glass cylinder, with stand and supports
of gold enamel.

It was taken away secretly by the Catholics after
it had been there a year, and was found quite bare.
The only parts that were covered with skin and
flesh were the thumb and finger, which had been
anointed at his ordination with the holy oil, and
made still more holy by the touch of the Blessed
Sacrament. So his brother, another pious priest,
kept the thumb himself, and gave the finger to me.[2]

I had given me about the same time a silver head
of St. Thomas of Canterbury; also his mitre set
with precious stones. The head, though neither
large nor costly, is very precious from having in it
a piece of the skull of the same Saint, which we
think was the piece that was cut off when he was
so wickedly slain. It is of the breadth of two gold
crowns. The silver head was old and had lost
some stones, so the gentleman, in whose house I
was, had it repaired and better ornamented. On
this account, the Superior afterwards let him keep
it in his private chapel in trust for the Society.

In like manner another Catholic gentleman in
that county has by the same permission a large
piece of the arm of St. Vita, virgin, daughter of a
king in the west of England. Many churches in
England are dedicated in her honour under the
name of Whitchurch. This relic reached me by
God's will in this manner. The parson of the
place where the whole or great part of her body
used to be kept in olden times with due honour,
began to be troubled in his rest, insomuch that he
could not sleep. The annoyance had lasted for
some time, when one day the thought struck him
that his troubles came from his not paying proper

[2] It is however certainly the *thumb* of the holy Priest that is to
be seen among the relics at Stonyhurst.

respect to these bones which he had in his keeping;
and that he ought to give them to the Catholics,
the rightful owners. He did so, and his rest was
never again broken. A good priest told me this
story, and gave me a large bone, which a pious
Catholic is keeping at present for the Society.

There was also given me some beautiful altar
furniture, which I used to the great comfort and
increase of devotion as well of the Catholics of the
house as of visitors.

CHAPTER IX.

BEGINNINGS OF DANGER.

BUT there is a time for gathering stones together,
and a time for scattering them. The time had now
come for trying the servants of God, my hosts, and
myself along with them. And that they might be
more like in their sufferings to their Lord for Whom
they suffered, God allowed them to be betrayed by
their own servant whom they loved. He was not
a Catholic, nor a servant of the house, but had been
once in the service of the second brother, who when
he crossed the sea recommended him to his mother
and brother. He lived in London, but often used to
visit them, and knew nearly everything that happened in either of their houses. I had no reason for
suspecting one whom all trusted. Still I never let
him see me acting as a priest, or dressed in such
a way as to give him grounds to say that I was
one. However, as he acknowledged afterwards, he
guessed what I was from seeing his master treat me
with such respect; for he nearly always set me two

or three miles on my journeys. Often too my host
would bear me company to London, where we used
at that time to lodge in this servant's house. I
had not yet found by experience, that the safest plan
was to have a lodging of my own. Such were the
facts which, as the traitor afterwards stated, gave
rise to his suspicions. Feeling sure that he could
get more than thirty pieces of silver from the sale of
his master, he went to the magistrates and bar-
gained to betray him. They, it seems, sent him for
a while to spy out who were priests, and how many
there were of them haunting the houses of the
widow and her son.

The widow's house was first searched. The priest
that usually dwelt there was then at home, but
escaped for that time by taking refuge in a hiding-
place. As for the pious widow, they forced her to
go to London, there to appear before the judges who
tried cases concerning Catholics. At her appearance
she answered with the greatest courage, more like a
free woman than a grievously persecuted prisoner.
She was thrown into jail, where she so united piety
with patience, as to do her own work like a menial,
cook her food with her own hands, and wash the
dishes. Her aim in this was to find her way by hu-
miliations to true humility of heart, and also to save
expense so as to be able to support more Catholics.
During her imprisonment she always used to send
me one half of her yearly income, to wit six hundred
florins (60*l.*); with the other half, besides many other
good works, she maintained a priest, to bring her
Holy Communion at stated times, and assist her
fellow-prisoners. She spent all her time either in
prayer or in working with her own hands, making
altar furniture which she sent to divers persons. The

holy woman persevered in these good works, till in
two years' time God called her to higher things.

It was His will that the heretics should come to
know that she received visits from a priest. If I
remember well, the priest was Father Jones, a
Franciscan Recollect, afterwards martyred. They
resolved therefore to use the law against the widow.
She was brought up, and the usual false witnesses
appeared, to accuse her of being privy to the maintenance of priests, contrary to the law of the land.
The judges at once empanelled a jury, to pronounce
her guilty or not guilty. The godly woman seeing
that the consciences of the jury would be stained
with her blood, if she let them give their verdict in
the case, made up her mind to hold her peace and
answer nought to the judges' demand whether she
was guilty or not guilty. At the same time she
knew well the provision of the law, that men or
women who refused to plead in a matter of life and
death should have far more keen and dreadful
torments than convicted felons. They are laid on
their backs upon a sharp stone; then a heavy
weight is put upon their breasts, which crushes the
sufferer to death. Till the time of which I treat
we had only had two female martyrs, not counting
the Queen of Scots. One named Clitherow, at
York, chose the same sort of martyrdom as the
widow, and for the same reason, namely to spare
the consciences of the jury, who she was sure would
find her guilty as usual to please the judges, even
though conscious of the injustice they were doing.
The godly widow of whom I am speaking, resolved
to follow this holy martyr's example. She had
made up her mind to take the same course and bear
the same punishment. So for her silence she was

sentenced to be crushed to death. She went from the court rejoicing that she had been held worthy to quit life in this manner for the name of Jesus. However on account of her rank, and the good name which she had, the Queen's councillors would not let such barbarity be practised in London. So they transferred her after her condemnation to a more loathsome prison, and kept her there, They wanted at the same time to seize her income for the Queen. Now if she had been dead, this income would not have gone to the Queen, but to the widow's son, my host. The godly woman therefore lived in this prison, reft of her goods but not of her life, of which she most desired to be reft. She pined in a narrow and filthy cell till the accession of King James, when, as is usual at the crowning of a new king, she received a pardon, and returned home; where she now serves the servants of God, and has two of Ours with her in the house. So much then for the good widow; to return to ourselves.

The hidden traitor, wholly unknown to his master, was watching his chance of giving us up without betraying his own treachery. At first he settled to have me seized in a house, which had been lately hired in London to answer my own and my friend's purposes. From his master's employing him in many affairs, he could not help knowing the place which his master had hired for my use. Consequently he promised the magistrates to tell them when I was coming, so that they might surround the house during the night with their officers, and cut off my escape. The plan would have succeeded, had not God brought it to pass otherwise through an act of obedience.

My Superior had lately come to live four or five miles from London. I had gone to see him, and had been with him a day or two, when, having business in London, I wrote to those who kept the house to expect me on such a night, and bring in certain friends whom I wanted to see. The traitor, who was now often seen in the house, which belonged ostensibly to his master, learnt the time, and got the priest-hunters to come there at midnight with their band.

Just before mounting my horse to depart, I went to take leave of my Superior. He would have me stay that night. I told him my business, and my wish to keep my appointment with my friends; but the blessed Father would not allow it, though as he said afterwards, he knew no reason, nor was it his wont to act in this manner.[1] Without doubt he was guided by the Holy Ghost; for early next morning we heard that some Papists had been

[1] An extract from a letter of Father Garnet which is copied in one of the Stonyhurst MSS., will not be uninteresting. It is dated, Sep. 6, 1594, and is written to Father Persons at Rome " The Friday night before Passion Sunday was such a hurly-burly in London as never was seen in man's memory ; no, not when Wyatt was at the gates. A general search in all London, the Justices and chief citizens going in person ; all unknown persons taken and put in churches till the next day. No Catholics found, but at one poor tailor's house at Golding-lane end, which was esteemed such a booty as never was got since this Queen's days. The tailor and divers others there taken lie yet in prison, and some of them have been tortured. That mischance touched us near ; they were our friends and chiefest instruments. That very night had been there *long John* with the little beard, once your pupil, [in the margin is written *John Gerard,*] if I had not more importunely stayed him than ever before. But soon after he was apprehended, being betrayed we know not how : he will be stout I doubt not." There will be opportunities of giving more from this and other letters as we proceed.

seized in that house, and the story ran that a priest was among them. The fact was that my servant, Richard Fulwood, was caught trying to hide himself in a dark place, there being as yet no regular hiding-places, though I meant to make some. As he cut a good figure, and neither the traitor nor any one else that knew him was there, he was taken for a priest. Three Catholics and one schismatic were seized and thrown into prison. The latter was a Catholic at heart, but did not refuse to go to the heretics' churches. As he was a trusty man, I employed him as keeper of the house, to manage any business in the neighbourhood. At their examination they all showed themselves steadfast and true, and answered nothing that could give the enemy any inkling that the house belonged to me instead of to my host. It was well that it was so; for things would have gone harder with the latter had it been otherwise. The magistrates sent him a special summons, in the hope that my arrest would enable them to make out a stronger case against him. As soon as he arrived in London, he went straight to the house, never dreaming what had happened there, in order to treat with me as to the reason of his summons, and how he was to answer it. So he came and knocked at the door. It was opened to him at once; but, poor sheep of Christ, he fell into the clutches of wolves, instead of the arms of his shepherd and friend. For the house had been broken into the night before, and there were some ministers of Satan still lingering there, to watch for any Catholics that might come, before all got scent of the danger. Out came these men then; the good gentleman found himself ensnared, and was led prisoner to the magistrates.

" How many priests do you keep in your house ? "
—" Who are they ? " were the questions poured in
upon him on all sides. He made answer, that
harbouring priests was a thing punishable with
death, and so he had taken good care not to run
such a risk. On their still pressing him, he said
that he was ready to meet any accusation that
could be brought against him on this head. However they would not hint anything about me,
because though disappointed this time, they still
hoped to catch me later, as the traitor was as yet
unsuspected.

My host had on hand a translation of a work of
Father Jerome Platus, "On the happiness of a Religious State." He had just finished the second
part, and had brought it with him to see me about it.
When he was seized, these papers were seized too.
Being asked what they were, he said it was a book
of devotion. Now the heretics are wont to pry
into any writings that they find, because they are
afraid of any thing being published against themselves and their false doctrine. Not having time to
go on with the whole case, they were very earnest
about his being answerable for those papers. He
said that there was nothing contained in them
against the state or against sound teaching ; and
offered on the spot to prove the righteousness and
holiness of everything that was there set down. In
so doing, as he told me afterwards, he felt great
comfort at having to answer for so good a book.
He was thrown into prison, and kept in such close
confinement that only one of his servants was allowed to go near him, and that was the traitor.
Knowing that his master had no inkling of his bad
faith, they hoped by his means to find out my

F

retreat, and seize my person much sooner than they could otherwise have done.

On learning the seizure of our house at London and my host's imprisonment, I went down to his country-house to settle with his wife and friends what was to be done, and put all our effects in safe keeping. As we wanted the altar furniture for the approaching Easter, we sent very little of it to our friends. Of course I could not stay away from my entertainers at so holy a time, especially as they were in sorrow and trouble. In Holy Week the treacherous servant came from London with a letter from his master, wherein the latter set forth all that had befallen him, the questions that had been put to him, and his answers. This letter, though seen, had been let pass for the credit of the bearer, to give him a chance of seeing whether I was in the house at this solemn season. He brought me another letter from my servant, whose capture I spoke of above. When by the traitor's information they knew him to be my servant, hoping to wrest from him the disclosure of his friends and abettors, they kept him in solitary confinement in the loathsome prison of Bridewell. The purport of the letter was how he had denied everything,[2] what threats had been held out to him, and what his sufferings were in prison. He had, he said, hardly

---

[2] It was of the last importance for the friends of a prisoner to know, if possible, what replies he had really given, not only that they might take measures, if necessary, for their own safety, but also that they might know how far to go in their own answers when summoned. The persecutors were in the habit of publishing all sorts of pretended replies which they said had been given by prisoners in their secret examinations, so that prisoners seized every possible opportunity of communicating the truth to their friends; often, as we shall see, in the most ingenious way.

enough black bread to keep him from starving ; his abode was a narrow strongly-built cell, in which there was no bed, so that he had to sleep sitting on the window-sill, without taking off his clothes. There was a little straw in the place, but it was so trodden down and swarming with vermin that he could not lie on it.   But what was most intolerable to him was their leaving all that came from him in an open vessel in that narrow den, so that he was continually distressed and almost stifled by the smell.   Besides all this he was daily awaiting an examination by torture.   While reading the letter to my hostess in presence of the traitor, I chanced to say at this last part, " I wish I could bear some of his tortures, so that there might be less for him." It 'was these words of mine that let us know later on who was the traitor, and author of all our woes. For when I was taken and questioned, those who were examining me forgot their secret, and asked, " Did you not say so and so before such a lady, as you read your servant's letter ?"   But to take up the thread of my story.

CHAPTER X.

THE traitor on his return to London informed our enemies of everything. Forthwith they sent two of their best messengers, or pursuivants as they call them, to two gentlemen of the county who were justices of the peace, bidding them search the house carefully with their men. The traitor also returned on Easter Sunday on pretence of bringing a fresh letter from London, but in reality to play into the hands of our enemies and acquaint them with our plans. On Easter Monday, on account of the dangers that threatened us, we rose before our usual hour, and were trying to get ready for Mass before sun-rise, when suddenly we heard the noise of horses galloping, and of a multitude of men coming to surround the house and cut off all escape. Seeing what was going to happen, we had the doors kept fast. Meanwhile the ornaments were pulled off the altar, the hiding-places thrown open, my books and papers carried into them, and an effort was made to hide me and all my effects together. I wanted to get into a hiding-place near the dining-room, as well to be further from the chapel and the more suspicious part of the house, as because there was store of provisions there, to wit, a bottle of wine, and certain light but strengthening food, such as biscuit made to keep. Moreover I hoped

to hear there our enemies' talk, wherein there might
be something perchance which bore upon our interests. These reasons then moved me to choose
that place, and in sooth it was very fit and safe
for hiding in. But God so willed it, that the mistress of the house should in no wise agree. She
would have me go into a place near the chapel,
where the altar furniture could sooner be stowed
with me. I yielded, though there was nothing there
for me to eat in case the search should last long. I
went in then, after everything was safe that needed
putting away.

Scarcely had I done so, when the searchers broke
down the door and forcing their way in, spread
through the house with great noise and racket.
Their first step was to lock up the mistress of the
house in her own room with her two daughters;
and the Catholic servants they kept locked up in
divers places in the same part of the house. They
then took to themselves the whole house, which
was of a good size, and made a thorough search
in every part, not forgetting even to look under the
tiles of the roof. The darkest corners they examined
with the help of candles. Finding nothing whatever, they began to break down certain places that
they suspected. They measured the walls with
long rods, so that if they did not tally, they might
pierce the part not accounted for. Thus they
sounded the walls and all the floors, to find out and
break into any hollow places that there might be.

They spent two days in this work without finding
anything. Thinking therefore that I had gone on
Easter Sunday, the two magistrates went away on
the second day, leaving the pursuivants to take the
mistress of the house, and all her Catholic servants

of both sexes to London, to be examined, and imprisoned. They meant to leave some who were not
Catholics to keep the house, the traitor being one of
them. The good lady was pleased at this, for she
hoped that he would be the means of freeing me, and
rescuing me from death : for she knew that I had
made up my mind to suffer and die of starvation
between two walls, rather than come forth and save
my own life at the expense of others. In fact
during those four days that I lay hid, I had nothing
to eat but a biscuit or two and a little quince jelly,
which my hostess had at hand and gave me as I
was going in. She did not look for any more, as
she supposed that the search would not last beyond
a day. But now that two days were gone, and
she was to be carried off on the third with all her
trusty servants, she began to be afraid of my dying
of sheer hunger. She bethought herself then of
the traitor, who she heard was to be left behind.
He had made a great fuss and show of eagerness in
withstanding the searchers, when they first forced
their way in. For all that, she would not have let
him know of the hiding-places, had she not been
in such straits. Thinking it better however to rescue
me from certain death, even at some risk to herself, she charged him, when she was taken away,
and everyone had gone, to go into a certain room,
call me by my wonted name, and tell me that the
others had been taken to prison, but that he was left
to deliver me. I would then answer, she said, from
behind the lath and plaster where I lay concealed.

The traitor promised to obey faithfully, but he
was faithful only to the faithless,[1] for he unfolded

---

[1] Fidelis tantum erat infidelibus.—*MS.*

the whole matter to the ruffians who had remained behind. No sooner had they heard it, than they called back the magistrates who had departed. These returned early in the morning, and renewed the search. They measured and sounded everywhere, much more carefully than before, especially in the chamber above mentioned, in order to find out some hollow place. But finding nothing whatever during the whole of the third day, they purposed on the morrow to strip off all the plaster of that room. Meanwhile they set guards in all the rooms about, to watch all night lest I should escape. I heard from my hiding-place the pass-word which the captain of the band gave to his soldiers, and I might have got off by using it, were it not that they would have seen me issuing from my retreat : for there were two on guard in the chapel where I got into my hiding-place, and several also in the large plastered room which had been pointed out to them.

But mark the wonderful providence of God. Here was I in my hiding-place. The way I got into it was by taking up the floor, made of wood and bricks, under the fire-place. The place was so constructed that a fire could not be lit in it without damaging the house ; though we made a point of keeping wood there, as if it were meant for a fire. Well, the men on the night watch lit a fire in this very place, and began chatting together close to it. Soon the bricks, which had not bricks but wood underneath them, got loose and nearly fell out of their places, as the wood gave way. On noticing this and probing the place with a stick, they found that the bottom was made of wood ; whereupon they remarked that this was something curious. I

·thought that they were going there and then to break open the place and enter, but they made up their minds at last to put off further examination till next day. Meanwhile, though nothing was further from my thoughts than any chance of escaping, I besought the Lord·earnestly, that ·if it were for the glory of His Name, I might not be taken in that house, and so endanger my entertainers; nor in any other house, where others would share my disaster. My prayer was heard. I was preserved in that house in a wonderful manner; and when, a few days after, I was taken, it was without prejudice to any one, as shall be presently seen.

Next morning therefore they renewed the search most carefully, everywhere except in the top chamber which served as a chapel, and in which the two watchmen had made a fire over my head and had noticed the strange make of the grate. God had blotted out of their memory all remembrance of the thing. Nay, none of the searchers entered the place the whole day, though it was the one that was most open to suspicion, and if they had entered, they would have found me without any search; rather, I should say, they would have seen me, for the fire had burnt a great hole in my hiding-place, and had I not got a little out of the way, the hot embers would have fallen on me. The searchers, forgetting or not caring about this room, busied themselves in ransacking the rooms below, in one of which I was said to be. In fact they found the other hiding-place, which I thought of going into, as I mentioned before. It was not far off, so I could hear their shouts of joy when they first found it. But after joy comes grief: and so it was with them. The only thing that they found, was a goodly store of provision laid up. Hence they may have thought that this was the place that the mistress of the house meant; in fact an answer might have been given from it to the call of a person in the room mentioned by her.

They stuck to their purpose however, of stripping off all the plaster work of the other large room. So they set a man to work near the ceiling, close to the place where I was: for the lower part of the walls was covered with tapestry, not with plaster. So they stripped off the plaster all round, till they came again to the very place where I lay, and there they lost heart and gave up the search. My hiding-place was in a thick wall of the chimney, behind a finely inlaid and carved mantelpiece. They could not well take the carving down without risk of breaking it. Broken however it would have been, and that into a thousand pieces, had they any conception that I could be concealed behind it. But knowing that there were two flues, they did not think that there could be room enough there for a man. Nay, before this, on the second day of the search they had gone into the room above, and tried the fireplace through which I had got into my hole. They then got into the chimney by a ladder to sound with their hammers. One said to another in my hearing, " Might there not be a place here for a person to get down into the wall of the chimney below, by lifting up this hearth ? " " No," answered one of the pursuivants, whose voice I knew, " you could not get down that way into the chimney underneath but there might easily be an entrance at the back of this chimney." So saying, he gave the place a kick. I was afraid that he would hear the hollow sound of the hole where I was. But God who set bounds to the sea, said also to their dogged obstinacy, "Thus far shalt thou go and no further;" and He spared His sorely-stricken children, and gave them not up into their persecutors' hands, nor allowed utter ruin to light upon them for their great charity towards me.

Seeing that their toil availed them naught, they thought that I had escaped somehow, and so they went away at the end of four days, leaving the mistress and her servants free. The yet unbetrayed traitor stayed after the searchers were gone. As soon as the doors of the house were made fast, the mistress came to call me, another four-days-buried Lazarus, from what would have been my tomb had the search continued a little longer. For I was all wasted and weakened, as well with hunger, as with want of sleep, and with having to sit so long in such a narrow place. The mistress of the house too had eaten nothing whatever during the whole time, not only to share my distress, and to try on herself how long I could live without food, but chiefly to draw down the mercy of God on me, herself, and her family, by this fasting and prayer. Indeed her face was so changed when I came out, that she seemed quite another woman, and I should not have known her but for her voice and her dress. After coming out I was seen by the traitor, whose treachery was still unknown to us. He did nothing then, not even send after the searchers, as he knew that I meant to be off, before they could be recalled.

CHAPTER XI.

MY CAPTURE AND EXAMINATIONS.

As soon as I had taken a little refreshment and rest, I set out and went to a friend's house, where I kept still for a fortnight. Then knowing that I had left my friends in great distress, I proceeded to London to aid and comfort them. I got a safe lodging with a person of rank.[1] A year ago it had been Father Southwell's abode, before his seizure and imprisonment in the Tower of London, where he now was. I wanted however to hire a house where I might be safe and unknown, and be free to treat with my friends; for I could not manage my business in a house that was not my own, especially in such a one as I then dwelt in. I had recourse to a servant of Father Garnet, named Little John,[2] an excellent man and one well able to help me. He it was that used to make our hiding-places; in

[1] This was the unfortunate Countess of Arundel, whose husband Philip Howard, Earl of Arundel, was at this time (1594) in the tenth year of his imprisonment in the Tower. He died the following year in the same prison, the noblest victim to the jealous and suspicious tyranny of Elizabeth, *non sine veneni suspicione*, as his coffin-plate still testifies.

[2] This holy martyr's true name was Nicholas Owen. Father Gerard speaks at length about him farther on. In those times every priest and priest's servant had a *sobriquet* or *alias*, to baffle the persecutors. Father Gerard has already mentioned two of his own; he also very commonly went by the name of Thomson; and it is under this name that he is spoken of by Tanner.

fact he had made the one to which I owed my safety. Thanks to his endeavours I found a house well suited for my purpose. The next thing was to agree with the landlord about the rent, a matter which was soon settled. Till the house was furnished, I hired a room in my landlord's own house. There I resolved to pass two or three nights in arranging my affairs, getting letters from my friends in distress, and writing back letters of comfort in return. Thus it was that the traitor got sent to the place, which was only known to a small circle of friends. It was God's will that my hour should then come.

One night the traitor had to bring a letter that needed an answer, and left with the answer about ten o'clock. I had only come in about nine, sore against the will of the lady, my entertainer, who was uncommonly earnest that I should not leave her house that night. Away went the traitor then, and gave information to the priest-hunters both when and where he had left me. They got together a band, and came at midnight to the house, just as I had gone to sleep. Little John and I were both awakened by the noise outside. I guessed what it was, and told John to hide the letter received that night in the ashes where the fire had been. No sooner had he done so and got into bed again, than the noise which we had heard before seemed to travel up to our room. Then some men began knocking at the chamber-door, ready to break it in if it was not opened at once. There was no exit except by the door where our foes were; so I bade John get up and open the door. The room was at once filled with men, armed with swords and staves; and many more stood outside, who were not able to enter. Among the rest stood two pursuivants, one of whom knew me well, so there was no chance of my passing unknown.

I got up and dressed, as I was bid. All my effects were searched, but without a single thing being found that could do harm to any man. My companion and I were then taken off to prison. By God's grace we did not feel distressed, nor did we show any token of fear. What I was most afraid of, was that they had seen me come out of that lady's house, and had tracked me to the room that I had hired; and so that the noble family that had harboured me would suffer on my account. But this fear was unfounded; for I learnt afterwards that the traitor had simply told them where he had left me, and there it was that they found me.

The pursuivant who knew me, kept me in his house two nights; either because those who were to examine me were hindered from doing so on the first day, or (as it struck me afterwards) because they wished first to examine my companion, Little John. I noticed the first night, that the room where I was locked up was not far from the ground; and that it would be easy to let myself down from the window, by tearing up the bed-clothes and making a rope of them. I should have done so that very night, had I not heard some one stirring in the next room. I thought that he was put there to watch me, and so it turned out. However I meant to carry my plan out the night after, if the watchman went away; but my keeper forestalled me; for to save the expense of a guard, he put irons on my arms, which hindered me both from bringing my hands together and from separating them.

Then in truth I was more at ease in mind though less in body; for the thought of escape vanished, and there came in its place a feeling of joy that I had been vouchsafed this suffering for the sake of Christ, and I thanked the Lord for it as well as I could.

Next day I was brought before the Commissioners,[8] at the head of whom was one who is now Lord Chancellor of the realm. He had been a Catholic, but went over to the other side, for he loved the things of this world.

They first asked me my name and calling. I gave them the name I passed by; whereupon one called me by my true name, and said that I was a Jesuit. As I was aware that the pursuivant knew me, I answered that I would be frank and open in everything that belonged to myself, but would say nothing that could affect others. So I told them my name and calling, to wit that, though most unworthy, I was a priest of the Society of Jesus.

"Who sent you into England?" they asked.

"The Superiors of the Society."

"To what end?"

"To bring back stray souls to their Creator."

"No, no:" said they, "you were sent for matters of State: and to lure people from the obedience of the Queen to the obedience of the Pope."

"As for matters of State," I replied, "we are

---

[8] Honorarios arbitros seu examinatores.—*MS.* The rendering is conjectural. Perhaps the words are intended to signify some members of the Privy Council. Sir Thomas Egerton, afterwards Lord Ellesmere, was Attorney General at this date, 1594, and later on became Chancellor. It is not easy to see whom else Father Gerard can allude to as presiding at his examination, although Lord Campbell, in his Lives of the Chancellors, says nothing of Egerton's having been a Catholic.

forbidden to have anything to say to them, as they do not belong to our Institute. This prohibition indeed extends to all the members of the Society; but on us missioners it is particularly enjoined in a special instruction. As for the obedience due to the Queen and the Pope, each is to be obeyed in that wherein they have jurisdiction; and one obedience does not clash with the other, as England and all Christian realms have hitherto experienced."

"How long have you been doing duty as a priest in this country?"

"About six years."

"How and where did you land, and where have you lived since your landing?"

"I cannot in conscience answer any of these questions," I replied, "especially the last, as it would bring mischief on others; so I crave pardon for not satisfying your wishes."

"Nay," said they, "it is just on these heads that we chiefly desire you to satisfy us, and we bid you in the Queen's name to do so."

"I honour the Queen," said I, "and will obey her and you in all that is lawful, but here you must hold me excused: for were I to mention any person or place where I have been lodged, the innocent would have to suffer, according to your laws, for the kind service they have done me. Such behaviour on my part would be against all justice and charity, and therefore I never will be guilty of it."

"You shall do so by force, if not by good will."

"I hope," I said, "by the grace of God, it shall not be as you say. I beg you therefore to take this my answer; that neither now nor at any other time will I disclose what you demand of me."

Thereupon they wrote a warrant for my impri-

sonment, and gave it to the pursuivants, bidding
them take me to prison. As we were leaving, he
who is now Chancellor said that I must be kept in
close confinement, as in cases of high treason:
" But tell the gaolers," he added, "to treat him well
on account of his birth." It seems however that
the head gaoler gave orders at variance with this
humane recommendation: for I was lodged in a
garret [4] where there was nothing but a bed, and no
room to stand up straight, except just where the bed
was. There was one window always open, through
which foul air entered and rain fell on to my bed.
The room door was so low, that I had to enter not
on my feet, but on my knees, and even then I was
forced to stoop. However I reckoned this rather an
advantage, inasmuch as t helped to keep out the
stench (certainly no small one) that came from the
privy close to my door, which was used by all the
prisoners in that part of the house. I was often
kept awake, or woke up, by the bad smell.

In this place I passed two or three days of true
repose. I felt no pain or anxiety of mind, and
enjoyed, by the blessing of God, that peace which
the world does not and cannot give.

On the third or fourth day, I was taken for a
second examination to the house of a magistrate
called Young. He it was who had the management
of all the searches and persecutions that the
Catholics in the neighbourhood of London had to
endure; and it was to him that the traitor had
given his information. Along with him was another,
who had for many years conducted the examina-

---

[4] Father Gerard was first confined in the Counter, as he tells us
later. Father Garnet in one of his letters speaks of the Counter
as "a very evil prison and without comfort."

tions by torture, Topcliffe by name. He was a man of cruelty, athirst for the blood of the Catholics, and so crafty and cunning, that all the wily wit of his companion seemed abashed into silence by his presence; in fact the justice spoke very little during the whole examination. I found the two of them alone; Young in a civilian's dress, Topcliffe with a sword by his side and in a court dress.[5] He was an old man, grown grey in wickedness. Young began questioning me as to my place of abode, and the Catholics that I knew. I answered that I neither could nor would make disclosures that would get any one into trouble, for reasons already stated. He turned then to Topcliffe and said: "I told you how you would find him."

Topcliffe looked frowningly at me and said:

"Do you know me? I am Topcliffe, of whom I doubt not you have often heard."

He meant this to frighten me. To heighten the effect, he had laid his sword on the table near his hand, as though he were ready to use it on occasion. But he failed certainly, and caused me not the least alarm; and whereas I was wont to answer with deference on other occasions, this time I did quite the contrary, because I saw him making a show to scare me. Finding that he could get no other manner of reply from me than what I had given, he took a pen and wrote an artful and malicious form of examination.

"Here," says he, "read this paper; I shall show it to the Privy Council, that they may see what a traitor you are to the realm, and how manifestly guilty."

---

[5] This brutal officer was a Queen's messenger, or pursuivant, as they were sometimes called.

The contents of the paper were as follows :

" The examinee was sent by the Pope and the Jesuit Persons, and coming through Belgium there had interviews with the Jesuit Holt and Sir William Stanley: thence he came into England, on a political errand, to beguile the Queen's subjects, and lure them from their obedience to their Sovereign. If therefore he will not disclose the places and persons with whom he has lived, it is presumed that he has done much mischief to the state, etc."

On reading this, I saw that I could not meet so many falsehoods with one single denial ; and as I was desirous that he should show my way of answering to the Council, I said that I also wished to answer in writing. Hereat Topcliffe was over-joyed, and cried out, " Oh! now you are a reasonable man : " but he was disappointed. He had hoped to catch me in my words, or at least to find out my hand-writing, so that some of the papers found in the houses of the Catholics might be proved to be mine. I foresaw this, and therefore wrote in a feigned hand as follows :

" I was sent by my Superiors. I never was in Belgium ; I have not seen Father Holt since the time that I left Rome. I have not seen Sir Wil-liam Stanley since he left England with the Earl of Leicester. I am forbidden to meddle with matters of State ; I never have done so, and never will. I have tried to bring back souls to the knowledge and love of their Creator, and to make them show obedience to the laws of God and man ; and I hold this last point to be a matter of conscience. I humbly crave that my refusal to answer anything concerning the persons that I know, may not be set down to contempt of authority ; seeing that God's commandment forces me to follow this course, and to act otherwise would be against charity and justice."

While I was writing this, the old man waxed wroth. He shook with passion, and would fain have snatched the paper from me.

" If you don't want me to write the truth," said I, "I'll not write at all."

"Nay," quoth he, " write so and so, and I'll copy out what you have written."

"I shall write what *I* please," I answered, "and not what *you* please. Show what I have written to the Council, for I shall add nothing but my name."

This I signed so near the writing, that nothing could be put in between. The hot-tempered man, seeing himself disappointed, broke out into threats and blasphemies :

" I'll get you put into my power, and hang you in the air, and show you no mercy ; and then I shall see what God will rescue you out of my hands."

From the abundance of his heart he poured forth these evil words; but by this he raised my hopes, just the opposite effect to what he wanted.[6] Neither then nor since have I ever reckoned aught of a blasphemer; and in sooth I have found by experience, that God increases the confidence of His servants, when He allows strife to rise up against them. I gave therefore this short answer:

[6] Even the gentle Father Southwell could not but show his estimate of this reprobate man. We translate the following from Father More's *History of the English Province*: Lib. V. n. 15.— "Though he readily answered the questions of others, yet if Topcliffe interposed he never deigned him a reply : and when asked the cause of this, he answered : ' Because I have found by experience that the man is not open to reason.' "

"You will be able to, do nothing, without the leave of God, Who never abandons those that hope in Him. The will of God be done."

Thereupon Young called the gaoler who had brought me, to take me back to prison. As he was leading me off, Topcliffe addressed him and bade him put irons on my legs. Both then fell a-chiding him for having brought me by himself, fearing perchance lest I should escape from his hands.

When I had crept back to my little closet, my legs were garnished according to order. The man seemed grieved that put the fetters on. For my part instead of grief I felt very much joy, such is God's goodness to the most unworthy of His creatures. To pay the man for the kind turn that he had done me, I gave him some money for his job; and told him it was no punishment to suffer in so good a cause.

CHAPTER XII.

A DIGRESSION.

HERE I stayed upwards of three months. During the first month I made from memory, as well as I could, the Spiritual Exercises; giving four and sometimes five hours a day to meditation. God lavished His goodness on me throughout, and I had proof that He opens His bounteous hand to His servants most of all, when He has closed up the sources of earthly comfort to them.

While I was quietly lodged in prison, without being brought out or undergoing any further examination for many days, they examined and put to the torture Richard Fulwood whom the traitor had pointed out as my servant, and Little John who had been taken with me. Unable, either by coaxing or bribery, to draw anything from them that would compromise others, they had recourse to threats and then to force: but the force of the Holy Ghost in them was too great to be overcome by men. They were both hung up for three hours together, having their arms fixed into iron rings, and their bodies hanging in the air; a torture which causes frightful pain and intolerable extension of the sinews. It was all to no purpose; no disclosure could be wrested from them that was hurtful to others; no rewards could entice, no threats or punishments force them, to discover where I or

any of Ours had been harboured, or to name any of
our acquaintance or abettors.

Here I ought not to pass over in silence God's
great goodness and mercy to me, the most unworthy of all his servants. It was shown in this,
that there was not a single traitor, either among
those that were then seized in my house or in the
house of the good gentleman, my entertainer; no,
nor even among those that in the other persecutions,
which by God's providence afterwards befel me,
were imprisoned, tortured, and treated with the
utmost cruelty. Not one of them, I say, ever
yielded, but all by the grace of God held steadfast
through everything. Those whom I used as companions, or the servants I entrusted with commis-
sions to the gentlemen of my acquaintance, as they
necessarily knew all my friends, would have been
able to do very great mischief, and enrich themselves by ruining others: yet no one of them ever
caused any harm either by word or deed, wittingly
or unwittingly; nor, as far as I remember, did they
ever give any one matter of complaint. On many
of them, God, in His goodness, poured the choicest
gifts of His Holy Spirit.

John Lasnet, the first that I had, died in Spain
a Lay-brother of the Society. The second that I
had for some little while, was Michael Walpole,
who is now a priest of the Society and labouring in
England. The third was named Willis. He had
a vocation, so I sent him to study in the seminary
at Rhemes, where he went through his course of
philosophy. His behaviour there was orderly, but
afterwards at Rome he joined a turbulent party,
thus returning evil for good. He was the only one
of my helpmates that walked at all awry. He was

however made Priest, and sent into England. There he was seized, and condemned to death for the faith, and answered unflinchingly before the tribunal; but instead of losing his life, he was kept some time in prison; whence he effected his escape, and is still labouring in England.

After him I had a godly man of the name of John Sutton, the brother of three priests, one of whom was a martyr, and another died in the Society. Father Garnet kept him in his house for many years, up to the time of his own arrest.

The next that I had was Richard Fulwood, of whom I have spoken above. He managed to make his escape, and during my imprisonment was employed by Father Garnet until that Father's happy death. He managed nearly all his master's business with strangers, not without the knowledge of the persecutors, who offered a handsome sum for his capture, and were still more earnest about it after Father Garnet was taken. In fact they gave the poor man no peace until they drove him into banishment, where he yet remains, doing good service to our mission notwithstanding.

After him I had John Lilly, a man well-known at Rome; he died lately in England, a lay-brother of the Society. Next came two other godly men, whom I did not take to keep, but merely as makeshifts, till I could get a man every way suited to my wants, and endowed with a religious spirit. I found one at length; and when I quitted England, I took him with me, and left him at St. Omer's. There he was well grounded in Greek and Latin, and became a great favourite with all the Fathers, who sent him into Spain with the highest recommendations. He still remains there, growing always in virtue and learning. Not long ago I had a letter from the Father Prefect of Studies, in which he tells me that he is the best student in his course.

Such were the mercies of God vouchsafed to me His unworthy servant, in answer to my constant prayers. Many gentlemen entrust themselves and their interest to our servants' good faith no less than to ours; so that there could be no greater let or hinderance to our good work, than any treachery on their part: indeed the defection of such a one would be likely to cause the most frightful ruin among Catholics. For if one servant, and he neither a Catholic nor one of the household, like the traitor of whom I have spoken, made such havoc in his master's family, what mischief could a priest's servant do to the many persons of high rank, that had harboured him and his master! God has hitherto kept me free from the like betrayal.

To return to my story. They could wrest nothing out of Little John and Fulwood; and none of my host's Catholic servants would make any avowal, or own that they knew me. Seeing that they could bring no witness against him (Mr. Wiseman), the heretics gradually lost the hope they had of seizing all his chattels and revenue.

CHAPTER XIII.

SOMETIMES they would bring me up for examination, when they had anything new against me. Once they, called me to try on a suit of clothes, which had been found in my host's house, and which the traitor said were mine. I put them on and they were just a fit, for the truth was that they had been made for me; however I would not own them, nor admit them to be mine. Hereupon Young flew into a passion, calling me a headstrong and unreasonable man. He was so barefaced as to add:

"How much more sensible is Southwell, who after long wilfulness is now ready to conform, and wishes to treat with some man of learning."

"Nay," I answered, "I will never believe that Father Southwell wishes to treat with any one from any wavering in his faith, or to learn what to believe from a heretic: but he might perchance challenge any heretic to dispute with him that dared, as Father Campian did, and as many others would do if you would let them, and appoint proper umpires."

Then Young, seizing hold of the book and kissing it, cried:

"I swear upon this book that Southwell has offered to treat, with a view of embracing our religion."

"I do not believe he ever did so," said I.

"What," said an officer of the court, "do you not believe his oath?"

"No," was my reply, "I neither can nor will believe him; for I have a better opinion of Father Southwell's firmness than of his truthfulness; since perhaps he thinks that he is allowed to make this statement to beguile me."

"No such thing," said Young: "But are you ready to conform if he has done so?" (To conform in the Protestant sense, means to embrace their deformed religion.)

"Certainly not," I answered; "for if I keep myself free from heresy and heretical meetings, it is not because he or any man on earth does the same; but because to act otherwise would be to deny Christ, by denying His faith, which may be done by deed as well as by word. This is what our Lord forbade under pain of a heavier punishment than man can inflict, when He said, 'He that shall deny Me before men, him will I deny before My Father Who is in Heaven.'"

To this the heretic answered not a word, save that I was stiff-necked, (a word that was applicable rather to himself,) and bade them take me back to prison.

Another time I was sent for to be confronted with three witnesses, servants of a certain nobleman named Lord Henry Seymour, son of the Duke of Somerset. They were heretics, and avouched that on a certain day I had dined with their mistress and her sister, whilst they among others waited at table. The two sisters were daughters of the Earl of Northumberland. One of them was a devout Catholic, and had come to London a little before my imprisonment, to get my help in passing over to Belgium, there to consecrate herself to God. She was staying at the house of her sister, the wife of the aforesaid lord. She wanted to bring back this sister to the Catholic faith, which the latter had abandoned after her good father's death. I dined with them on the day the witnesses mentioned. It was in Lent; and they told how their mistress ate meat, while the Lady Mary and I ate nothing but fish. Young flung this charge in my teeth with an air of triumph, as though I could not help acknowledging it, and thereby disclosing some of my acquaintances. I answered that I did not know the men whom he had brought up.

" But we know you," said they, " to be the same that was at such a place on such a day."

"You wrong your mistress," said I, "in saying so. I however will not so wrong her."

"What a barefaced fellow you are! " exclaimed Young.

"Doubtless," I answered, "were these men's statement true : as for me, I cannot speak positively in the matter, for reasons that I have often alleged ; let them look to the truth and justice of what they say."

Young then, in a rage, remanded me to prison.

CHAPTER XIV.

AFTER three months, some of my friends made efforts to have me removed to another more comfortable prison, seeing that nothing could be proved against me except my priesthood; and this they obtained by means of a handsome bribe to Young. So they sent to my prison, which was called the Counter, and took off my fetters. These were rusty when they were first put on; but by wearing and moving about in them every day, I had rendered them quite bright and shining. My cell was so small, that a man who had his legs free, might take the whole length of it in three steps. I used to shuffle from one end to the other, as well for exercise, as because the people underneath used to sing lewd songs and Geneva psalms; and I wanted to drown by the clanking of my chain, a noise that struck still harsher on my ear. My fetters then being removed, and my expenses paid, (which were not great, as I had had little but butter and cheese to season my bread withal,) they brought me before Young, who, making a show of anger, began to chide and upbraid me more than was his wont, and asked me whether I was yet willing to acknowledge where and with whom I had lived? I answered that I could not do so with a safe conscience, and therefore would not.

"Well then," said he, "I will put you in closer confinement, where you shall be safer lodged, and have iron bars before your window."

Forthwith he wrote a warrant and sent me to the prison that is called the Clink.[1] He made all this show, that he might not appear to have taken money for what he did. The fact was, that the prison to which I was now sent was far better than the other, and more comfortable for all prisoners; but to me it afforded especial comfort, on account of the great number of Catholics whom I found there.

They could not now hinder me from approaching the sacraments, and being comforted in divers other ways, as I shall afterwards show; for when I had been there a few months, the place was by God's grace so improved, that as for discharging all the duties of the Society, I should never wish to be at large in England, provided I could always live in the like prison and after the like fashion. So my my being shut up in the Clink, seemed like a change from purgatory to paradise. Instead of lewd songs and blasphemies, the prayers of some Catholic neighbours in the next room met my ear. They came to my door to cheer me up, and showed me a way by which we could open a freer communication. This was through a hole in the wall, which they had covered with a picture, that it might not be seen. By means of it, they gave me, on the morrow, a letter from my friends; and at the same time furnished me with materials for writing back.

[1] This was a prison in Southwark. In Father More's Latin narrative it appears as *Atrium Wintoniense.* Southwark is in the Diocese of Winchester, and much property in that neighbourhood belonged of old to the Bishop.

I wrote therefore to Father Garnet, and told him
the whole truth of what had happened to me, and
what manner of replies I had made, as I have set
forth above.

I also confessed, and received the Most Holy
Body of Christ, through the same hole. But I had
not to do this long, for the Catholics contrived to
fashion a key that would open my door; and then
every morning, before the gaoler got up, they
brought me to another part of the prison, where I
said Mass, and administered the sacraments to the
prisoners lodged in that quarter; for all of them
had got keys of their cells.

I had just such neighbours as I would have
picked out, had I had my choice. My next door
neighbour was our brother, Ralph Emerson, of
whom Father Campian in a letter to Father General
makes mention in these terms, " My little man and
I." He was indeed small in body, but in steadfastness and endurance he was great. He had been
already many long years in bonds, ever keeping
godly and devout, like a man of the Society : and
after my coming to the Clink, he remained six or
seven years more. At last he was sent off, with
other confessors of Christ, to the castle of Wisbech,
where he was attacked with palsy. One half of
his body was powerless, so that he could not move
about or do the least thing for himself. He lived
notwithstanding, to add by his patience fresh jewels
to the crown that awaited him. Being driven into
banishment with the same company, he came to
St. Omer's, and died a holy death there, to the
great edification of the by-standers. I found this
good Brother my next door neighbour in the Clink;
overhead I had John Lilly, whom God's providence

had shut up there for his own good and mine. I
had other godly men around me, all true to their
faith.

These having the free run of the prison, any one
might visit them without danger. I arranged therefore, that when any of my friends came to the
prison, they should ask to see one of these; and
thus they got to have talk with me without its
being noticed. I did not however let them into
my room, but spoke to them through the aforesaid
hole.

So I passed some time in great comfort and
repose; striving the while to gather fruit of souls,
by letter and by word of mouth. My first gaoler
was a sour-tempered man, who watched very closely
to see that there were no unlawful doings amongst
us. This called for great wariness on our part, to
avoid discovery: but ere long God summoned him
from the wardenship of the prison, and from the
prison of his body at the same time.

His successor was a younger man of a milder
turn. What with coaxing, and what with bribes, I
got him not to look into our doings too nicely, and
not to come when he was not called for, except at
certain fixed times, at which he always found me
ready to receive him.

I used the liberty thus granted me for my neighbours' profit. I began to hear many confessions,
and reconciled many persons to the Catholic Church.
Some of these were heretics, but the greater number
were only schismatics, as I could deal more freely
with these than with the others. It was only
after long acquaintance, and on the recommendation
of trusty friends, that I would let any heretics know
how little restraint was put upon me. I do not

remember above eight or ten converts from heresy, of whom four entered religion. Two joined our Society, and the other two went to other Orders. As for schismatics, I brought back a goodly number of them to the bosom of the Church. Some became religious; and others gave themselves to good works in England during the persecution. Of these last, was Mr. John Rigby, afterwards martyred. His martyrdom was on this wise.

On one occasion he appeared before the judges, to plead the cause of a Catholic lady. They, unwilling to grant any boon to a Catholic family, asked the advocate of what religion he was himself, that he pleaded so boldly in behalf of another; was he a priest?

"No," he answered.

"Are you a Papist?"

"I am a Catholic."

"Indeed; how long have you been one?"

"For such a time."

"Who made you a Catholic?"

Not to implicate me, he gave the name of a priest who had been martyred shortly before, [Father Jones, *alias* Buckley, a Franciscan].

"So you have been reconciled to the Church of Rome?"

Such a reconciliation is high treason by their unjust laws, and it was of this that they wanted to make him out guilty. He did not notice the snare. He had been taught that it was sinful to say that one was not a Catholic; and thought perchance that it was forbidden also to throw the burden of proof on the persecutors, as is the custom of those that are wary. So like a right-hearted, godly, and courageous man as he was, he frankly

answered that he had been reconciled. He was at
once hand-cuffed, and thrown into prison. At his
trial he made another good confession of his faith,
declaring that he gloried in being a Catholic. He
received the sentence of death with joy. Whilst it
was being pronounced, and he standing before the
judges the while, of a sudden the gyves were
loosened of themselves, and dropped off his legs.
They were replaced by the gaoler, and, if I mistake
not, dropped off a second time. He was led back
to prison, whence, shortly before his martyrdom, he
wrote me a letter full of thanks for having made
him a Catholic, and helped (though little indeed)
to place him in those dispositions, which he hoped
would soon meet with their reward from God. He
also sent me the purse which he was used to bear
about with him : I use it now, in honour of the
martyr, to carry my reliquary in.

As he was being drawn to the place of execution, he was met by a certain Earl,[2] in company
with other gentlemen. The Earl seeing him dragged
on the hurdle, asked what he had been guilty of.
The martyr overheard him, and answered :

"Of no offence against the Queen or the State.
I am to die for the Catholic faith."

The Earl, seeing him to be a stalwart and comely
man, said :

"By my troth, thou wast made rather for gallantry than for martyrdom."

"As for the matter of gallantry," the martyr
answered, "I call God to witness, that I die a
virgin."

The Earl was much struck at what he heard ; and

---

[2] The Earl of Rutland. See Challoner's " Missionary Priests."

H

from that time began to look upon Catholics and their religion in a better light, as he has often since given proof. So the holy man went to heaven, where I doubt not that he pleads before the throne of God for his unworthy father in Christ.

CHAPTER XV.

MARTYRDOM OF MISTRESS ANN LINE.

DURING my stay in this prison, I found means to give the Spiritual Exercises. The gaoler did as I wished him to do; he never came to me without being called, and never went into my neighbours' rooms at all. So we fitted an upper chamber to serve as a chapel, where six or seven made the Exercises, all of whom resolved to follow the counsels of Christ our Lord, and not one of them flinched from his purpose.

I found means also to provide for a very pressing need. Many priests of my acquaintance, being unable to meet with safe lodgings when they came to London, used to put up at inns till they had settled the business that brought them. Again, as my abode was fixed, and easy to find, the greater part of the priests that were sent from the seminaries abroad had instructions to apply to me, that through me they might be introduced to their Superior, and might receive other assistance at my hands. Not having always places prepared, nor houses of Catholics to which I could send them, I rented a house and garden in a suitable spot, and furnished it as far as was wanted, by the help of my friends. Thither I used to send those who brought letters of recommendation from our Fathers, and who I was assured led a holy life and seemed well fitted for the mission. I maintained them there, till I had supplied them, through the aid of certain friends, with clothes and necessaries, sometimes even with a residence, or with a horse to go to their friends and kinsmen in the country. I covered all the expenses of this house with the alms that were bestowed on me. I did not receive alms from many persons, still less from all that came to see me; indeed, both out of prison and in prison, I often refused such offers. I was afraid that if I always accepted what was offered, I might scare from me souls that wished to treat with me on the business of their salvation; or receive gifts from those that could either ill afford it, or would afterwards repent of it. I made it a rule therefore, never to take alms except from a small number of persons, whom I knew well. Most of what I got was from those devoted friends, who offered me not only their money but themselves, and looked upon it as a favour when I took their offer.

I gave charge of this house to a very godly and discreet matron of good birth, whom the Lord honoured with martyrdom. Her maiden name was Heigham, but she bore the name of Line from her deceased husband. Both she and her husband were beloved by God, and had much to suffer for His sake. This lady's father was a Protestant, and when he heard of his daughter's becoming a Catholic, he withheld the dower which he had promised her. He disinherited one of his sons for the same reason. This son, called William Heigham, is now in Spain, a lay-brother of the Society. It is twenty-six years since I knew him. He was then a well-educated gentleman, finely dressed like other high-born Londoners. He supported a priest named Thomson, whom I afterwards saw martyred. As soon as his father learned that he too had become a Catholic, he went and sold his estate, the rents of which were reckoned at 6,000 florins (600*l.*) yearly, that it might not pass to his son. The son was afterwards arrested for the faith: and he and his priest together, if I mistake not, were thrown into the prison of Bridewell, where vagrants are shut up and put to hard labour under the lash. I paid him a visit there, and found him toiling at the tread-mill, all covered with sweat. On recovering his freedom, he hired himself out as a servant to a gentleman, that had to wife a Catholic lady whom I knew. She entrusted her son to his care: he taught the boy the ground-work of the Latin tongue, besides giving him lessons on the harp, which he himself touched admirably. I went to see him in this situation, and had a long talk with him about his call to his present state. Mistress Line, his sister, married a good husband and a staunch Catholic. He had been heir to a fine estate: but his father or uncle (for he was heir to both) sent a message from his death-bed to young Line, then a prisoner for the faith, asking him to conform and go to some heretical church for once; otherwise he would have to give up his inheritance to his younger brother. "If I must either give up God or the world," was his courageous answer, "I prefer to give up the world, for it is good to cleave unto God." So both his father's and his uncle's estate went to his younger brother. I saw this latter once in his elder brother's room, dressed in silk and other finery, while his brother had on plain and mean clothes.

This good man afterwards went into Belgium, where he obtained a pension from the King of Spain, part of which he sent to his wife; and thus they lived a poor and holy life. His death, which happened in Belgium, left his widow friendless, so that she had to look to Providence for her support. Before my imprisonment, she had been charitably taken by my entertainers into their own house. They furnished her with board and lodging, and I made up the rest.

She was just the sort of person that I wanted as head of the house that I have spoken of, to manage the money matters, take care of the guests, and meet the inquiries of strangers. She had good store of charity and wariness; and in great patience she possessed her soul. She was nearly always ill from one or other of many divers diseases, which purified her and made her ready for heaven. She used often to say to me: " Though I desire above all things to die for Christ, I dare not hope to die by the hand of the executioner; but perhaps the Lord will let me be taken some time in the same house with a priest, and then be thrown into a chill and filthy dungeon, where I shall not be able to last out long in this wretched life." Her delight was in the Lord, and the Lord granted her the desires of her heart.

When I was rescued out of prison, she gave up the management of my house; for then so many people knew who she was, that her being in a place was enough to render it unsafe for me. So a room was hired for her in another person's house, where she often used to harbour priests. One day, (it was the feast of the Purification of the Blessed Virgin) she let in a great many Catholics to hear Mass, a

thing which she would never have done in my
house. Good soul, she was more careful of me
than of herself. Some neighbours noticed the
throng, and called the constables. They went
upstairs into the room, which they found full of
people. The celebrant was Father Francis Page, of
the Society of Jesus, who was afterwards martyred.
He had pulled off his vestments before the priest-
hunters came in ; so that they could not readily
make out which was the priest. However from the
father's grave and modest look, they thought that
he must be their man. Accordingly they laid hold
of him, and began questioning him and the others
also. No one would own that there was a priest
there : but as the altar had been found ready for
Mass, they acknowledged that they had been
waiting for a priest to come. While the Catholics
and their persecutors were wrangling on this point,
Father Francis Page, taking advantage of some
one's opening the door, got away from those that
held him and slipped out, shutting the door behind
him. He then went upstairs to a place that he
knew, where Mrs. Line had had a hiding-place
made, and there he ensconced himself. Search
was made for him the whole house over, to no
purpose.

So they took Mrs. Lines and the richer ones of
the party to prison, and let the others go on bail.
God lengthened out the martyr's life beyond her
expectation. It was some months before she was
brought to trial, on a charge of harbouring and
supporting priests. To the question of "guilty or
not guilty," she made no direct answer, but cried
out in a loud voice, so that all could hear her:
"My Lords, nothing grieves me, but that I could

not receive a thousand more."[1]   She listened to the sentence of death with great show of joy and thanksgiving to the Lord God.   She was so weak, that she had to be carried to court in a chair, and sat there during the whole of the trial.   After her return to prison, a little before her death, she wrote to Father Page, who had escaped.   The letter is in my hands at present.   She disposed therein of the few things that she had, leaving to me a fine large Cross of gold that had belonged to her husband.   She mentioned me thrice in the letter, calling me her father.   She also left some few debts which she begged me to see paid.   Afterwards she bequeathed me her bed by word of mouth.   I wanted to purchase it from the gaolers, who had plundered everything found in her cell after her death; but I could only get the coverlet, which I used ever after during my stay in London, and reckoned it no small safeguard.

Being arrived at the place of execution, some preachers wanted to tease her, as usual, with warnings to abandon her errors; but she cut them short, saying, "Away! I have no dealings nor communion with you."   Then kissing the gallows with great joy, she knelt down to pray, and kept on praying till the hangman had done his duty.   So she gave up her soul to God, along with the martyr Father Filcock, of the Society of Jesus, who had often been her confessor, and had always been her friend.   Her martyrdom however happened six or seven years after the time of which I am now speaking.   She managed my house for three years, and received therein many holy priests.

[1] These words are given in English in the MS.

CHAPTER XVI

I ALWAYS had a priest residing in this house, whom I used to send to assist and console my friends, as I was unable to visit them myself. The first I had there was Father Jones, a Franciscan, afterwards martyred, but then newly arrived in England. I was glad to be able to provide for him there, as I hoped thereby to establish a good feeling between his order and ours. He, however, finding a number of friends whom he was desirous of assisting, after thanking me for the hospitality afforded him, in a few months betook himself to his own connexions. A little later he was taken, and suffered martyrdom with great constancy.

After him I received another priest, lately arrived from Spain, and formerly known to me, Robert Drury by name. He was of gentle birth and well educated, and could consequently associate with gentlemen without causing any suspicion. I introduced him therefore to my chief friends; and he assisted them well and zealously for two years and more that he tarried in my house. This good priest also God chose to be His witness and martyr. For after my escape from England, two years ago from this present writing, he was taken, found guilty of high treason, and executed accordingly; although they had nothing to bring against him, save only that he was a priest, and refused to take the new-invented oaths. At his martyrdom happened a noteworthy circumstance. When he had arrived at the scaffold, some of the principal officers pressed him to have pity on himself, to conform to the King's laws, to go to the Protestant church, and to save his life.

" Well, my masters," said the martyr, " can you warrant me that I shall truly be saved from death, if I consent to go to your churches ? "

" Aye, verily can we," they replied, " and we promise you this in the King's name, that you shall not die."

Then the martyr turned him to the people, and said aloud :

" You see now what sort of high treason they find us guilty of. You see that religion is the only cause for which I and other priests are put to death."

Hereupon the officers were enraged, and revenged themselves by cutting him down directly he was turned off, and disembowelling him while he was still alive. But they killed his body only, and had nothing more they could do to him.

In that house of mine, while I was in prison, there lived a while one of our fathers, who was in ill health, Father John Curry. There also he died, and there he lies buried in some secret corner. For those priests who live secretly on the mission, we are obliged also to bury secretly when they die.

All this while my good host [Mr. Wiseman], who had been taken a little before me, was kept imprisoned ; and for the first four months so straitly, that neither his wife nor any of his friends were allowed to have any access to him. After this,

however, the persecutors, seeing that they could
not produce any proof against him, because none of
the Catholic servants would acknowledge anything,
and the traitor had never seen me in priest's guise,
and was only one witness after all, by degrees relaxed a little of their harshness, and permitted him
to be visited and cared for, though they still kept
him in strict custody.

He no-wise regretted that he had during four
years given me a home, though he found himself
in consequence exposed to such extreme distresses,
and saw his family and fortune made a mark for
the persecutors as a result of having harboured me.
Nay, it was not only that he bore all these trials
patiently, but he really thought it all joy to suffer
thus for the good cause. His wife also, though she
loved her husband most tenderly, and was of a pecu-
liarly sensitive mind, yet in this juncture bore everything with a singular sweetness and patience. After
I was transferred to the Clink, where there was more
chance of communicating with me either by word
or letter, she took a house in the immediate neighbourhood of my prison, in order that she might
consult me constantly, and provide me with everything I needed. In this house she and her husband,
who obtained his release after a time by large
payments of money, resided, while I remained in
that prison. But after my escape from the Tower,
they betook themselves back to their country seat,
in order that they might have me with them there
again.

In the meantime I was so fully taken up in the
prison with business, and with the visits of Catholics, that in the next room, which was Brother
Emerson's, there were often six or eight persons

at once, waiting their turn to see me. Nay, many of my most intimate and attached friends have oft-times had to wait many hours at a stretch, and even then I have been obliged to ask them to come another time.

Among other occupatiohs I heard many general confessions. One case was that of a Catholic gentleman of great wealth, who had always lived quietly, cautiously avoiding anything that savoured of danger. At length however, God so willing, he was taken and thrown intó the same prison with me, an occurrence which was certainly the very last he looked for. He was all the more perplexed because the persecutors alleged so slight and trivial a cause for his imprisonment. When he spoke to me of this, I replied that all things indeed happened by permission of God, but especially things of this sort: that He often warned men by such means "to agree with their adversary quickly" while time allowed, and that this was our Lord's own advice, Who wished to be rather a Father than a Judge. I advised him then to take the opportunity of this forced retirement, to enter into himself, and take account of his soul, how much he owed his Lord; and that the rather, as he knew not whether he should ever after have the like opportunity. This was, I told him, sent him perhaps as a sort of last summons to hold himself prepared for death. He yielded to my advice, read the book called "Memoriale," by Father Louis of Granada, prepared himself for confession, and made it with great exactness, much to his own consolation and mine. At this time he was in strong and perfect health, but a few days later, being released from prison, he took ill and died within two months.

About this time I assisted several persons to turn their minds from secular things, and by God's grace to follow the counsels of our Lord. Among these were two young men, friends, who were writers in a certain office in London, an occupation which gave them a considerable income. One was Father Francis Page, afterwards enrolled in the glorious army of martyrs. His friend a man of excellent parts, gave himself to the study of Theology, with the view of becoming a priest and entering the Society; but he died during his studies, leaving behind him a reputation for great virtue and holiness.

Mr. Francis Page was the son of well-to-do parents, and being both handsome and very winning in manner, was beloved by the daughter of his employer, a man of great wealth. The love was mutual ; indeed it was by the lady's means that he had become a Catholic ; and they had engaged with each other to marry when the consent of their parents might be had. The young lady was herself a good and devoted soul ; she used frequently to come to me for direction, and at last introduced Mr. Page to me. He was already a Catholic, but was, as I have said, looking forward to live in the married state. There shone in him however so singular a modesty and candour of mind, and I found him so powerfully drawn to virtue, that I could not doubt that he was intended for higher things. I began therefore to speak with him of the uncertainty of riches, and of the delusive hopes of happiness in this world, and put before him the possibility of a more perfect life. I did this the rather, because I thought it unlikely that the parents of the young lady would consent to her marrying below her degree. After this I gave him some meditations, and some writings to copy out which treated of the spiritual life ; and God in His goodness gradually weaned his mind from the love of transitory things and fixed it on things eternal. In fact he came to the determination of giving up both his place in the office and the thought of marrying ; and, in order that he might be nearer to me for a time, he came to live as a servant in the house of the lady my hostess, though such a position was of course far below that which he was leaving. But he wished to prepare himself for greater things which he hoped for, and in this he was much helped by Father Edward Coffin, who was then residing in my hostess' family. This same Father often visited me, and consoled me much. I shall have occasion to speak more of Father Francis Page hereafter.

CHAPTER XVII.

WHILE I remained in this prison, I sent over numbers of boys and young men to Catholic seminaries abroad. Some of these are, at this present, priests of the Society, and engaged on the English Mission : others still remain in the Seminaries, in positions of authority, to assist in training labourers for the same field. On one occasion I had sent two boys on their way to St. Omers, and had given them letters of recommendation, written with lemon-juice, so that the writing was not visible on the paper. In the paper itself I wrapped up a few collars, so that it might seem that its only use was to keep the collars clean. The boys were taken, and, on being questioned, confessed that I had sent them. They let out also that I had given them this letter, and had told them, when they came to a certain college of Ours, by which they had to pass to reach St. Omers, to bid the Fathers steep the paper in water, and they would be able to read what I had written. On this information, then, the paper was steeped by the authorities, and two letters of mine were read, written on the same paper. One was written in Latin to our Belgian Fathers; this I had consequently signed with my own proper name. The other was addressed to our English

Fathers at St. Omers. The letters having been thus discovered, I was sent for to be examined.

Young however was no longer to be my examiner. He had died in his sins, and that most miserably. As he lived, so he died:[1] he lived the devil's confessor, he died the devil's martyr; for not only did he die in the devil's service, but he brought on his death through that very service. He was accustomed to work night and day to increase the distress of the Catholics, and to go forth frequently in inclement weather, at one or two o'clock in the morning, to search their houses. By these labours he fell into a consumption, of which he died. He died moreover overwhelmed with debt, so that it might be clear that he abandoned all things for the devil's service. Notwithstanding all the emoluments of his office, all the plunder he took from the persecuted Catholics, and the large bribes they were constantly giving him to buy off his malicious oppression, his debts were said to amount to no less a sum than a hundred thousand florins [10,000*l.*]; and I have heard even a larger sum mentioned than this. Perhaps he expected the Queen would pay his debts; but she did nothing of the sort. All she did, was to send a gentleman from Court to visit him, when he was confined to his bed, and near death; and this mark of favour so delighted him, that he seemed ready to sing *Nunc dimittis.* But it was a false peace, and the lifting up of the soul that goes before a fall; and like another Aman he was bidden, not to a banquet, but to execution, and that for ever. So with his mouth full of the Queen's praises, and his great

---

[1] "Qualis vita, finis ita."—*MS.*

obligations to Her Majesty, he died a miserable death, and anguish took the place of his joy. The joy of the hypocrite is but for an instant.

This man's successor in the office of persecuting and harassing the servants of God, was William Wade, now Governor of the Tower of London, but at that time Private Secretary of the Lords of the Council. For the members of the Council choose always to have a man in their service, to whose cruelty anything particularly odious may be attributed, instead of its being supposed to be done by their warrant. This Wade then sent for me, and first of all showed me the blank paper that I had given the boys, and asked me if I recognized it. I answered: "No, I do not." And in fact I did not recognize it, for I did not know the boys had been taken. Then he dipped the paper in a basin of water, and showed me the writing, and my name subscribed in full. When I saw it, I said:

"I do not acknowledge the writing: Any one may easily have counterfeited my handwriting and forged my signature; and if such boys as you speak of have been taken, they may perhaps in their terror say anything that their inquisitors want them to say, to their own prejudice and that of their friends; a thing I will never do. At the same time, I do not deny that it would be a good deed to send such boys abroad to be better educated; and I would gladly do it, if I had the means; but closely confined as I am in prison, I cannot do anything of the kind, though I should like to do it."

He replied to me with a torrent of abuse for denying my signature and handwriting, and said:

"In truth, you have far too much liberty; but you shall not enjoy it long."

Then he rated the gaoler soundly, for letting me have so much freedom.

I was sent for on two or three other occasions, to be examined; and whenever I came out of this prison I always wore a Jesuit's cassock and cloak, which I had had made as soon as I came among Catholic fellow-prisoners.[2] The sight of this dress raised mocks from the boys in the streets, and put my persecutors in a rage. On the first occasion, they said I was a hypocrite. I replied: "When I was arrested, you called me a courtier, and said that I had dressed myself in that fashion in order to disguise my real character, and to be able to deal with persons of rank in safety and without being recognized. I told you then, that I did not like a layman's dress, and would much rather wear my own. Well, now I am doing so; and you are in a rage again. In fact, you are not satisfied with either piping or mourning, but you seek excuses for inveighing against me."

To this they answered: "Why did you not go about in this dress before, instead of wearing a disguise, and taking a false name? A thing no good man would do."

I replied: "I am aware you would like us not

---

[2] Father Bartoli in his "Inghilterra," Book V. ch. 13., has the following passage about Father Gerard, whom he knew personally at Rome:

"At his first entrance into this prison (the Clink) he procured himself a habit of the Society, and continued to wear it from that time forward, even in the face of all London when he was being taken to his different examinations; so that the people crowded to see a Jesuit in his habit, while the preachers were all the more exasperated at what they thought an open defiance of them."

Father Bartoli embodies a great deal of this narrative of Father Gerard in different parts of his History of the Society in England.

I

to do so, in order that we might be arrested at once, and not be able to do any good in the work of rescuing and gaining souls. But do you not know that St. Raphael personated another, and took another name, in order that, not being known, he might better accomplish God's work for which he had been sent?"

At another time I was examined before the Dean of Westminster, the dignitary who has taken the place of the former Abbot of the great royal monastery there. Topcliffe and some other commissioners were present. Their object was to confront me with the good widow, my host's mother, of whom I have before spoken; and who was confined at this time in a prison near the church at Westminster;[3] for she was not yet condemned to death; that happened later. They wanted to see if she recognized me. So when I came into the room where they brought me, I found her already there. When she saw me coming in with the gaolers, she almost jumped for joy: but she controlled herself, and said to them:

"Is that the person you spoke of? I do not know him; but he looks like a priest."

Upon this she made me a very low reverence, and I bowed in return. Then they asked me if I did not recognize her.

I answered: "I do not recognize her.[4] At the same time, you know this is my usual way of answering; and I will never mention any places, or give the names of persons that are known to me

---

[3] The Gatehouse prison.

[4] It will be noticed that when such answers as the above are given, the speaker often adds something to show the questioner that he has no right to expect a true answer, and consequently no ground for trusting the present answer to be a true one.

(which this lady however is not); because to do so, as I have told you before, would be contrary both to justice and charity."

Then Topcliffe said: "Tell the truth: have you reconciled any persons to the Church of Rome."

I quite understood his bloodthirsty intention, that being a thing expressly prohibited under penalty of high treason, as I mentioned before in the case of Master Rigby who was martyred; but then I knew I was already as much compromised on account of my priesthood, and therefore I answered boldly:

"Yes, in truth I have received some persons, and I am sorry that I have not done this good service to more."

"Well," said Topcliffe, "how many would you like to have reconciled, if you could? A thousand?"

"Certainly," I said, "a hundred thousand, and many more still, if I could."

"That would be enough," said Topcliffe, "to levy an army against the Queen."

"Those whom I reconciled," said I, "would not be against the Queen, but all for her; for we hold that obedience to superiors is of obligation."

"No such thing," said Topcliffe, "you teach rebellion. See, I have here a Bull of the Pope, granted to Sanders [5] when he went to Ireland to stir up the Queen's subjects to rebellion. See, here it is. Read it."

I answered: "There is no need to read it. It is likely enough that the Pontiff, if he sent him, gave him authority. But *I* have no power to meddle at all in such matters. We are forbidden to have

[5] The celebrated Theologian and controversialist, Dr. Sanders, was sent as Papal Legate into Ireland by Gregory XIII. in 1579.

anything to do with such things. I never have, and never will."

"Take and read it," he said: "I will have you read it."

So I took it, and seeing the Name of JESUS on the top, I reverently kissed it.

"What," said Topcliffe, "you kiss a Bull of the Pope, do you?"

"I kissed," said I, "the Name of JESUS, to which all love and honour are due. But if it is a Bull of the Pope, as you say, I reverence it also on that score."

And so saying, I kissed the printed paper again. Then Topcliffe, in a furious passion, began to abuse me calumniously, in words which I cannot repeat.

At this insolence, to own the truth, I somewhat lost command of myself; and though I knew that he had no grounds which seemed probable even to himself for what he said, but had uttered it from pure malice, I exclaimed:

"I call the Great and Blessed God to witness, that all your insinuations are false."

And, as I spoke, I laid my hand on the book that was open before me on the table. It was a copy of the Holy Bible, but according to their corrupt translation into the vulgar tongue. Then Topcliffe held his peace; but the Dean took up the word.

"Are you willing," said he, "to be sworn on our Bible?" (The better instructed Catholics, who can show the dishonesty of that translation, usually refuse this.)

I replied: "In truth, under the necessity of rebutting this man's false charges at once, I did not take notice what version this was. However, there are some truths, as for instance the Incarnation and

Passion of Christ, that have not been corrupted by mis-translation; and by these I call the truth of God to witness. There are many other things falsely rendered, so as to involve heresies; and these I detest and anathematize."

So saying, I laid my hand again upon the book, and more firmly than before. Then the old man was angry, and said:

"I will prove that you are a heretic."

I replied: "You cannot prove it."

"I will prove it," he said, "thus: Whoever denies Holy Scripture is a heretic: you deny this to be Holy Scripture: *Ergo.*"

I replied; "This is no true syllogism; it shifts from general to particular, and so has four terms."

The old man answered: "I could make syllogisms before you were born."

"Very likely," I said; "but the one you have just produced is not a true one."

However the good old man would not try a new middle-term, and made no further attempt to prove me a heretic. But one urged one thing, and another another, not in the way of argument, but after their usual plan, asking me such questions as they knew very well I did not like to answer; and then, in the end, they sent me back to prison.

CHAPTER XVIII.

On another occasion they examined me, and all the other Catholics that were confined in the same prison with me, in a public place called Guildhall, where Topcliffe and several other Commissioners were present. When they had put their usual questions and received from me the usual answers, they came to the point; intending I imagine, to sound us all as to our feelings towards the State; or else to entrap us in some expressions about the State that might be made matter of accusation. They asked me then, whether I acknowledged the Queen as the true Governor and Queen of England.

I answered: "I do acknowledge her as such."

"What," said Topcliffe, "in spite of Pius the Fifth's excommunication?"

The fact was, I knew that the operation of that excommunication had been suspended for all in England by a declaration of the Pontiff, till such time as its execution became possible.

Topcliffe proceeded: "What would you do in case the Pope sent an army into England, asserting that the object was solely to bring back the kingdom to the Catholic religion, and protesting that there was no other way left of introducing the Catholic faith, and moreover commanding all in virtue of his

Apostolical authority to aid his cause? Whose side would you then take, the Pope's or the Queen's?"

I saw the man's malicious cunning, and that his aim was, that whichever way I answered I might injure myself, either in soul or body; and so I worded my reply thus :

"I am a true Catholic, and a true subject of the Queen. If then this were to happen, which is unlikely, and which I think will never be the case, I would act as became a true Catholic and a true subject."

"Nay, nay," said he, "answer positively and to the point."

"I have declared my mind," said I, "and no other answer will I make."

On this he flew into a most violent rage, and vomited out a torrent of curses; and ended by saying :

"You think you will creep to kiss the Cross this year; but before the time comes, I will take good care you do no such thing."

He meant to intimate, in the abundance of his charity, that he would take care I should go to Heaven by the rope before that time. But he had not been admitted into the secrets of God's sanctuary, and did not know my great unworthiness. Though God had permitted him to execute his malice on others, whom the Divine Wisdom knew to be worthy and well-prepared, as on Father Southwell, and others, whom he pursued to the death, yet no such great mercy of God came to me from his anger. Others indeed, for whom a kingdom was prepared by the Father, were advanced to Heaven by our Lord Jesus through his means ; but

this heavenly gift was too great for an angry man
to be allowed to bestow on me.   However he was
really in some sort a prophet in uttering these words ;
though he meant them differently from the sense in
which they were fulfilled.

What I have mentioned happened about Christmas.   In the following Lent he himself was thrown
into prison for disrespect to the members of the
Queen's Council, on an occasion, if I mistake not,
when he had pleaded too boldly in behalf of his
only son, who had killed a man with his sword in
the great hall of the Court of Queen's Bench.
This took place about Passion Sunday.   We then,
who were in prison for the Faith, seeing our enemy
Aman about to be hanged on his own gibbet, began
to lift up our heads, and to use what liberty we had
a little more freely, and we admitted a greater
number to the Sacraments, and to assist at the
services and holy rites of the Church.   Thus it was
that on Good Friday a large number of us were
together in the room over mine, in fact all the
Catholics in the prison, and a number of others
from without.   I had gone through all the service,
and said all the prayers appointed for the day, up
to the point where the priest has to lay aside his
shoes.   I had put them off, and had knelt down,
and was about to creep towards the Cross and make
the triple adoration of it : when lo! just as I had
moved two paces, the head gaoler came and knocked
at the door of my room underneath, and as I did
not answer from within he began to batter violently
at the door and make a great noise.   As soon as I
heard it, I knew that the chief gaoler was there,
because no other would have ventured to behave in
that way to me : so I sent some one directly, to say

that I would come without delay, and then, instead
of going on with the adoratiou of the material
cross, I hastened to the spiritual cross that God
presented to me, and taking off the sacred vestments
that I was wearing I went down with speed, for
fear the gaoler might come up after me, and find a
number of others, who would have thus been brought
into trouble. When he saw me, he said in a loud
tone of voice:

" How comes it that I find you out of your room,
when you ought to be kept strictly confined to it ? "

As I knew the nature of the man, I pretended in
reply to be angry, that one who professed to be a
friend should have come at such a time as that,
when if ever we were bound to be busy at our
prayers.

" What," said he, " you were at Mass, were you ?
I will go up and see."

" No such thing," I said : "you seem to know
very little of our ways. there is not a single Mass
said to-day throughout the whole Church. Go up
if you like ; but understand that, if you do, neither
I nor any one of the Catholics will ever pay anything for our rooms. You may put us all, if you
like, in the common prison of the poor who do not
pay. But you will be no gainer by that ; whereas,
if you act in a friendly way with us, and do not
come upon us unawares in this manner, you will
not find us ungrateful, as you have not found us
hitherto."

He softened down a little at this; and then I
said:

" What have you come for now, I pray."

" Surely," said he, " to greet you from Master
Topcliffe."

"From him?" I said, "and how is it that he and I are such great friends? Is he not in prison? He cannot do anything against me just now I fancy."

"No," said the gaoler, "he cannot. But he really sends to greet you. When I visited him to-day, he asked me how you were. I replied that you were very well. 'But he does not bear his imprisonment,' said Master Topcliffe, 'as patiently as I do mine. I would have you greet him then in my name, and tell him what I have said.' So I have come now for the purpose of repeating his message to you."

"Very well," I replied. "Now tell him from me, that by the grace of God I bear my imprisonment for the cause of the Faith with cheerfulness, and I could wish his cause were the same."

Thereupon the gaoler went away, rating his servant however for not having kept me more closely confined. And thus Topcliffe really accomplished what he had promised, having checked me in the very act of adoration, although without thinking of what he said, and with another intent at the time. Thus was Saul among the prophets. However he did not prevent my going up again and completing what I had begun.

The man who had charge of my room would not do anything in our rooms without my leave. And after my first gaoler, who soon died, the others who succeeded were well disposed to oblige me. One of them, who had the gaolership by inheritance, I made a Catholic. He immediately gave up his post and sold the right of succession, and became the attendant of a Catholic gentleman, a friend of mine, and afterwards accompanied his son to Italy,

and got a vocation to the religious state. At
present he is a prisoner in the very prison where he
had been my gaoler. The next who had the charge
of me after him, being a married man with children,
was kept by fear of poverty from becoming a
Catholic; but yet he was afterwards so attached
to myself and all our friends, that he received us
into his own house, and sometimes concealed there
such Catholics as were more sorely pressed than
others by the persecution. And when I was to
be got out of the Tower of London, with serious
risk to all who aided the enterprise, he himself in
person was one of three who exposed themselves to
such great danger. And although he was nearly
drowned the first night of the attempt, he rowed
the boat the next night as before, as I shall hereafter relate. For not long after what I just now
mentioned, I was removed from that prison to the
Tower of London; the occasion of which was the
following.

CHAPTER XIX.

THERE was in the prison with me a certain priest, to whom I had done many good services. When he first came to England, I had lodged him in an excellent house with some of my best friends; I had made Catholics of his mother and only brother; I had secured him a number of friends when he was thrown into prison, and had made him considerable presents. I had always shown him affection, although, perceiving that he was not firm and steady in spirit, but rather hankered too much after freedom, I did not deal confidently with him, as with others in the prison, especially Brother Emerson and John Lilly. Nevertheless this good man, from some motive or other, procured my removal; whether in the desire and expectation, that if I were gone, all whom he saw coming to me would henceforth come to him, or in order to curry favour with our enemies, and obtain liberty or some such boon for himself, is not certain. Be that as it may, he reported to our enemies, that he was standing by when I handed a packet of letters dated from Rome and Brussels to a servant of Father Garnett's of the name of Little John, about whom I have before spoken. This latter, after having been arrested in my company, as I have related, and subjected to various examinations, but without disclosing anything, had been released for a sum of money which some Catholic gentlemen paid. For his services were indispensable to them and many others, as he was a first-rate hand at contriving priests' hiding-places. The priest then reported that I had given this man letters, and that I was in the habit of receiving letters from beyond the sea addressed both to my Superior and to myself.

Acting on this information, the persecutors sent a Justice of the Peace to me one day, with two Queen's messengers, or pursuivants as they call them. These came up to my room on a sudden with the head-gaoler; but by God's Providence they found no one with me at the time except two boys, whom I was instructing with intention to send them abroad : one of whom, if I remember right, escaped, the other they imprisoned for a time. But they found nothing else in my room that I was afraid of being seen : for I was accustomed to keep all my manuscripts and other articles of importance in some holes made to hide things. All these holes were known to Brother Emerson; and so after my removal he took out everything, and among the rest a reliquary that I have with me now, and a store of money that I had in hand for the expenses of my house in town, of which I have before spoken, to the amount of thirteen hundred florins [130*l.*]. This money he sent to my Superior, who took charge of the house from that time till I was got out of prison.

When these officials came in they began to question me; and when the examination was over, which it soon was, as they could get nothing from me of what they wanted to know, they began to search the room all over, to find letters or some-thing else, that might serve their turn and injure me. While the Justice of the Peace was rummag-ing my books, one of the pursuivants searched my person, and opening my doublet, he discovered my hair-shirt. At first he did not know what it was, and said:

" What is this ? "

" A shirt," I replied.

" Ho, ho ! " said he, " It is a hair-shirt." And he caught hold of it, and wanted to drag it off my body by force.

This insolence of the varlet, to confess my imper-fection honestly, excited me more than anything that I have ever had to endure from my enemies, and I was within a little of thrusting him violently back;[1] but I checked myself by God's grace, and claimed the Justice's protection, who immediately made him give over. So they sought, but found nothing that they sought for in my room except myself; and me they took at once, and went straight to the Tower of London with me, and there handed me to the Governor, whose title is King's Lieu-tenant. He was a Knight of the name of Barkeley. He conducted me at once to a large high tower of three stories, with a separate lock-up place in each, one of a number of different towers contained within the whole enclosure. He left me for the night in the lowest part, and committed the custody of my person to a servant in whom he placed great confidence. The servant brought a little straw at once, and throwing it down on the ground went

---

[1] Father Gerard was a very tall man, and at this time about thirty-three years of age; so that most probably, if he had allowed himself, he could have given a good account of his assailant.

away fastening the door of my prison, and securing the upper door both with a great bolt and with iron bars. I recommended myself therefore to God, Who is wont to go down with His people into the pit, and Who never abandoned me in my bondage, as well as to the most Blessed Virgin, the Mother of Mercy, and to my Patron Saints and Guardian Angel; and after prayer I lay down with a calm mind on the straw, and slept very well that night.

The next day I examined the place, for there was some light though dim; and I found the name of Father Henry Walpole, of blessed memory, cut with a knife on the wall, and not far from there I found his oratory, which was a space where there had been a narrow window, now blocked up with stones. There he had written on either side with chalk the names of the different choirs of Angels, and on the top above the Cherubim and Seraphim the name of Mary Mother of God, and over that the name of JESUS, and over that again in Latin, Greek, and Hebrew, the name of GOD. It was truly a great consolation to me, to find myself in this place, hallowed by the presence of so great and so devoted a martyr, the place too in which he was frequently tortured, to the number, as I have heard, of fourteen times. Probably they were unwilling to torture him in public and in the ordinary place, because they did it oftener than they would have it known. And I can well believe that he was racked that number of times, for he lost through it the proper use of his fingers. This I can vouch for from the following circumstance. He was carried back to York, to be executed in the place where he was taken on his first landing in England, and while in prison there he had a discussion with some

ministers which he wrote out with his own hand.
A part of this writing was given to me, together
with some meditations on the Passion of Christ,
which he had written in prison before his own
passion. These writings however I could scarcely
read at all, not because they were written hastily,
but because the hand of the writer could not form
the letters. It seemed more like the first attempts
of a child, than the handwriting of a scholar and a
gentleman, such as he was. Yet he used to be
at Court before the death of Father Campion, in
whose honour he also wrote some beautiful verses
in the English tongue, declaring that he and many
others had received the warmth of life from that
blessed martyr's blood, and had been animated by
it to follow the more perfect counsels of Christ.

When therefore I found myself in Father Walpole's
cell, I rejoiced exceedingly thereat : but I was not
worthy to be the successor of such a man in his place
of suffering. For on the day following my gaoler,
either because he thought to do me a favour, or in
consequence of his master's orders, brought me into
the upper room, which was sufficiently large and
commodious for a prisoner. I told him that I preferred to stay in the lower dungeon, and mentioned
the reason, but as he showed himself opposed to
this, I asked him to allow me to go there sometimes
and pray. This he promised me, and in fact frequently permitted. Then he inquired of me if he
could go for me anywhere to any friends of mine
who would be willing to send me a bed. For it is
the custom in this prison that a bed should not be
provided, but that a prisoner should provide himself
a bed and other furniture, which afterwards goes to
the Lieutenant of the Tower, even though the

prisoner should be liberated. I replied that I had no friend to whom I could send, except such as I left in the prison from which I had been brought[2] : these perhaps, if he would call there, would give me a plain bed by way of alms. The gaoler therefore went to the Catholics detained in the Clink, who immediately sent me a bed such as they knew I wished for; that is, a mattrass stuffed with wool and feathers after the Italian fashion. They sent also a coat and some linen for me; and asked him always to come there for anything I wanted, and promised to give money or anything else, provided he brought a note signed by me of things I needed. They also gave him money at that time for himself, and besought him to treat me kindly.

[2] This was said of course, because it was dangerous to mention the names of any friends who were still at liberty. It could do no harm to mention those already in prison.

CHAPTER XX,

MY FIRST TORTURE.

ON the third day immediately after breakfast came my gaoler to me, and with sorrowful mien told me that the Lords Commissioners had come, and with them the Queens Attorney General,[1] and that I must go down to them.

" I am ready," I replied, " I only ask you to allow me to say a *Pater* and *Ave* in the lower dungeon."

This he allowed; and then we went together to the house of the Lieutenant, which was within the Tower walls. There I found five men none of whom had before examined me except Wade, who was there for the purpose of accusing me on all points.

The Queen's Attorney General then took a sheet of paper, and began to write a solemn form of juridical examination. They did not ask anything at that time about private Catholics, but only about matters of State, to which I answered as before in general terms; namely,— that all such things were strictly forbidden to us of the Society,—that I had consequently never mixed myself up with political matters, sufficient proof whereof I said was to be found in the fact that though they had had me in custody for three years, and had constantly examined

---

[1] Sir Edward Coke was Attorney General at this time, 1597.

me, they had never been able to produce a single line of my writing, nor a single trustworthy witness, to show that I had ever injured the State in a single point.

They then inquired what letters I had lately received from our Fathers abroad. Here it was I first divined the reason of my being transferred to the Tower;—I answered however that if I had ever received any letters from abroad, they never had any connexion with matters of State, but related solely to the money matters of certain Catholics who were living beyond seas.

" Did not you," said Wade, " receive lately a packet of letters; and did you not deliver them to such a one for Henry Garnett ? "

" If I have received any such," I answered, " and delivered them as you say, I only did my duty. But I never received nor delivered any, but what related to the private money matters of certain religious or students, who are pursuing their studies beyond seas, as I have before said."

" Well," said they, " where is he to be found to whom you delivered the letters, and how is he called ? "

" I do not know," I answered, " and if I did know, I neither could nor would tell you : " and then I alleged the usual reasons.

" You tell us," said the Attorney General, " that you do not wish to offend against the State. Tell us then where this Garnett is. For he is an enemy of the State, and you are bound to give information of such people."

" He is no enemy of the State ; " I replied, " but on the contrary I am sure that he would be ready to lay down his life for the Queen and the State.

However I do not know where he is, and if I did know I would not tell you." '

" But you shall tell us," said they, " before we leave this place."

" Please God," said I, " that shall never be."

They then produced the warrant which they had for putting me to the torture, and gave it me to, read; for it is not allowed in this prison to put any one to the torture without express warrant. I saw the document was duly signed, so I said ;—

" By the help of God I will never do what is against justice, and against the Catholic Faith. You have me in your power; do what God permits you, for you certainly cannot go beyond."

Then they began to entreat me not to force them to do what they were loth to do; and told me they were bound not to desist from putting me to the torture day after day, as long as my life lasted, until I gave the information they sought from me.

" I trust in God's goodness," I answered, "that He will never allow me to do so base an act as to bring innocent persons to harm. Nor indeed do I fear what you can do to me, since all of us are in God's hands."

Such was the purport of my replies, as far as I can remember.

Then we proceeded to the place appointed for the torture. We went in a sort of solemn procession; the attendants preceding us with lighted candles, because the place was underground and very dark, especially about the entrance. It was a place of immense extent, and in it were ranged divers sorts of racks, and other instruments of torture. Some of these they displayed before me, and told me I should have to taste them every one. Then again they asked me if I was willing to satisfy them on the points on which they had questioned me. "It is out of my power to satisfy you;" I answered: and throwing myself on my knees I said a prayer or two.

Then they led me to a great upright beam or pillar of wood which was one of the supports of this vast crypt. At the summit of this column were fixed certain iron staples for supporting weights. Here they placed on my wrists gauntlets of iron, and ordered me to mount upon two or three wicker steps;[3] then raising my arms they inserted an iron bar through the rings of the gauntlets and then through the staples in the pillar, putting a pin through the bar so that it could not slip. My arms being thus fixed above my head, they withdrew those wicker steps I spoke of, one by one, from beneath my feet, so that I hung by my hands and arms. The tips of my toes however still touched the ground:[4] so they dug away the ground beneath; for they could not raise me higher, as they had suspended me from the topmost staple in the pillar.

Thus hanging by my wrists I began to pray, while those gentlemen standing round asked me again if I was willing to confess. I replied, "I neither can nor will:" but so terrible a pain began to oppress me that I was scarce able to speak the words. The worst pain was in my breast and belly, my arms and hands. It seemed to me that all the

---

[3] "Scirpicula quædam duo vel tria ex juncis facta."—*MS.* It is not easy to understand exactly what these were.

[4] Father Gerard's great stature could not be more clearly indicated. This would of course involve a greater weight of body, and consequently greater severity in this mode of torture. "Erat enim," says Father More in his History, "pleno et procero corpore."

blood in my body rushed up my arms into my hands; and I was under the impression at the time that the blood actually burst forth from my fingers and at the back of my hands. This was however a mistake; the sensation was caused by the swelling of the flesh over the iron that bound it.

I felt now such intense pain (and the effect was probably heightened by an interior temptation), that it seemed to me impossible to continue enduring it. It did not however go so far as to make me feel any inclination or real disposition to give the information they wanted. For as the eyes of our merciful Lord had seen my imperfection, He did *not suffer me to be tempted above what I was able, but with the temptation made also a way of escape.* Seeing me therefore in this agony of pain and this interior distress, His infinite mercy sent me this thought: "the very furthest and utmost they can do is to take away thy life; and often hast thou desired to give thy life for God: thou art in God's hands, Who knoweth well what thou sufferest, and is all-powerful to sustain thee." With this thought our good God gave me also out of His immense bounty the grace to resign myself and offer myself utterly to His good pleasure, together with some hope and desire of dying for His sake. From that moment I felt no more trouble in my soul, and even the bodily pain seemed to be more bearable than before, although I doubt not that it really increased from the continued strain that was exercised on every part of my body.

Hereupon those gentlemen, seeing that I gave them no further answer, departed to the Lieutenant's house; and there they waited, sending now and then to know how things were going on in the crypt. There were left with me three or four strong men, to superintend my torture. My gaoler also remained, I fully believe out of kindness to me, and kept wiping away with a handkerchief the sweat that ran down from my face the whole time, as indeed it did from my whole body. So far indeed he did me a service; but by his words he rather added to my distress, for he never stopped entreating and beseeching me to have pity on myself, and tell these gentlemen what they wanted to know; and so many human reasons did he allege, that I verily believed he was either instigated directly by the devil under pretence of affection for me, or had been left there purposely by the persecutors to influence me by his show of sympathy. In any case these shafts of the enemy seemed to be spent before they reached me, for though annoying they did me no real hurt, nor did they seem to touch my soul or move it in the least. I said therefore to him, "I pray you to say no more on that point, for I am not minded to lose my soul for the sake of my body." Yet I could not prevail with him to be silent. The others also who stood by said: "He will be a cripple all his life, if he lives through it: but he will have to be tortured daily till he confesses." But I kept praying in a low voice, and continually uttered the Holy Names of JESUS and MARY.

I had hung in this way till after one of the clock as I think, when I fainted. How long I was in the faint I know not; perhaps not long; for the men who stood by lifted me up, or replaced those wicker steps under my feet, until I came to myself; and immediately they heard me praying they let me down again. This they did over and over again when the faint came on, eight or nine times before five of the clock. Somewhat before five came Wade again, and drawing near said : " Will you yet obey the commands of the Queen and the Council ? "

" No," said I, " what you ask is unlawful, therefore I will never do it."

" At least then," said Wade, " say that you would like to speak to Secretary Cecil."

" I have nothing to say to him," I replied, "more than I have said already : and if I were to ask to speak to him, scandal would be caused, for people would imagine that I was yielding at length, and was willing to give information."

Upon this Wade suddenly turned his back in a rage and departed, saying in a loud and angry tone, " Hang there then till you rot ! "

So he went away, and I think all the Commisioners then left the Tower : for at five of the clock the great bell of the Tower sounds, as a signal for all to leave who do not wish to be locked in all night. Soon after this they took me down from my cross : and though neither foot nor leg was injured, yet I could hardly stand.

CHAPTER XXI.

MY SECOND TORTURE.

I was helped back to my cell by the gaoler, and meeting on the way some of the prisoners who had the range of the Tower, I addressed the gaoler in their hearing, saying I wondered how those gentlemen could insist so on my telling them where Father Garnett was, since every one must acknowledge it to be a sin to betray an innocent man, a thing I would never do though I should die for it. This I said out loud, on purpose that the authorities might not have it in their power to publish a report about 'me, that I had made a confession, as they often did in other cases. I had also another reason, which was that word might reach Father Garnett (through these persons spreading abroad what they heard me say), that it was about him I was chiefly examined, in order that he might look to himself. I noticed that my gaoler was very unwilling I should speak thus before the others, but I did not stint for that. My gaoler appeared sincerely to compassionate my state, and when we reached my cell he laid me a fire, and brought me some food, as supper-time had nearly come. I scarcely tasted anything, but laid myself on my bed, and remained quiet there till the next morning.

Early next morning however, soon after the

Tower gates were opened, my gaoler came up to the cell and told me that Master Wade had arrived, and that I must go down to him. I went down therefore that time in a sort of cloak with wide sleeves, for my hands were so swollen that they would not have passed through ordinary sleeves. When I had come to the Lieutenant's house, Wade addressed me thus : " I am sent to you on the part of the Queen and of Master Secretary Cecil, the first of whom assures you on the word of a Sovereign, the other on his word of honour, that they know for certain that Garnett *is* in the habit of meddling in political matters, and that he is an enemy of the State. Consequently unless you mean to contradict them flatly, you ought to submit your judgment, and produce him."

" They cannot possibly know this," I replied, "by their own experience and of certain knowledge, since they have no personal knowledge of the man. Now I have lived with him and know him well, and I know him to be no such character as you say."

" Well then," returned he, " you will not acknowledge it, nor tell us what we ask ? "

" No, certainly not ; " said I, " I neither can nor will."

" It would be better for you if you did ; " he replied. And thereupon he summoned from the next room a gentleman who had been there waiting, a tall and commanding figure, whom he called the Superintendent of Torture. I knew there was such an officer, but this man was not really in that charge, as I heard afterwards, but was Master of the Artillery in the Tower. However Wade called him by this name to strike the greater terror into me, and said to him, " I deliver this man into your

hands. You are to rack him twice to-day, and
twice daily until such time as he chooses to confess." The officer then took charge of me, and
Wade departed.

Thereupon we descended with the same solemnity
as before into the place appointed for torture, and
again they put the gauntlets on the same part of
my arms as before : indeed they could not be put on
in any other part, for the flesh had so risen on both
sides that there were two hills of flesh with a valley
between, and the gauntlets would not meet anywhere but in the valley. Here then were they put
on, not without causing me much pain. Our good
Lord however helped me, and I cheerfully offered
Him my hands and my heart. So I was hung up
again as I before described ; and in my hands I felt
a great deal more pain than on the previous day,
but not so much in my breast and belly, perhaps
because this day I had eaten nothing.

While thus hanging I prayed, sometimes silently,
sometimes aloud, recommending myself to our
Lord JESUS and His Blessed Mother. I hung
much longer this time without fainting, but at
length I fainted so thoroughly that they could not
bring me to, and they thought that I either was
dead or soon would be. So they called the Lieutenant, but how long he was there I know not, nor
how long I remained in the faint. When I came
round however, I found myself no longer hanging
by my hands, but supported sitting on a bench, with
many people round me, who had opened my teeth
with some iron instrument and were pouring warm
water down my throat. Now when the Lieutenant
saw I could speak, he said :

" Do you not see how much better it is for you to

yield to the wishes of the Queen than to lose your life this way ? "

By God's help I answered him with more spirit than I had ever before felt ; " No, certainly I do not see it.   I would rather die a thousand times than do what they require of me."

" You will not, then ? " he repeated.

" No, indeed I will not," I answered, "while a breath remains in my body."

" Well then," said he, and he seemed to say it sorrowfully, as if reluctant to carry out his orders, " we must hang you up again now, and after dinner too."

" Let us go then in the name of God," I said, " I have but one life ; and if I had more I would offer them all for this cause."   And with this I attempted to rise in order to go to the pillar, but they were obliged to support me, as I was very weak in body from the torture.   And if there was any strength in my soul, it was the gift of God ; and given, I am convinced, because I was a member of the Society, though a most unworthy one.   I was suspended therefore a third time, and hung there in very great pain of body, but not without great consolation of soul, which seemed to me to arise from the prospect of dying.   Whether it was from a true love of suffering for Christ, or from a sort of selfish desire to be with Christ, God knows best : but I certainly thought that I should die, and felt great joy in committing myself to the will and good pleasure of my God, and contemning entirely the will of men. Oh that God would grant me always to have that same spirit (though I doubt not that it wanted much of true perfection in His eyes), for a longer life remains to me than I then thought, and He

granted me.a reprieve to prepare myself better for
His Holy Presence.

After a while the Lieutenant seeing that he made
no way with me by continuing the torture, or
because the dinner-hour was near at hand, or
perhaps through a natural feeling of compassion,
ordered me to be taken down. I think I hung not
quite an hour this third time. I am rather inclined
to think that the Lieutenant released me from compassion ; for, some time after my escape, a gentleman of quality told me he had it from Sir Richard
Barkeley himself (who was this very Lieutenant of
whom I speak), that he had of his own accord
resigned the office he held, because he would no
longer be an instrument in torturing innocent men
so cruelly. And in fact he gave up the post after
holding it but three or four months, and another
Knight was appointed in his stead, in whose time it
was that I made my escape.[1]

So I was brought back to my room by my gaoler,
who seemed to have his eyes full of tears, and he

---

[1] Among the extracts from Father Garnett's letters in the Stonyhurst MSS. occur the following. They seem to be written to
Father Persons at Rome.

"Apr. 23, 1597. John Gerard hath been sore tortured in ye
Tower : it is thought it was for some letters directed to him out of
Spain."

Between this date and the next, some of Father Gerard's
correspondence probably reached Father Garnett, for on June 10,
1597, he writes :—

"I wrote unto you heretofore of ye remove of Mr. Gerard to
ye Tower: he hath been thrice hanged up by ye hands, every
time until he was almost dead, and that in one day twice. The
cause was (as now I understand perfectly) for to tell where his
superior was, and by whom he had sent him letters which were
delivered him from Father Persons. He was discovered by one of
his fellow prisoners. The Earl of Essex saith he must needs
honour him for his constancy."

assured me that his wife had been weeping and
praying for me the whole time, though I had never
seen the good woman in all my life. Then he
brought me some food, of which I could eat but
little, and that little he was obliged to cut for me
and put into my mouth. I could not hold a knife
in my hands for many days after, much less now
when I was not even able to move my fingers, nor
help myself in anything, so that he was obliged to
do everything for me. However by order of the
authorities he took away my knife, scissors, and
razors, lest I should kill myself, I believe : for they
always do this in the Tower as long as the prisoner
is under warrant for torture. I expected therefore
daily to be sent for again to the torture-chamber,
according to order ; but our merciful God, while to
other stronger champions, such as Father Walpole
and Father Southwell, He gave a sharp struggle
that they might overcome, gave His weak soldier
but a short trial that he might not be overcome.
They indeed being perfected in a short time fulfilled
a long space ; but I, unworthy of so great a good,
was left to run out my days, and so supply for my
defects by washing my soul with my tears, since I
deserved not to wash it with my blood. God so
ordained it, and His Holy Will be done.

CHAPTER XXII.

I REMAINED therefore in my cell, spending my time principally in prayer. And now again I made the Spiritual Exercises, as I had done at the beginning of my imprisonment, giving four or five hours a day to meditation for a whole month. I had a breviary with me, so that I was able to say my Office; and every day I said a dry Mass, (i.e. such as is said by those who are practising Mass before the priesthood), and that with great reverence and desire of communicating, especially at that part where I should have communicated if the Sacrifice had been real. And these practices consoled me in my tribulation.

At the end of three weeks, as far as I can remember, I was able to move my fingers, and help myself a little, and even hold a knife. So when I had finished my retreat I asked leave to have some books, but they only allowed me a Bible, which I obtained from my friends in my former prison. I sent to them for some money, by means of which I saw that I should be able to enlist the sympathies of my gaoler, and induce him to allow me things, and even to bring me some books. My friends sent me by him all that I asked for. I got my gaoler to buy some large oranges, a fruit of which he was very fond. But besides gratifying him with a present of them, I meditated making another use of them in time.

I now began to exercise my hands a little after dinner. Supper I never took, though it was allowed : indeed, there was no stint of food in the prison, all being furnished at the Queen's expense : for there were given me daily six small rolls of very good bread. There are different scales of diet fixed in the prison according to the rank of the prisoner; the religious state indeed they take no account of, but only human rank, thus making most of what ought to be esteemed the least. Well, the exercise which I gave my hands was to cut the peels of these oranges into the form of crosses, and sew them two and two together. I made many of these crosses, and many rosaries also strung on silken cord. Then I asked my gaoler if he would carry some of these crosses and rosaries to my friends in my old prison. He, seeing nothing in this to compromise him, readily undertook to do so. In the meanwhile I put by some of the orange-juice in a small jug. I was now in want of a pen, but I dared not openly ask for one : nay, even if I had asked and obtained my request, I could at this time scarcely have written, or but very badly ; for though I could hold a pen, yet I could hardly feel that I had anything in my fingers. The sense of touch was not recovered for five months, and even then not fully, for I was never without a certain numbness in my hands up to the time of my escape, which was more than six months after the torture. So I begged for a quill to make myself a tooth-pick, which he readily brought me. I made this into a pen fit for writing, then cutting off a short piece of the pointed end, I fixed it on a small stick. With the rest of the quill I made a tooth-pick, so long that nothing appeared to have been cut off, and this I afterwards showed my gaoler. Then I begged for some paper to wrap up my rosaries and crosses, and obtained his leave also to write a line or two with pencil on the paper, asking my friends to pray for me. All this he allowed, not suspecting that he was carrying anything but what he knew. But I had managed to write on the paper with some orange-juice, telling my friends to write back to me in the same way, but sparingly at first ; asking them also to give the bearer a little money and promise him some as often as he should bring any crosses or rosaries from me with a few words of my writing to assure them that I was well.

When they received the paper and the rosaries, knowing that I should if possible have written something with orange-juice, as I used to do with them, they immediately retired to a private room and held the paper to a fire. Thus they read all I had written, and wrote back to me in the same way, sending me some comfits or dried sweetmeats wrapped up in the paper on which they had written. We continued this method of communication for about half a year; but we soon proceeded with much greater confidence when we found that the man never failed to deliver our missives faithfully. For full three months however he had no idea that he was carrying letters to and fro. But after three months I began to ask him to allow me to write with a pencil at greater length, which he permitted. I always gave him these letters open, that he might see what I wrote : and I wrote nothing but spiritual matters that he could see, but on the blank part

K

of the paper I had written with orange-juice directions and particular advice for my different friends,
about which he knew nothing.

As it happened indeed, I need not have been so
circumspect ; for the man, as I found out after some
time, could not read. He pretended however that
he was able, and used to stand and look over my
shoulder while I read to him what I had written
with pencil. At length it occurred to me that possibly he could not read ; so in order to make the
trial, while he was looking over the paper I read it
altogether in a different way from what I had written
it. After doing this on two or three occasions without
his taking any notice, I said openly to him with a
smile, that he need not look over my shoulder any
more. He acknowledged indeed that he could not
read, but said that he took great pleasure in hearing
what I read to him. After this he let me write what
I would, and carried everything as faithfully as ever.
He even provided me with ink, and carried closed
letters to and fro between my friends and me. For
seeing that I had to do with very few, and those
discreet and trustworthy people, and thinking that
neither I nor they were likely to betray him, he did
just what we asked him for a consideration, for he
always received a stipulated payment. He begged
me however not to require him to go so often to the
Clink prison, lest suspicion should arise from these
frequent visits, which might cause harm not only to
him but to me : he proposed therefore that some
friend of mine should meet him near the Tower
and deliver the letters to him. But I was loth to
risk the safety of any one by putting him thus in
the man's power. It made no difference to those
already in custody ; they could without much addi-

tional danger hold correspondence with me, and send me anything for my support by way of alms. Besides I knew that my messenger would not be likely to speak of the letter he carried, as this would be as dangerous for himself as for those to whom he carried them.

Nay even if he had wished he could not have done much injury either to me or my friends, because I took good care never to name any of them in my letters. Both before I was in prison and after, I invariably used pseudonyms which were understood by those to whom I wrote : thus, I called one "brother," another "son," another "nephew" or "friend," and so of their wives, calling this one "sister," that "niece," or "daughter." In this way no one not in the secret could possibly tell whom I meant, even if the letters had been intercepted, which they never were. I may add that even had the letters been betrayed and read, they could never have been made further use of by the enemy, in allowing them to be carried to their destination to lure the correspondents on till they should compromise themselves, as was sometimes done. For I never wrote now with lemon-juice, as I did once in the Clink; which letter was betrayed to the persecutor Wade, as I before related. The reason of my doing so then was because that was a kind of circular letter which had to be read in one place and then carried to another. Now lemon-juice has this property, that what is written in it can be read by water quite as well as by fire, and when the paper is dried the writing disappears again till it is steeped afresh, or again held to the fire. But anything written with orange-juice is at once washed out by water and cannot be read at all in that way; and if held to the fire, though the characters are thus made to appear and can be read, they will not disappear again; so that a letter of this sort once read can never be delivered to any one as if it had not been read. The party will see at once that it has been read, and will certainly refuse and disown it if it should contain anything dangerous. It was in this way I knew that my letters always reached my friends and that theirs reached me in safety. And so our correspondence continued,—I obtaining sure information of all my friends, and they receiving at my hands the consolation they sought.

In order however that matters might go on still more securely, I managed through some of my friends that John Lilly's release should be purchased: and from that time I always got him to bring to my gaoler everything that reached me from the outside. It was through his means too a little later that I escaped from the Tower, although nothing certainly was farther from my thoughts when I thus secured his services : all I had in view was to be able to increase my correspondence with safety. This went on for about four months, and after the first month I gave a good time to study by means of books secretly procured. But at this time an event occurred which caused :me great anxiety.

Master Francis Page, of whom I have before spoken, was now living with my former host [Mr. Wiseman], who had been released from prison. After my removal to the Tower, he got to learn in what part of it I was confined : and out of respect for me used to come daily to a spot from whence he could see my window, in order to get the chance some day of seeing me there. At last it so happened that going one day to the window (it was a warm day in summer), I noticed a gentleman at some distance pull off his hat as if to me; then he walked to and fro, and frequently stopped and made pretence of arranging his hair or doing something about his head, in order to have the opportunity of doffing his hat to me without attracting the attention of others. At last I recognized him by the clothes that he was accustomed to wear, and made him a sign of recognition, and giving him my blessing I withdrew at once from the window, lest others should see me and have suspicion of him. But the good man was not content with this; daily did he come for my blessing, and stopped some time walking to and fro, and ever as he turned he doffed his hat, though I frequently made signals to him not to do so. At length he was noticed doing this, and one day as I was looking I saw him to my great grief seized and led away. He was brought to the Lieutenant of the Tower, who examined him about me and my friends. But he denied everything, and said that he simply walked there for his amusement, it being a fine open space close to the River Thames. So they kept him a prisoner for some days, and meanwhile by inquiry found that he was living with my former host. This increased their suspicion that he had been sent there to give me some sign. But as he constantly denied everything, they at last had recourse to me, and sent for me to be examined. Now as I was going to the examination Master Page was walking up and down with my gaoler in the hall, through which I was taken to the chamber where the authorities awaited me. Immediately I was introduced the examiners said to me;

" There is a young man here named Francis Page who says he knows you and desires to speak with you."

"He can do so if he wishes," I replied; "but who is this Francis Page? I know no such person."

"Not know him?" said they, "he at any rate knows you so well that he can recognize you at a distance, and has come daily to salute you."

I however maintained I knew no one of the name. So when they found they could twist nothing out of me either by wiles or threats, they sent me back. But as I passed again through the hall where Master Page was with the others, I looked round from one to another, and said with a loud voice,

" Is there any one here of the name of Francis Page, who says he knows me well, and has often come before my window to see me? Which of all these is he? I know no such person, and I wonder that any one should be willing to injure himself by saying such things."

All this while the gaoler was trying to prevent my speaking, but was unable. I said this not because I had any idea that he had acknowledged that he knew me, but for fear they might afterwards tell him of me what they had told me of him. And so it turned out. For they had told him already that I had acknowledged I knew him, and they had only sent for me then that he might see me go in, intending to tell him I had confirmed all I said before. But now they could not so impose on him. For when he was summoned, he immediately told them what I had said publicly in the hall as I passed through. The men in their disappointment stormed against the gaoler and me, but being thus baffled could not carry out their deception.

A little later they released Master Page for money, who soon crossed the sea, and after going through his studies in Belgium was made priest. Thence he returned afterwards to England and remained mostly in London, where he was much beloved, and useful to many souls. One of his penitents was that Mistress Line whose martyrdom I have above related. In her house he was once taken as I said, but that time he escaped. A little after he obtained his desire of being admitted into the Society, but before he could be sent over to Belgium for his noviceship, he was again taken, and being tried like gold in the furnace, and accepted as the victim of a holocaust, he washed his robe in the blood of the Lamb, and is now in the possession of his reward. And he sees me now no longer detained in the Tower while he is walking by the water of the Thames, but rather he beholds me on the waters still tossed by various winds and storms while he is secure of his own eternal happiness, and solicitous, as I hope, for mine. Before all this however he used to say that he was much encouraged and cheered by hearing what I said as I passed through the hall, as it enabled him to detect and avoid the snares of the enemy.

During the time I was detained in the Tower, no one was allowed to visit me, so I could afford no help to souls by my words; by letter however I did what I could with those to whom I could venture to trust the secret of how they might correspond with me. Once however after John Lilly's release, as he was walking in London streets, two ladies, mother and daughter, accosted him, and begged him if it was by any means possible to bring them where they could see me. He knowing the extreme danger of such an attempt endeavoured to dissuade them, but they gave him no peace till he promised to open the matter to the gaoler, and try to get him to admit them, as if they were relations of his. Gained over by large promises the man consented; the ladies had also made a present of a new gown to his wife. They therefore dressing themselves as simple London citizens, the fashion of whose garments is very different from that of ladies of quality, came with John Lilly under pretence of visiting the gaoler's wife, and seeing the lions that are kept in the Tower, and the other animals there which the curious are in the habit of coming to see. After they had seen all the sights, the gaoler led them within the walls of the Tower, and when he found a good opportunity introduced them into my room, exposing himself to a great danger for a small gain. When they saw me they could not restrain themselves from running and kissing my feet, and even strove with one another who should first kiss them. For my part I could not deny them what they had bought so dear, and then begged for so earnestly, but I only allowed them to offer this homage to me as to the prisoner of Christ, not as to the sinner that I am. We conversed a little, then leaving with me what they had brought for my use, they returned in safety much consoled, for they thought they should never see my face again, inasmuch as they had heard in the city that I was to be brought to trial and executed.

CHAPTER XXIII.

MASS IN THE TOWER.

ONCE also Father Garnett sent me similar happy
news, warning me in a letter full of consolation to
prepare myself for death. And indeed I cannot
deny that I rejoiced at the things that were said to
me : but my great unworthiness prevented me from
going into the House of the Lord. In fact the good
Father, though he knew it not, was to obtain this
mercy before me; and God grant that I may be able
to follow him even at a distance to the cross which
he so much loved and honoured. God gave him
the desire of his heart ; for it was on the Feast of
the Invention of the Holy Cross that he found Him
Whom his soul loved. On this same Feast of the
Holy Cross and anniversary day of this holy Father's
martyrdom, I received, by his intercession I fully
believe, two great favours of which I will speak
further at the close of this narration ; to which close
indeed it behoves me to hasten, for I am conscious
that I have already been more diffuse than such
small matters warranted.

What Father Garnett warned me of by letter the
enemy threatened also by words and acts about
that time. For those who had come before with
authority to put me to the torture, now came again,
but with another object, viz., to take my formal

examination in preparation for my trial. So the
Queen's Attorney-General questioned me on all
points, and wrote everything down in that order
which he meant to observe in prosecuting me at
the assizes, as he told me. He asked me therefore
about my priesthood, and about my coming to
England as a priest and a Jesuit, and inquired
whether I had dealt with any to reconcile them to
the Pope, and draw them away from the faith and
religious profession which was approved in England.
All these things I freely confessed that I had done ;
answers which furnished quite sufficient matter for
my condemnation according to their laws. When
they asked however with whom I had communicated in political matters, I replied that I had
never meddled with such things. But they urged
the point, and said it was impossible that I, who
so much desired the conversion of England, should
not have tried these means also, as being very well
adapted to the end. To this I replied as far as I
recollect in the following way :

" I will tell you my mind candidly in this matter,
and about the State, in order that you may have
no doubt about my intent, nor question me any more
on the subject ; and in what I say, lo ! before God
and His holy Angels I lie not, nor do I add aught
to the true feeling of my heart. I wish indeed that
the whole of England should be converted to the
Catholic and Roman Faith, that the Queen too
should be converted and all the Privy Council,
yourselves also, and all the Magistrates of the
realm : but so that the Queen and you all without
a single exception should continue to hold the same
powers and dignities that you do at present, and
that not a single hair of your head should perish,

that so you may be happy both in this life and the next. Do not think however that I desire this conversion for my own sake in order to regain my liberty, and follow my vocation in freedom. No; I call God to witness that I would gladly consent to be hung to-morrow, if all this could be brought about by that means. This is my mind and my desire, consequently I am no enemy of the Queen's nor of yours, nor have I ever been so."

Hereupon Mr. Attorney kept silence for a time, and then he began afresh to ask me what Catholics I knew; did I know such and such? I answered; "I do not know them." And I added the usual reasons why I should still make the same answer even if I did know them.

The Attorney-General wrote everything down, and said he should use it against me at my trial in a short time. But he did not keep his word. For I was not worthy to enter under God's roof, where nothing defiled can enter. I have therefore still to be purified by a prolonged sojourn in exile, and so at length, if God please, be saved as by fire.

This my last examination was in Trinity Term, as they call it. They have four terms in the year, during which many come up to London to have their causes tried, for these are times that the Law Courts are open. It is during these terms, on account of the great confluence of people, that they bring those priests to trial whom they have determined to prosecute; and probably this was what they proposed to do in my case—but man proposes and God disposes, and He had disposed otherwise. When this time therefore had passed away, there was no longer any probability that they would proceed against me publicly. I turned my attention consequently to study in this time of enforced leisure as I thought they had now determined only to prevent my communication with others, and that this was the reason they had transferred me to my present prison as being more strict and more secure.

I thus endeavoured to conform myself to the decrees of God and the tyranny of man; when lo! on the last day of July, the anniversary of Our Holy Father Ignatius' departure from this life, while I was in meditation and was entertaining a vehement desire of an opportunity for saying Mass, it came into my head that this really might be accomplished in the cell of a certain Catholic gentleman, which lay opposite mine on the other side of a small garden within the Tower. This gentleman [1] had been detained ten years in prison. He had been indeed condemned to death, but the sentence was not carried out. He was in the habit of going up daily on the leads of the building in which he was confined, which he was allowed to use as a place of exercise; here he would salute me, and wait for my blessing on bended knees.

On examining this idea of mine more at leisure, I concluded that the matter was feasible, if I could prevail on my gaoler to allow me to visit this gentleman. For he had a wife who had obtained

---

[1] We find from an extract of one of Father Garnett's letters in the Stonyhurst MSS. that this gentleman's name was Arden. "Oct. 8. 1597. Upon St. Francis day at night broke out of ye Tower one Arden, and Mr. Gerard the Jesuit: there is yet no great inquiry after him."

Bartoli also and Father More mention Arden as the name of Father Gerard's companion. One Edward Arden was put to death in 1583, fourteen years before this, for some pretended plot against the Queen. Father Gerard's companion was John Arden, no doubt a relation of this Edward.

permission to visit him at fixed times, and bring him changes of linen and other little comforts in a basket; and as this had now gone on many years, the officers had come to be not so particular in examining the basket as they were at first. I hoped therefore that there would be a possibility of introducing gradually by means of this lady all things necessary for the celebration of Mass, which my friends would supply. Resolving to make the trial, I made a sign to the gentleman to attend to what I was going to indicate to him. I then took pen and paper and made as if I was writing somewhat; then after holding the paper to the fire I made a show of reading it, and lastly I wrapped up one of my crosses in it, and made a sign of sending it over to him. I durst not speak to him across the garden as what I said would easily have been heard by others. Then I began treating with my gaoler to convey a cross or a rosary for me to my fellow-prisoner, for the same man had charge of both of us, as we were near neighbours. At first he refused, saying that he durst not venture, as he had had no proof of the other prisoner's fidelity in keeping a secret. "For if," said he, "the gentleman's wife were to talk of this, and it should become known I had done such a thing, it would be all over with me." I reassured him however, and convinced him that such a result was not likely, and, as I added a little bribe, I prevailed upon him as usual to gratify me. He took my letter, and the other received what I sent; but he wrote me nothing back as I had requested him to do. Next morning when he made his appearance on the leads he thanked me by signs, and showed the cross I had sent him.

After three days as I got no answer from him, I
began to suspect the real reason, viz., that he had
not read my letter. So I called his attention again,
and went through the whole process in greater
detail. Thus, I took an orange and squeezed the
juice into a little cup, then I took a pen and wrote
with the orange-juice, and holding the paper some
time before the fire, that the writing might be
visible, I perused it before him, trying to make him
understand that this was what he should do with
my next paper. This time he fathomed my meaning, and thus read the next letter I sent him. He
soon sent me a reply, saying that he thought the
first time I wanted him to burn the paper as I had
written a few visible words on it with pencil ; therefore he had done so. To my proposal moreover
he answered that the thing could be done, if my
gaoler would allow me to visit him in the evening
and remain with him till next day ; and that his
wife would bring all the furniture that should be
given her for the purpose.

As a next step I sounded the gaoler about allowing me to visit my fellow-prisoner, and proposed he
should let me go just once and dine with him, and
that he, the gaoler, should have his share in the
feast. He refused absolutely, and showed great
fear of the possibility of my being seen as I crossed
the garden, or lest the Lieutenant might take it
into his head to pay me a visit that very day. But
as he was never in the habit of visiting me, I argued
that it was very improbable that the thing should
happen as he feared ; after this, the golden arguments I adduced proved completely successful, and
he acceded to my request. So I fixed on the
Nativity of the Blessed Virgin ; and in the mean-

while I told my neighbour to let his wife call at such a place in London, having previously sent word to John Lilly what he should give her to bring. I told him moreover to send a pyx and a number of small hosts, that I might be able to reserve the Blessed Sacrament. He provided all I told him, and the good lady got them safely to her husband's cell. So on the appointed day I went over with my gaoler, and stayed with my fellow-prisoner that night and the next day; but the gaoler exacted a promise that not a word of this should be said to the gentleman's wife. The next morning then I said Mass, to my great consolation; and that Confessor of Christ communicated, after having been so many years deprived of that favour. In this Mass I consecrated also two and twenty particles, which I reserved in the pyx with a corporal; these I took back with me to my cell, and for some days renewed the divine banquet with ever-fresh delight and consolation.

CHAPTER XXIV.

Now while we were together that day, I,—though nothing was less in my thoughts when I came over than any idea of escape, (for I sought only our true deliverer Jesus Christ, as He was prefigured in the little ash-baked loaf of Elias, that I might with more strength and courage travel the rest of my way even to the mount of God,)—seeing how close this part of the Tower was to the moat by which it was surrounded, began to think with myself that it were a possible thing for a man to descend by a rope from the top of the building to the other side of the moat. I asked my companion therefore what he thought about it, and whether it seemed possible to him.

"Certainly," said he, "it could be done, if a man had some true and real friends to assist him, who would not shrink from exposing themselves to danger to rescue one they loved."

"There is no want of such friends," I replied, "if only the thing is feasible, and worth while trying."

"For my part," said he, "I should only be too glad to make the attempt; since it would be far better for me to live even in hiding, where I could enjoy the Sacraments and the company of good men, than to spend my life here in solitude between four walls."

"Well then," I answered, "let us commend the matter to God in prayer; in the meanwhile I will write to my Superior, and what he thinks best we will do."

I returned that night to my cell; and wrote a letter to Father Garnett by John Lilly, putting all the circumstances before him. He answered me that the thing should be attempted by all means, if I thought it could be done without danger to my life in the descent.

Upon this I wrote to my former host [Mr. Wiseman], telling him that an escape in this way could be managed, but that the matter must be communicated to as few as possible, lest it should get noised abroad and stopped. I appointed moreover John Lilly and Richard Fulwood, the latter of whom was at that time serving Father Garnett, if they were willing to expose themselves to the peril, to come on such a night to the outer bank of the moat opposite the little tower in which my friend was kept, and near the place where Master Page was apprehended, as I described before. They were to bring with them a rope, one end of which they were to tie to a stake; then we from the leads on the top of the tower would throw over to them a ball of lead with a stout string attached, such as men use for sewing up bales of goods. This they would find in the dark by the noise it would make in falling, and would attach the string to the free end of their rope, so that we who retained one end of the string would thus be able to pull the rope up. I ordered moreover that they should have on their breasts a white paper or handkerchief, that we

L

might recognize them as friends before throwing out our string, and that they should come provided with a boat in which we might quickly make our escape.

When these arrangements had been made and a night fixed, yet my host wished that a less hazardous attempt should first be made, viz., by trying whether my gaoler could be bribed to let me out, which he could easily do by permitting a disguise. John Lilly therefore offered him on the part of a friend of mine a thousand florins on the spot, and a hundred florins yearly for his life, if he would agree to favour my escape. The man would not listen to anything of the kind, saying he should have to live an outcast if he did so, and should be sure to be hung if ever he was caught. Nothing therefore could be done with him in this line. So we went on with our preparations according to our previous plan; and the matter was commended to God with many prayers by all those to whom the secret was committed. One gentleman indeed, heir to a large estate, made a vow to fast once a week during his life if I escaped safely.

When the appointed night came, I prevailed on the gaoler by entreaties and bribes to allow me to visit my friend. So he locked us both in together with bolts and bars of iron as usual, and departed. But as he had also locked the inside door that led to the roof, we had to loosen the stone, into which the bolt shot, with our knives, or otherwise we could not get out. This we succeeded in doing at length, and mounted the leads softly and without a light, for a sentinel was placed in the garden every night, so that we durst not even speak to each other but in a very low whisper.

About midnight we saw the boat coming with our friends, namely, John Lilly, Richard Fulwood, and another who had been my gaoler in the former prison, through whom they procured the boat, and who steered the boat himself. They neared the shore; but just as they were about to land, some one came out of one of the poor cottages thereabouts to do somewhat, and seeing their boat making for the shore, hailed them, taking them for fishermen. The man indeed returned to his bed without suspecting anything, but our boatmen durst not venture to land till they thought the man had gone to sleep again. They paddled about so long however that the time slipped away, and it became impossible to accomplish anything that night; so they returned by London Bridge. But the tide was now flowing so strongly that their boat was forced against some piles there fixed to break the force of the water, so that they could neither get on nor get back. Meanwhile the tide was still rising, and now came so violently on the boat that it seemed as if it would be upset at every wave. Being in these straits they commended themselves to God by prayers, and called for help from men by their cries. All this while we on the top of the tower heard them shouting, and saw men coming out on the bank of the river with candles, running up and getting into their boats to rescue those in danger. Many boats approached them but none durst go up to them, fearing the force of the current.[1] So they stood

[1] The piers of Old London Bridge were so numerous, and offered so great an obstruction to the water, that it was always a service of danger to pass under the arches while the tide was running: and often the river formed a regular cataract at this part.

there in a sort of circle round them, spectators of
their peril, but not daring to assist.   I recognized
Richard Fulwood's voice in the shouts, and said,
" I know it is our friends who are in danger."   My
companion indeed did not believe I could distinguish
any one's voice at that great distance ;[2] but I knew
it well, and groaned inwardly to think that such
devoted men were in peril of their lives for my sake.
We prayed fervently therefore for them, for we saw
that they were not yet saved, though many had
gone to assist them.   Then we saw a light let down
from the bridge,[3] and a sort of basket attached to a
rope, by which they might be drawn up, if they
could reach it.   This it seems they were not able
to do.   But God had regard to the peril of His
servants, and at last there came a strong sea boat
with six sailors, who worked bravely, and bringing
their boat up to the one in danger, took out Lilly
and Fulwood.   Immediately they had got out, the
boat they had left capsized before the third could
be rescued, as if it had only kept right for the sake
of the two who were Catholics.   However by God's
mercy the one who was thrown into the river caught
a rope that was let down from the bridge, and was
so dragged up and saved.   So they were all rescued
and got back to their homes.

> [2] The distance would be something over half a mile.
> [3] Our readers will remember that at this time each side of the
> bridge was lined with houses, which looked sheer down into the
> river.

CHAPTER XXV.

ESCAPE FROM THE TOWER.

ON the following day John Lilly wrote me by the gaoler as usual. What could I expect him to say but this :—' We see, and have proved it by our peril, that it is not God's will we should proceed any further in this business.' But I found him saying just the contrary. For he began his letter as follows :—" It was not the will of God that we should accomplish our desire last night, still He rescued us from a great danger, that we might succeed better the next time. What is put off is not cut off :[1] so we mean to come again to-night with God's help."

My companion on seeing such constancy joined with such strong and at the same time pious affection, was greatly consoled and did not doubt success. But I had great ado to obtain leave from the gaoler to remain another night out of my cell; and had misgivings that he would discover the loosening of the stone when he locked the door again. He however remarked nothing of it.

In the meantime I had written three letters to be left behind. One was to the gaoler, justifying myself for taking this step without a word to him; I told him I was but exercising my right, since I was

---

[1] "Quod differtur non aufertur."—*MS.*

detained in prison without any crime, and added that I would always remember him in my prayers, if I could not help him in any other way. I wrote this letter with the hope that if the man were taken into custody for my escape it might help to show that he was not to blame. The second letter was to the Lieutenant, in which I still further exonerated the gaoler, protesting before God that he knew nothing whatever about my escape, which was of course perfectly true, and that he certainly would not have allowed it if he had suspected anything. This I confirmed by relating the very tempting offer which had been made him and which he had refused. As to his having allowed me to go to another prisoner's cell, I said I had extorted it from him with the greatest difficulty by repeated importunities, and therefore it would not be right that he should suffer death for it. The third letter was to the Lords of the Council, in which I stated first the causes which moved me to the recovery of my liberty of which I had been unjustly deprived. It was not so much the mere love of freedom, I said, as the love of souls which were daily perishing in England that led me to attempt the escape, in order that I might assist in bringing them back from sin and heresy. As for matters of state, as they had hitherto found me averse to meddling with them, so they might be sure that I should continue the same. Besides this, I exonerated the Lieutenant and gaoler from all consent to or connivance at my escape, assuring them that I had recovered my liberty entirely by my own and my friends' exertions. I prepared another letter also, which would be taken next morning to my gaoler, not however by John Lilly, but by another, as I shall narrate presently.

At the proper hour we mounted again on the leads. The boat arrived and put to shore without any interruption. The schismatic, my former gaoler at the Clink, remained with the boat, and the two Catholics came with the rope. It was a new rope, for they had lost the former one in the river on occasion of their disaster. They fastened the rope to a stake, as I had told them ; they found the leaden ball which we threw, and tied the string to the rope. We had great difficulty however in pulling up the rope, for it was of considerable thickness, and double too. In fact Father Garnett ordered this arrangement, fearing lest otherwise the rope might break by the weight of my body. But now another element of danger showed itself, which we had not reckoned on : for the distance was so great between the tower and the stake to which the rope was attached, that it seemed to stretch horizontally rather than slopingly ; so that we could not get along it merely by our weight, but would have to propel ourselves by some exertion of our own. We proved this first by a bundle which we had made of books and some other things wrapped up in my cloak. This bundle we placed on the double rope to see if it would slide down of itself, but it stuck at once. And it was well it did ; for if it had gone out of our reach before it stuck, we should never have got down ourselves. So we took the bundle back and left it behind.

My companion, who had before spoken of the descent as a thing of the greatest ease, now changed his mind, and confessed it to be a thing very difficult and full of danger. "However," said he, " I shall most certainly be hung if I remain now, for we cannot throw the rope back without its falling into the water, and so betraying both us and our friends. I will therefore descend, please God, preferring to expose myself to danger with the hope of freedom, rather than to remain here with good certainty of being hung." So he said a prayer, and took to the rope, He descended fairly enough, for he was strong and vigorous, and the rope was then taut; his weight however slackened it considerably, which made the danger for me greater, and though I did not then notice this, yet I found it out afterwards when I came to make the trial.

So commending myself to God, to our Lord Jesus, to the Blessed Virgin, to my Guardian Angel, and all my Patrons, particularly Father Southwell, who had been imprisoned near this place for nearly three years before his martyrdom, and Father Walpole, I took the rope in my right hand and held it also with my left arm; then I twisted my legs about it, to prevent falling, in such a way that the rope passed between my shins. I descended some three or four yards face downwards, when suddenly my body swung round by its own weight and hung under the rope. The shock was so great that I nearly lost my hold, for I was still but weak, especially in the hands and arms. In fact, with the rope so slack and my body hanging beneath it, I could hardly get on at all. At length I made a shift to get on as far as the middle of the rope, and there I stuck, my breath and my strength failing me, neither of which were very copious to begin with. After a little time, the Saints assisting me, and my good friends below drawing me to them by their prayers, I got on a little further and stuck again, thinking I should never be able to accomplish it. Yet I was loth to drop into the water as long as I could possibly hold on. After another rest therefore I summoned what remained of my strength, and helping myself with legs and arms as well as I could, I got as far as the wall on the other side of the moat. But my feet only touched the top of the wall, and my whole body hung horizontally, my head being no higher than my feet, so slack was the rope. In such a position, and so exhausted as I was, it was hopeless to expect to get over the wall by my own unaided strength. So John Lilly got on to the wall somehow or other (for, as he afterwards asserted, he never knew how he got there), took hold of my feet, and by them pulled me to him, and got me over the wall on to *terra firma*. But I was quite unable to stand, so they gave me some cordial waters and restoratives, which they had brought on purpose. By the help of these I managed to walk to the boat, into which we all entered. They had however before leaving the wall untied the rope from the stake and cut off a part of it, so that it hung down the wall of the tower. We had previously indeed determined to pull it away altogether, and had with this object passed it round a great gun on the tower without knotting it. But God so willed it that we were not able by any exertion to get it away; and if we had succeeded it would certainly have made a loud splash in the water, and perhaps have brought us into a worse danger.

CHAPTER XXVI.

HOW THE GAOLER ESCAPED TOO.

On entering the boat we gave hearty thanks to God, Who had delivered us from the hand of the persecutor, and from all the expectation of the people: we returned our best thanks also to those who had exposed themselves to such labours and perils for our sakes. We went some considerable distance in the boat before landing. After we had landed I sent the gentleman, my companion, with John Lilly, to my house, of which I have before spoken, which was managed by that saintly widow, Mistress Line. I myself however with Richard Fulwood went to a house which Father Garnett had in the suburbs; and there Little John and I, a little before daylight, mounted our horses, which he had ready there for the purpose, and rode straight off to Father Garnett who was then living a short distance in the country.[1] We got there to breakfast, and great rejoicing there was on my arrival, and much thanksgiving to God at my having thus escaped from the hands of my enemies in the name of the Lord.

In the meanwhile I had sent Richard Fulwood with a couple of horses to a certain spot, that he might be ready to ride off with my gaoler, if he

---

[1] This was at Uxbridge. The house in the suburbs previously mentioned was in Spitalfields.

wished to consult his immediate safety. For I had
a letter written, of which I made previous mention,
which was to be taken to him early in the morning
at the place where he was accustomed to meet John
Lilly. Lilly however did not carry the letter, for
I had bidden him remain quiet within doors, until
such time as the storm which was to be expected
had blown over. So another person took the letter,
and gave it to the gaoler at the usual meeting place.
He was indeed surprised at another's coming, but
took the letter without remark, and was about to
depart with the intention of delivering it to me as
usual; but the other stopped him saying,

" The letter is for you, and not for any one else."

" For me ? " said the gaoler: " from whom does it
come ? "

" From a friend of yours," replied the other, " but
who he is I dont know."

The gaoler was still more astonished at this, and
said,

" I cannot myself read: if then it is a matter
which requires immediate attention, pray read it for
me."

So the man that brought the letter read it for
him. It was to the effect, that I had made my
escape from prison ; and here I added a few words
on the reasons of my conduct, for the purpose of
calming his mind: then I told him that though I
was no wise bound to protect him from the consequences, as I had but used my just right, yet as I
had found him faithful in the things which I had
entrusted him with, I was loth to leave him in the
lurch: if therefore he was inclined to provide for
his own safety immediately, there was a horse
waiting for him with a guide who would bring him

to a place of safety, sufficiently distant from London, where I would maintain him for life, allowing him two hundred florins yearly, which would support him comfortably. I added that if he thought of accepting this offer, he had better settle his affairs as quickly as possible and betake himself to the place which the bearer of the letter would show him.

The poor man was, as may well be supposed, in a great fright, and accepted the offer: but as he was about to return to the Tower to settle matters and get his wife away, a mate of his met him, and said, "Be off with you, as quick as you can; for your prisoners have escaped, and Master Lieutenant is looking for you everywhere. Woe to you, if he finds you!" So returning all in a tremble to the bearer of the letter, he besought him for the love of God to take him at once to where the horse was waiting for him. He took him therefore, and handed him over to Richard Fulwood who was to be his guide. Fulwood took him to the house of a friend of mine residing at the distance of a hundred miles from London, to whom I had written, asking him, if such a person should come, to take him in and provide for him : I warned him however not to put confidence in him, nor to acknowledge any acquaintance with me. I told him that Richard Fulwood would reimburse him for all the expenses, but that he must never listen to the man if at any time he began to talk about me or about himself.

Everything was done as I had arranged; my friend received no damage, and the gaoler remained there out of danger. After a year he went into another county, and becoming a Catholic, lived there comfortably for some five years with his family on the annuity which I sent him regularly

according to promise. He died at the end of those
five years, having been through that trouble rescued
by God from the occasions of sin, and, as I hope,
brought to heaven. I had frequently in the prison
sounded him in matters of religion; and though
his reason was perfectly convinced, I was never
able to move his will. My temporal escape then,
I trust, was by the sweet disposition of God's
merciful Providence the occasion of his eternal
salvation.

The Lieutenant of the Tower, when he could not
find either his prisoners or their gaoler, hastened
to the Lords of the Council with the letters which
he had found. They wondered greatly that I should
have been able to escape in such a way: but one
of the chief members of the Council, as I afterwards
heard, said to a gentleman who was in attendance,
that he was exceedingly glad I had got off. And
when the Lieutenant demanded authority and assistance to search all London for me, and any suspected
places in the neighbourhood, they all told him it
would be of no use. "You cannot hope to find
him," said they; "for if he had such determined
friends as to accomplish what they have, depend
upon it they will have made further arrangements,
and provided horses and hiding-places to keep him
quite out of your reach." They made search however in one or two places, but no one of any mark
was taken that I could ever hear of.

For my part, I remained quietly with Father
Garnett for a few days, both to recruit myself, and
to allow the talk about my escape to subside.
Then my former hosts, who had proved themselves
such devoted friends, urged my return to them, first
to their London house close to the Clink prison,

where they were as yet residing. So I went to them, and remained there in secrecy, admitting but very few visitors : nor did I ever leave the house except at night, a practice I always observed when in London, though at this time I did even this very sparingly, and visited only a few of my chief friends.

CHAPTER XXVII.

FORTUNATE PRECAUTIONS.

At this time I also visited my house, which was then under the care of Mistress Line, afterwards martyred. Another future martyr was then residing there of whom I have previously spoken, namely, Mr. Robert Drury, priest. In this house about this time I received a certain parson who had been chaplain to the Earl of Essex in his expedition against the Spanish King, when he took Cadiz. He was an eloquent man and learned in languages ; and when converted to the Catholic faith he had abandoned divers great preferments, nay, had likewise endured imprisonment for his religion. Hearing that he had an opportunity of making his escape, I offered that he should come to my house. There I maintained him for two or three months, during which time I gave him the Spiritual Exer-cises. In the course of his retreat he came to the determination of offering himself to the Society : upon which I asked him to tell me candidly how he, who had been bred up in Calvin's bosom as it were, had been accustomed to military life, and had learnt in heresy, and had long been accustomed, to prefer his own will to other people's, could bring himself to enter the Society, where he knew, or certainly should know, that the very opposite principles prevailed. To this he replied,

"There are three things in fact which have especially induced me to take this step. First, because I see that heretics and evil livers hold the Society in far greater detestation than they do any other religious order; from which I judge that it has the Spirit of God in an especial degree, which the spirit of the devil cannot endure, and that it has been ordained by God to destroy heresy, and wage war against sin in general. Secondly, because all ecclesiastical dignities are excluded by its Constitutions, whence it follows that there is in it a greater certainty of a pure intention; and as its more eminent members are not taken from it for the Episcopate, it is more likely to retain its first fervour and its high estimation for virtue and learning. Thirdly, because in it Obedience is cultivated with particular care, a virtue for which I have the greatest veneration, not only on account of the excellent effects produced thereby in the soul, but also because all things must needs go on well in a body where the wills of the members are bound together, and all are directed by God."

These were his reasons; so I sent him into Belgium, that he might be forwarded to Rome by Father Holt, giving him three hundred florins for his expenses. I gave the Spiritual Exercises also to some others in that house before I gave it up, among whom was a good and pious priest, named Woodward, who also found a vocation to the Society, and afterwards passed into Belgium with the intention of entering it; but as there was a great want of English priests in the [Spanish] army at the time, he was appointed to that work, and died in it, greatly loved and reverenced by all.

I did not however keep that house long after the recovery of my liberty, because it was now known to a large number of persons, and was frequented during my imprisonment by many more than I should have permitted if I had been free. My principal reason however for giving it up was because it was known to the person who had been the cause of my being sent to the Tower. He had indeed expressed his sorrow for his act, and had written to me to beg my pardon, which I freely gave him; yet as he was released from prison soon after my escape, and I found that those among whom he had lived had no very good opinion of his character, I did not think it well that a thing involving the safety of many should remain within his knowledge. Mistress Line also, a woman of singular prudence and virtue, was of the same mind. So I determined to make other arrangements as soon as possible.

Now a little before this had begun the movement of opposition against the Arch-priest. Hence it happened that some priests who were in the habit of resorting to my house and residing there for a time, began to swerve somewhat from the more perfect course, and yet always expected to be received to board and lodging in a house where they knew Mistress Line resided. The consequence was that this asylum of mine, which should have been reserved for the use of myself and my chief friends, was the resort of a great number of persons, many of whom were no great friends of mine, nor too much to be trusted. These circumstances, no less than those I mentioned above, confirmed me in my resolution of making a total change in my arrangements.

It seemed best therefore, in order to remove all idea of so general a place of resort, that Mistress Line should lodge for a space by herself in a hired room of a private house; while I, who did not wish to be without a place in London where I could safely admit some of my principal friends, and perhaps house a priest from time to time, joined with a prudent and pious gentleman, who had a wife of similar character, in renting a large and spacious house between us. Half the house was to be for their use, and the other half for mine, in which I had a fair chapel well provided and ornamented. Hither I resorted when I came to London, and here also I sent from time to time those I would, paying a certain sum for their board. In this way I expended scarce half the amount I did formerly under the other arrangement, when I was obliged to maintain a household whether there were any guests in the house or not; though indeed it was seldom that the house was empty of guests.

I made this new provision for my own and my friends' accommodation just in good time; for most certainly had I remained in my former house I should have been taken again. The thing happened in this wise. The priest who, as I have related, got me promoted from a more obscure prison to a nobler one, began to importune me with continual letters that I would grant him an interview. Partly by delaying to answer him, partly by excusing myself on the score of occupation, I put him off for about half a year. At length he urged his request very pressingly, and complained to me by letter

M

that I showed contempt of him. I sent him no
answer, but on a convenient occasion, knowing
where he lodged, I despatched a friend to him to
tell him that if he wished to see me, he must come
at once with the messenger. I warned the messenger however not to permit any delay, nor to
allow him to write anything nor address any one
on the way if he wished to have an interview with
me. I arranged moreover that he should be brought
not to any house, but to a certain field near one of
the Inns of Court, which was a common promenade,
and that the messenger should walk there alone
with him till I came. It was at night, and there
was a bright moon. I came there with a couple of
friends, in case any attempt should be made against
me, and making a half circuit outside, entered the
field near the house of a Catholic which adjoined
it ; and our good friend catching first sight of me
near this house, thought perhaps that I came out
of it, and in fact the Arch-priest was lodging in it
at the time. However that may be, I found him
there walking and waiting for me, and when I had
heard all he had to say, I saw there was nothing
which he had not already said in his letters, and
to which he had not had my answer. My suspicion
was therefore increased, and certainly not without
reason. For within a day or two that corner house
near which he saw me enter the field, and my old
house which I had lately left (though he knew not
I had left it), were both of them surrounded and
strictly searched on the same night and at the same
hour. The Arch-priest was all but caught in the
the one ; he had just time to get into a hiding-place,
and so escaped. The search lasted two whole days
in the other house, which the priest knew me to

have occupied at one time. The Lieutenant of the Tower and the Knight-Marshal conducted the searches in person, a task they never undertake unless one of their prisoners has escaped. From these circumstances it is sufficiently clear, both whom they were in search of, and from whom they got their information.

But when they found me not, (nor indeed did they find the priest who was then in the house living with a Catholic to whom I had let it,) they sent pursuivants on the next day to the house of my host, who had by this time returned to his country seat, but by God's mercy they did not find me there either. It was well therefore that I acted cautiously with the above-mentioned priest, and also that I had so opportunely changed my residence in London.

CHAPTER XXVIII.

A CHANGE OF QUARTERS.

I saw also that it would soon be necessary for me to give up my present residence in the country, and betake myself elsewhere; otherwise those good and faithful friends of mine would always be suffering some annoyance for my sake. I proposed the matter therefore to them, but they refused to listen to me in this point, though in all other things most compliant. But I thought more of their peace than of their wishes, however pious these wishes were; and therefore I laid the matter before my Superior, who approved my views. So I obtained from Father Garnett another of Ours, a pious and learned man whom I had known at Rome, and who at present was companion to Father Oldcorne of blessed memory: this was Father Richard Banks, now professed of four vows. I took him to live with me for a time, that I might by degrees introduce him into the family in my place; and in the meantime I made more frequent excursions than usual.

In one of these excursions I visited a noble family, by whom I had long been invited and often expected, but had never yet been able to visit them on account of my pressing occupations. Here I

found the lady of the house,[1] a widow, very pious
and devout, but at this present overwhelmed with
grief at the loss of her husband. She had indeed
been so affected by this loss that for a whole year
she scarce stirred out of her chamber, and for the
next three years which had intervened before my
visit, had never brought herself to go to that part
of the mansion in which her husband had died.
To this grief and trouble were added certain
anxieties about the bringing up of her son, who was
yet a child under his mother's care. He was one
of the first Barons of the realm; but his parents
had suffered so much for the Faith, and had mort-
gaged so much of their property to meet the
constant exactions of an heretical government,
that the remaining income was scarcely sufficient
for their proper maintenance. But a wise woman
builds up a house and is proved in it.

I found residing with this family one of our
Fathers, a learned man and a good preacher: he
had been a year in the house, but some of the
household were prejudiced against him. The
mistress however always showed him the utmost
reverence, and was assiduous in approaching the
Sacraments. On my arrival this good widow
seemed to see her wishes fulfilled, and not only
welcomed me most charitably, but appeared so
changed from grief to joy, that some of her household represented to me that if I would come there
oftener, still more if I could reside there perma-
nently, they were assured she would lay aside that
long-continued grief, and that both she herself and

---

[1] This lady was the widow of George Vaux, second son of Lord
Vaux of Harrowden. The elder brother dying unmarried, the
boy here mentioned became fourth Baron.—M.

her affairs would soon be in a better condition. This I think they had from the mistress herself. For she soon took an opportunity of praising the happiness of my hosts, of whom she had heard much not only about their domestic chapel and altar-furniture, but also about their virtue and patience, which had been so tried in the fire of persecution. She added that she marvelled not that they went forward so steadfastly since they had such a guide; she also would be able to do the like, had she but like opportunity; then all her affairs would go well.

I saw how much she was deceived in me, and how she thought of me above what was in me; I answered her therefore that she had even more and greater helps than they had, which was indeed but the truth. She rejoined that she had indeed a good and pious director whom she both much reverenced and loved; but that as he had never lived in the world, having always been with those who gave themselves to study, he was not so well able to judge what was best to be done in worldly affairs, and consequently some in the house were opposed to him.

"These persons," said I, "are evidently not possessed of the true spirit, which supposes obedience and subordination : and they would treat me in like fashion were I living in the house."

"They should soon quit it then," she replied, "even if they were ten times as necessary to me as they are." In fact they had the principal charge of the household under their mistress.

She besought me to make trial of her, whether or no she would be obedient and compliant in all that I might judge to be for the greater glory of God. I felt it impossible to reject such an offer from such a

person, made as it was at a time when good reasons
made it expedient that I should change my residence.
Nay it seemed to me clearer than noon-day that
God's good providence had arranged this, as from
the first day of my arrival in England it had directed
me hither and thither, but always changing my
position for the better, continually affording me
additional means of becoming acquainted with
greater numbers of persons, and those of higher
rank, and of strengthening and guiding them in His
service. I replied to her therefore, that I returned
her my best thanks, and that I would mention
her pious wish to my Superior: I added that there
was one thing that inclined me to listen to her proposal, and this was that whereas elsewhere I had
only a secular priest as companion, in her house I
should have a member of the same Society with
myself, and a person whom I much loved.

On my return to London therefore I proposed the
matter to Father Garnett, who was much rejoiced
at the offer, knowing the place to be one where good
might be done both directly and indirectly. He
said too that the offer had occurred most opportunely, for that there were some Catholics in
another county more to the north, where there was
no priest of the Society, who had been long peti-
tioning for this very father, at present stationed at
that house, and who would much rejoice at the
prospect of having him among them. To this I
urged that the place was large enough for two,
and that I very much desired to have a companion
of the Society with me. Father Garnett however
had already determined to place another father in
that residence, on account of the opposition of which
I have spoken; and was therefore unwilling to let

me have him for companion. I then requested that
he would assign me Father John Percy, with whom
I had become acquainted during my imprisonment,
not indeed personally but by frequent interchange
of letters. This father had been taken prisoner by
English soldiers in Holland, where he was recognized and tortured; he was afterwards thrown into
the foul gaol of Bridewell, and after remaining
there some time made a shift to escape from a
window with another priest, letting himself down
with a rope. Mistress Line made him welcome in my
house, where he tarried for a time; but soon after
went down into the county of York, and dwelt there
with a pious Catholic. In this part he made himself
so dear to every one, that though I had Father
Garnett's consent, it was a full year before I could
get him away from them.

Since now to the desire of this noble widow was
added the approval of Father Garnett, I so settled
my affairs as to provide amply for the security and
advantage of my former hosts. For I left with them
Father Banks, a most superior man in every respect:
and although at first my old friends did not value
him so much, yet as they became better acquainted
they found that the good account I had given them
was no more than the truth, and soon came to
esteem him as a father. I often afterwards visited
their house, where I found so great faith and piety.

When I was domiciled in my new residence, I
began by degrees to wean my hostess' mind from
that excessive grief; showing how that we ought
to mourn moderately only over our dead, and not
to grieve like those who have no hope. I added
that as her husband had become a Catholic before
his death, one little prayer would do him more good

than many tears :—that our tears should be reserved
for our own and others' sins, for our own souls
stood in need of floods of that cleansing water, and
it was to the concerns of our own souls that all our
thoughts and labours should be turned. I then
taught her the use of meditation, finding her quite
capable of profiting by it, for her mental powers
were of a very high order. I thus gradually brought
her first to change that old style of grief for a more
worthy one;—then to give eternal concerns the
preference over worldly matters; and to consider
how she might transform her life, which before was
good and holy, into better and holier, by endeavour-
ing as much as she could to imitate the life of our
Lord and of His Saints.

In the first place therefore she resolved to lead
an unmarried life; secondly to aim at poverty in
this sense, that all her actual fortune, and all that
she might ever have, should be devoted to the
service of God and His ministers, while she herself
should be but their servant to provide them with
what was necessary : lastly, she gave herself above
all to obedience, and determined to reduce her love
of it to practice no less perfectly than if she had
taken a vow : nay, it was her only trouble that it
was forbidden to priests of our Society to receive
such vows. In a word, it was her fixed resolve to
imitate as closely as possible the life of Martha and
the other holy women who followed our Lord, and
ministered to Him and His Apostles. Consequently
she was ready to set up her residence wherever I
judged it best for our purposes, whether at London
or in the most remote part of the island, as she
often protested to me. I considered however that
though a residence in or near London would be better

for the gaining of souls, yet that it was not at present very safe for me; nor indeed could she remain there in private, since she was well known for a Catholic, and the Lords of the Council demanded from her frequent accounts of her son, the Baron, where and how he was educated. Moreover as she had the management of her son's estate while he was a minor, stewards and bailiffs, and other such persons must have constant communication with her; so that it was quite out of the question her living near London under an assumed name; yet this was absolutely necessary if a person wished to carry on the good work in that neighbourhood. It was thus those ladies did with whom Father Garnett lived so long, who were in fact sisters of this lady's deceased husband, one unmarried, the other a widow. I saw therefore no fitter place for her to fix her residence than where she was among her own people, where she had the chief people of the county connected with her and her son, either by blood or friendship.

The only difficulty which remained was about the exact spot. The house in which she was actually living was not only old, but antiquated. It had been the residence of her husband's father, who had married a wife who was a better hand at spending than at gathering, and consequently the house was very poorly appointed for a family of their dignity. There was another and larger house of theirs at a distance of about three miles, which had been the old family seat. This had also been neglected, so that it was in some part quite ruinous, and not fit for our purpose, namely, to receive the Catholic gentry who might come to visit me. In addition to this, it was not well adapted for defence against any sudden intrusions of the heretics, and consequently we should not be able to be as free there as my hostess wished. Her desire was to have a house where we might as nearly as possible conform ourselves to the manner of life followed in our colleges: and this in the end she brought about.

She sought everywhere for such a house, and we looked at many houses in the country: but something or other was always wanting to her wishes. At last we found a house which had been built by the late Chancellor of England[2] who had died childless, and was now to be let for a term of years. It was truly a princely place, large and wellbuilt, surrounded by gardens and orchards, and so far removed from other houses that no one could notice our coming in or going out. This house she took on payment of fifteen thousand florins, and began to fit it up for our accommodation. She wished to finish the alterations before we removed thither; but man proposes, and God disposes as He wills, though always for the best, and for the true good of His elect.

[2] Sir Christopher Hatton, who died in 1591, had built a country seat at Stoke Pogis in Buckinghamshire.—M.

CHAPTER XXIX.

WHEN I came to this lady's house, she had a great
number of servants, some heretics, others indeed
Catholics, but allowing themselves too much liberty.
By degrees I got things into better order: some I
made Catholics of, others through public and private
exhortations, became by the grace of God more
fervent; in some cases where there did not appear
any hope of amendment, I procured their dismissal,
and among these was he who had chiefly opposed
the former priest of whom I spoke. There was
another also whom we could not correct as soon as
we wished, and who brought great trouble on us.
For on one occasion when we were in London,
either from thoughtlessness or loquacity, or because
the yoke of a stricter discipline, now begun in the
family, sat uneasily upon him, he said to a false
brother, that I had lately come to live at his lady's
house, and had carried on such and such doings
there; and that I was then in London at such a
house, naming the house of which I rented half, as
I have before said; he told him also that he had
gone to that house with his mistress, at a time when
she and I were in town on business connected with
her son. My hostess had now returned into the
country with this servant, leaving me for a short
time in town. But the man had left this tale

behind him, which soon came to the ears of the Council, how that I had my residence with such a lady, and was at this moment at such a house in London. They instantly therefore commissioned two justices of the peace to search the house.

I, who had no inkling of such a danger, had remained in town for certain business, and was giving a Retreat to three gentlemen in the house before mentioned. One of these three gentlemen was Master Roger Lee, now Minister in the English College of St. Omer's. He was a gentleman of high family, and of so noble a character and such . winning manners that he was a universal favourite, especially with the nobility, in whose company he constantly was, being greatly given to hunting, hawking, and all other noble sports. He was indeed excellent at everything, but he was withal a Catholic, and so bent on the study of virtue that he was meditating a retreat from the world, and a more immediate following of Christ. He used frequently to visit me when I was in the Clink prison, and I clearly saw that he was called to greater things than catching birds of the air; and that he was meant rather to be a catcher of men. I had now therefore fixed a time with this gentleman and good friend of mine, in which he should seek out by . means of the Spiritual Exercises the strait path that leads to life, under the guidance of Him Who is Himself the Way and the Life.

But while he and the others were engaged privately in their chambers in the study of this heroic philosophy, suddenly the storm burst upon us. I too, in fact, after finishing my business in town, had taken the opportunity of a little quiet to begin my own retreat, giving out that I had returned

into the country. I was now in the fourth day of
the retreat, when about three o'clock in the after-
noon John Lilly hurried up to my room and without
knocking entered with his sword drawn.

Surprised at this sudden intrusion, I asked what
was the matter.

"It is a matter of searching the house," he replied.

"What house?"

"This very house;—and they are in it already!"

In fact they had been cunning enough to knock
gently, as friends were wont to do; and the servant
opened readily to them, without the least suspicion
until he saw them rush in and scatter themselves in
all directions.

While John was telling me this, up came the
searching party, together with the mistress of the
.house, to the very room in which we were. Now
just opposite to my room was the chapel, so that
from the passage the door of the chapel opened on
the one hand, and that of my room on the other.
The magistrates then, seeing the door of the chapel
open, went in, and found there an altar richly
adorned, and the priestly vestments laid out close
by, so handsome as to cause expressions of admiration from the heretics themselves. In the meanwhile I in the room opposite, was quite at my wit's
end what to do; for there was no hiding-place in
the room, nor any means of exit except by the open
passage where the enemy were. However, I
changed the cassock which I was wearing for a
secular coat, but my books and manuscript meditations which I had there in considerable quantities I
was quite unable to conceal.

We stood there with our ears close to the chink

of the door, listening to catch what they said : and
I heard one exclaim from the chapel ; "Good God !
what have we found here ! I had no thoughts of
coming to this house to-day !" From this I con-
, cluded that it was a mere chance search, and that
they had no special warrant. Probably therefore,
I thought, they had but few men with them. So
we began to consult together whether it were not
better to rush out with drawn swords, seize the
keys from the searching party, and so escape ; for
we should have Master Lee and the master of the
house to help us, besides two or three men-servants.
Moreover, I considered that if we should be taken
in the house the master would certainly be visited
with a far greater punishment than what the law
prescribes for resistance to a magistrate's search.

While we were thus deliberating, the searchers
came to the door of my room and knocked. We
made no answer, but pressed the latch hard down,
for the door had no bolt or lock. As they continued
knocking, the mistress of the house said,

" Perhaps the man-servant who sleeps in that
room may have taken away the key. I will go and
look for him."

" No, no ; " said they, " you go no-where without
us ; or you will be hiding away something."

And so they went with her, not staying to
examine whether the door had a lock or not. Thus
did God blind the eyes of the Assyrians that they
should not find the place, nor the means of hurting
His servants, nor know where they were going.

When they had got below stairs, the mistress of
the house, who had great presence of mind, took
them into a room in which some ladies were, viz.
the sister of my hostess in the country, and Mistress

Line; and while the magistrates were questioning
these ladies she ran up to us saying, "Quick!
quick! get into the hiding-place!". She had scarce
said this and run down again, before the searchers
had missed her and were for remounting the stairs.
But she stood in their way on the bottom step, so
that they immediately suspected what the case was,
and were eager to get past. This however they
could not do without laying forcible hands on the
lady, a thing which as gentlemen they shrank from
doing. One of them however, as she stood there
purposely occupying the whole width of the stair-
way, thrust his head past her, in hopes of seeing
what was going on above stairs. And indeed he
almost caught sight of me as I passed along to the
hiding-place. For as soon as I heard the lady's
words of warning, I opened the door, and with the
least possible noise mounted from a stool to the
hiding-place, which was arranged in a secret gable
of the roof. When I had myself mounted, I bade
John Lilly come up also: but he more careful of
me than of himself, refused to follow me, saying;

"No, Father; I shall not come. There must be
some one to own the books and papers in your
room: otherwise, upon finding them, they will never
rest till they have found you too."

So spoke this truly faithful and prudent servant,
so full of charity as to offer his life for his friend.
There was no time for further words. I acquiesced
reluctantly, and closed the small trap-door by which
I had entered: but I could not open the door of
the inner hiding-place, so that I should infallibly
have been taken if they had not found John Lilly,
and mistaking him for a priest ceased from any
further search. For this was what happened; God

so disposing it, and John's prudence and intrepidity helping thereto.

For scarcely had he removed the stool by which I mounted, and had gone back to the room and shut the door, when the two chiefs of the searching party again came up stairs, and knocked violently at the door, ready to break it open if the key were not found. Then the intrepid soldier of Christ threw open the door and presented himself undaunted to the persecutors.

"Who are you?" they asked.

"A man, as you see:" he replied.

"But what are you? Are you a priest?"

"I do not say I am a priest," replied John; "that is for you to prove. But I am a Catholic certainly."

Then they found there on the table all my meditations, my breviary, and many Catholic books, and what grieved me most of all to lose, my manuscript sermons and notes for sermons, which I had been writing or compiling for the last ten years, and which I made more account of perhaps than they did of all their money. After examining all these, they asked whose they were.

"They are mine;" said John.

"Then there can be no doubt you are a priest. And this, cassock,—whose is this?"

"That is a dressing-gown, to be used for convenience now and then."

Convinced now that they had caught a priest, they carefully locked up all the books and writings in a box, to be taken away with them: then they locked the chapel-door, and put their seal upon it: and taking John by the arm, they led him down stairs, and delivered him into the custody of their

N

officers. Now when he entered with his captors into the room where the ladies were, he, who at other times was always wont to conduct himself with humility and stand uncovered in such company, now on the contrary after saluting them covered his head and sat down. Nay, assuming a sort of authority, he said to the magistrates : " These are noble ladies ; it is your duty to treat them with consideration. I do not indeed know them ; but it is quite evident that they are entitled to the greatest respect."

I should have mentioned that there was a second priest in the house with me, Father Pollen, an old man, who had quite lately made his noviceship at Rome. He luckily had a hiding-place in his room, and had got into it at the first alarm.

The ladies therefore now perceiving that I was safe, and that the other priest had also escaped, and seeing also John's assumed dignity, could scarce refrain from showing their joy. They made no account now of the loss of property, or the annoyance they should have to undergo from the suspicion of having had a priest in the house. They wondered indeed and rejoiced, and almost laughed to see John playing the priest ; for so well did he do it as to deceive those deceivers, and divert them from any further search.

CHAPTER XXX.

FURTHER HISTORY OF JOHN LILLY.

The magistrates who had searched the house took away John Lilly with them, and the master of the house also with his two men-servants, under the idea that all his property would be confiscated for harbouring a priest. The ladies however represented that they had merely come to pay an after-dinner visit to the mistress of the house, without knowing anything about a priest being there; so they were let off on giving bail to appear when summoned. The same favour was ultimately shown to Master Roger Lee, though it was with greater difficulty the magistrates could be persuaded that he was only a visitor. At last then they departed well satisfied, and locked up their prisoners for the night to wait their morrow's examination.

Immediately on their departure the mistress of the house and those other ladies came with great joy to give me notice; and we all joined in giving thanks to God Who had delivered us all from such imminent danger by the prudence and fidelity of one. Father Pollen and I removed that very night to another place, lest the searchers should find out their error and return.

The next day I made a long journey to my

hostess' house in the country, and caused much fear, and then much joy, as I related all that God had done for us. Then we all heartily commended John Lilly to God in prayer. And indeed there was reason enough to do so. For the magistrates, making full inquiries the next day, found that John had been an apothecary in London for six or seven years, and then had been imprisoned in the Clink for eight or nine more, and that he had been the person who had communicated with me in the Tower, for the gaoler's wife after her husband's flight had confessed so much. They saw therefore clearly that they had been tricked, and that John was not a priest, but a priest's servant; and they now began to have a shrewd suspicion, though rather too late, that I had been hidden at the time in the same house where they caught him, especially as they found so many books and writings which they did not doubt were mine. They sent therefore to search the house again, but they found only an empty nest, for the birds were flown.

John was carried to the Tower, and confined there in chains. Then they examined him about my escape, and about all the places he had been to with me since. He, seeing that his dealings with the gaoler were already known to them, and desirous (if God would grant him such a favour) to lay down his life for Christ, freely confessed that it was he who had compassed my deliverance, and that he took great pleasure in the thought of having done so; he added that he was in the mind to do the same again, if occasion required, and opportunity offered. The gaoler however he exonerated, and protested that he was not privy to the escape. With regard to the places where he had been with me, he answered (as he had often been taught to do), that he would bring no one into trouble, and that he would not name a single place, for to do so would be a sin against charity and justice. Upon this they said they would not press him any further in words, but would convince him by deeds that he must tell them all they wanted. John replied :

" It is a thing that, with the help of God, I will never do. You have me in your power; do what God permits you."

Then they took him to the torture-chamber, and hung him up in the way I have before described, and tortured him cruelly for the space of three hours. But nothing could they wring from him that they could use either against me or against others : so that from that time they gave up all hope of obtaining anything from him either by force or fear. Consequently they tortured him no more, but kept him in the closest custody for about four months to try and tire him into compliance. Failing also in this, and seeing that their pains availed them nothing, they sent him to another prison, where prisoners are usually sent who are awaiting execution : and probably it was their intention to deal that way with him, but God otherwise determined. For after a long detention here, and having been allowed a little communication with other Catholic prisoners, he was asked by a certain priest to assist him in making his escape. Turning his attention therefore to the matter, he found a way by which he delivered both the priest and himself from captivity.

I ought not however to omit an incident that happened during his detention in the Tower, since it is in such things that the dealings of God's

Providence are often to be very plainly recognized. While he was under examination about me and others of the Society, Wade, who was at that time the chief persecutor, asked him if he knew Garnett. John said he did not.

"No?" said Wade, with a sour smile; "And you don't know his house in the Spital either, I dare say! I don't mind letting you know," he continued, "now that I have you safe, that I am acquainted with his residence, and that we are sure of having him here in a day or two to keep you company. For when he comes to London he puts up at that house, and then we shall catch him."

John knew well that the house named was Father Garnett's resort, and was in great distress to find that the secret had been betrayed to the enemy; and though kept as close as possible, yet he managed to get an opportunity of sending some little article *wrapped up in blank paper* to a friend in London. His friend on receiving it carefully smoothed out the paper and held it to the fire, knowing that John would be likely to communicate by the means of orange-juice if he had the opportunity: and there he found it written that this residence of Father Garnett's had been betrayed, and that Father Garnett must be warned of it. This was instantly done, and in this way the father was saved, for otherwise he would assuredly, as Wade had said, have betaken himself to that house in a day or two. Now however he not only did not go, but took all his things away: so that when the house was searched a day or two later they found nothing. Had it not been for this providential warning from our greatest enemy, they would have found plenty: they would have found him, his books, altar-furniture, and other things of a similar nature. Father Garnett then escaped this time by John's good help as I had done previously.

After his escape John came to me : but though I desired much to keep him, it was out of the question, for he was now so marked a man that his presence would have been a continual danger for me and all my friends. For I was wont in the country to go openly to the houses of Catholic gentlemen, and it might well happen that John might come across persons that knew him, and would know me through him. Whereas but very few of the enemy knew me, for I was always detained in close custody, and none but Catholics saw me in prison : nay, such Catholics only as I knew to be specially trustworthy. I had indeed been examined publicly in London several times, but the persons concerned in the examinations very seldom left town ; and if they had done so I should have been warned of it instantly, and should have taken good care never to trust myself in their neighbourhood. So I put John with Father Garnett, to stay in quiet hiding for a time ; and when opportunity offered, sent him over to Father Persons, that he might obtain, what he had long hoped for, admission into the Society. He was admitted at Rome, and lived there for six or seven years as a lay-brother, much esteemed I believe by everybody. I can on my part testify about him to the Greater Glory of God,—and that the more allowably because I believe he has died in England before this present writing, whither he returned with a consumption on him,—I can, I say, testify that for nearly six years that he was with me in England, and had his hands full of business for me, though he had to do with all sorts of men

in all sorts of places (for while I was engaged upstairs with the gentry or nobility, he was associating
downstairs with the servants, often enough very
indifferent characters), yet the whole of this time
he so guarded his heart and his soul that I never
found him to have been even in danger of mortal
sin ; nay, most constantly in his confessions, unless
he had added some venial sins of his past life I
should not have had sufficient matter for the sacrament. Truly his was an innocent soul, and endowed
also with great prudence and cleverness.

But now that I have brought the history of John
Lilly to its close, it is time to return to myself, who
having just escaped one danger, had like to have
fallen into a second and still greater' one, had not
God again interposed His hand.

CHAPTER XXXI.

MORE DANGERS.

I MENTIONED just now that one of my hostess'
servants told a friend of his, but an enemy of ours,
that I habitually resided at his mistress' house, and
that at that particular time I was in such a house
in London. ' How this house was searched, and
how they seized my companion and my manuscripts, but missed me, I have related. The
Council therefore, now knowing my residence in
the country, issued a commission to some Justices
of the Peace in that county to search this lady's
house for a priest. It had in fact begun to be
talked of in 'the county that she had taken this
grand house in order that she might harbour priests

there in large numbers and with greater freedom, because it was more private; and in this people were not far wrong.

Now at this time, that is, soon after my return from London, we had driven over to the new house to make arrangements for our removal thither, and with the special object of determining where to construct hiding-places. To this end we had Little John with us, whom I have before mentioned as very clever at constructing these places, and whom Father Garnett had lent to us for a time for this purpose. Having made all the necessary arrangements, we left Little John behind, and Hugh Sheldon also to help him, who is now at Rome with Father Persons in the room of John Lilly. These two, whom we had always found most faithful, were to construct the hiding-places, and to be the only ones beside ourselves to know anything about them. The rest of us however returned the same day to our hostess' old house, and by the advice of one of the servants, God so disposing it, we came back a different way, as being easier for the carriage. Had we returned by the way we went, the searchers would have come early to the house where we were, and most probably catching us entirely unprepared would have found what they came to seek. The fact was that the road by which we went to the new house ran through a town, where some of the enemy were on the watch and had seen us pass: but not seeing us return, they concluded that we were spending the night at the new house, and went there the first thing in the morning to search.

But the house was so large, that although they had a numerous body of followers, they were not able to surround it entirely, nor to watch all the outlets so narrowly, but what Little John managed to make off safely. Hugh Sheldon they caught, but could get nothing out of him: so they sent him afterwards to prison at Wisbech, and from thence later to some other prison in company with many priests, and at last in the same good company into exile.

When however the Justices found that they were wrong, and that the lady had returned home the previous day, they retraced their steps and came as fast as their horses could carry them to the old house. They arrived at our dinner-hour, and being admitted by the carelessness of the porter got into the hall before we had any warning. Now as the lady of the house was a little indisposed that morning, we were going to take our dinner in my room, viz. Father Percy, myself, and Master Roger Lee, who had come down from London to finish his retreat which had been so rudely interrupted before. So when I heard who had come, that they were in the great hall, and that his lordship himself, who was indeed but a boy at that time, could not prevent them from intruding into his room, though he was also unwell, I made a pretty shrewd guess what they had come about, and snatching up such things as wanted hiding I made the best of my way to the hiding place, together with Father Percy and master Roger Lee. For it would not do for this latter to have been found here, especially as he had already been found in the house in London where I was known to have been, and would therefore have given good reason to think that I was here also. But we had to pass by the door of the room in which the enemy were as yet waiting, and exclaiming that they would wait no longer. Nay, one of the pursuivants opened the door and looked out ; and some of the servants said afterwards that he must have seen me as I passed. But God certainly interposed; for it was surely not to be expected from natural causes that men who had come eager to search the house at once, and were loudly declaring they would do so, should stay in a room where they were not locked in, just as long as was necessary for us to hide ourselves, and then come forth as if they had been let loose, intrude upon the lady of the house, and course through all the rooms like bloodhounds after their prey. I cannot but think that this was the finger of God, Who would not that the good intentions of this lady should be so soon frustrated, but rather wished by so evident a display of his Providence to confirm her in her determinations, and preserve her for many more good works.

The authorities searched the house thoroughly the whole day, but found nothing. At last they retired disappointed, and wrote to the Council what they had done. We soon discovered who had done the mischief (for he had not done it secretly) and discharged him, but without unkindness. I gave out also that I should quit the place altogether, and for a time we practised particular caution on all points.

CHAPTER XXXII.

SOME QUIET WORK.

IN consequence of this mishap it became impossible for us to remove to the new house. For those same Justices, who were pestilent heretics, and several others in the same county, Puritans, declared they would never suffer her ladyship to live at peace if she came there, as her only object was to harbour priests. Being deterred therefore from that place, but not from her design, she set about fitting up her own present residence for the same purpose, and built us separate quarters close to the old chapel, which had been erected anciently by former Barons of the family to hear Mass in when the weather might make it unpleasant to go to the parish church. Here then she built a little wing of three stories for Father Percy and me. The place was exceedingly convenient, and so free from observation that from our rooms we could step out into the private garden, and thence through spacious walks into the fields, where we could mount our horses and ride whither we would.

As we lived here safely and quietly, I frequently left Father Percy at home, and made excursions to see if I could establish similar centres of operation among other families : and in this Father Roger Lee (to give him his present title) helped me not a

little. He first took me to the house of a relation
of his, who lived in princely splendour, and whose
father was one of the Queen's Council. This young
nobleman [1] was a schismatic, that is, a Catholic
by conviction, but conforming externally to the
State Religion; and there seemed no hope of getting
him any further, for he contented himself with
velleities, and was fearful of offending his father.
His wife however, who was a heretic, had begun to
listen with interest to Catholic doctrine, so that
there was hope she might in time be brought into
the Church. Their house was full of heretic
servants, and there was a constant coming and
going of heretic gentry either on business or on
visit; it was therefore imperatively necessary that
as I could only go there publicly I should well
conceal my purpose.

We paid a visit then to this house, and were
made very welcome, Master Lee for his own sake,
as being much beloved and I for his. On the first
day I looked in vain for an opportunity of a conversation with the Lady of the house, for there was
always some one by. We were obliged to play at
cards to pass the time, as those are wont to do who
know not the eternal value of time, or at least care
not for it. On the next day however, as the lady
of the house stept aside once to the window to set
her watch, I joined her there, and after talking a
little about the watch, passed on to matters which
I had more in view, saying I wished that we took
as much pains to set our souls in order as we did

---

[1] This was Francis, son of Sir John Fortescue, Master of the
Wardrobe to Queen Elizabeth, who married Grace Manners,
grand-daughter of the first earl of Rutland. Roger Lee was first
cousin to Sir Francis Fortescue.—M.

our watches.   She looked up at me in pure surprise
to hear such things from my lips; and as I saw I
might never get a better opportunity than the
present, I began to open a little further, and told
her that I had come there with Master Lee specially
for her sake, hearing from him that she took interest
in matters of religion; and that I was ready to
explain the Catholic doctrine to her, and satisfy all
the doubts she could possibly have : moreover that
I could point out the way to a height of virtue
which she had hitherto never dreamt of, for that in
heresy she could neither find that way, nor any who
made account of it.   She was struck with what I
said, and promised to find some opportunity for
further conversation, when we might speak more
fully on the matter.   I gave her this hint of a higher
virtue, because she had been represented to me, as
she really was, as a lady of most earnest and
conscientious character.

She found the time according to her promise; all
her difficulties were removed, and she became a
Catholic.   After reconciling her to the Church, I
made some other converts in the same house; then
I got her a Catholic maid, and suggested that she
should keep a priest always in the house, to which
she gladly assented.   This was a thing that might
easily be managed, not indeed as it was in our
house, where the whole household was Catholic
and knew us to be priests ; but a priest could well
live in the upper part of the house, from which all
heretics might be kept away, especially now that
some of the servants were Catholics.   And indeed
the accommodation was such that I do not know
any place in England where a priest who wished to
be private could live more conveniently.   For he

could have in the first place a fine room to himself, opening on a spacious corridor of some eighty paces which looked on a garden most expensively laid out: in this corridor moreover was a separate room which would serve excellently as a chapel, and another for his meals, with fire-places and every convenience. It was a pity, I said, that such a place had not a resident priest, where the mistress was a devout Catholic, and the master no enemy to religion. Her husband indeed made no difficulty of receiving priests; nay, he sometimes came to hear me preach, and at last went so far as to be fond of dressing the altar with his own hands, and of saying the Breviary: yet with all this he still remains outside the Ark, liable to be swept off by the waters of the deluge when they break forth, for he presumes too much on an opportunity of doing penance before death.

The lady then readily fell in with my suggestion of having a priest in her house; so I brought thither Father Antony Hoskins, a man of great ability, who had lately come over from Spain, where he had spent ten years in the Society with remarkable success in his studies. Being placed there he did a great deal of good on all sides, and remained with them almost up to the present time, when at length he has been removed and put to greater things. He did not however stay constantly at home, for he is a man whom, when once known, many would wish to confer with, so that he was forced to go about at times. At present there is another father in the house, a most devoted man. But the lady directs herself chiefly by Father Percy, who this very week addressed me a letter in the following words:

"Such a one" (meaning this lady of whom I have been speaking) "is going on very well. She has offered her heart to our Lady of Loreto, to serve Her and Her Son for ever with all that she possesses; and in token of this she has had made a beautiful heart of gold, which she wishes to send to Loreto by the first opportunity. We desire therefore to hear from you by whom she can send this offering."

Thus he writes about this lady. In this way then, by the Grace of God, was this house, with its domestic church, established and confirmed in the Faith.

Master Roger also introduced me to some neighbours of his: among others to a gentleman of the Queen's court, who had inherited a large estate, and had married a lady who was sole heiress to all her father's property.[2] Not one of this family was a Catholic, nor even inclined to the Catholic Faith. The wife's father, who was the head of the house, was a thorough heretic, and had his thoughts entirely occupied in hoarding money for his daughter, and increasing her revenues. His son-in-law devoted himself wholly to juvenile sports. When in London, he attended at Court, being one of the Queen's gentlemen pensioners; but in the country he spent almost his whole time in hunting and hawking. Hence it happened that Master Roger Lee, who was a neighbour of his, and fond of similar sports, often joined him on such occasions, and brought his falcons to hawk in company. We two therefore took advantage of this acquain-

[2] This gentleman was Sir Everard Digby, afterwards concerned in the powder plot. The lady was Mary Mulshaw of Gothurst in Buckinghamshire.

tanceship, and I was introduced to this gentleman's house as a friend and intimate of Master Lee's. We made frequent visits there, and took every opportunity of speaking of Catholic doctrine and practice. I took care however that Master Lee should always speak more frequently and more earnestly than I, that no suspicion might arise about my real character. Indeed so far was this gentleman from having the least suspicion about me, that he seriously asked Master Lee whether he thought I was a good match for his sister, whom he wished to see married well, and to a Catholic, for he looked on Catholics as good and honourable men.

We had therefore, as I said, frequent converse on matters of salvation; and the wife was the first to listen with any fruit, at a time when she was living in the country but her husband was up in town. Her parents were now dead, and she was mistress of the house, so that we were able to deal more directly with her. At last she came to the point of wishing to be a Catholic, and told me she should be glad to speak with a priest. I could scarce forbear a smile at this, knowing that she was already speaking with one; I answered however, that the thing might be managed, and that I would speak with Master Lee on the subject. " In the meantime," I added, " I can teach you the way to examine your conscience, as I myself was taught to do it by an experienced priest." So I told Master Roger that as she was now determined and prepared, he might inform her of my being a priest. This he did, but she for some time refused to believe it, saying,

." How is it possible he can be a priest? Has

o

he not lived among us rather as a courtier? Has he not played at cards with my husband, and played well too, which is impossible for those who are not accustomed to the game? Has he not gone out hunting with my husband, and frequently in my hearing spoken of the hunt in proper terms, without tripping, which no one could do but one who has been trained to it?"

Many other things she adduced to show I could not be a priest : to all of which Master Lee replied,

"It is true that he said and did what you say; and unless he had done so, how could he have gained entrance here, and conversed with you, and by his conversation brought you to the Faith? For if he had presented himself as a priest (which he would much prefer, were it feasible), how would your father, who was then living, have allowed his introduction, or you yourselves?"

She could not but admit. the truth of this; yet she found it hard to believe that it was so. "I pray you," she said, "not to be angry with me, if I ask further whether any other Catholic knows him to be a priest but you.—Does So-and-so know him?"

"Yes," he answered, "and has often confessed to him."

Then she mentioned other names, and at last that of my hostess [the Lady Vaux], who lived in the neighbourhood, but ten miles off.

"Does she too know him as a priest, and deal with him as such?"

"Why," said Master Lee, "she not only knows him as a priest, but has given herself, and all her household, and all that she has, to be directed and governed by him, and takes no other guide but him."

Then at length she confessed herself satisfied.

" You will find him, however," added Master Lee, " quite a different man, when he has put off his present character."

This she acknowledged the next day, when she saw me in my cassock and other priestly garments, such as she had never before seen. She made a most careful confession, and came to have so great an opinion of my poor powers that she gave herself entirely to my direction, meditated great things, which indeed she carried out, and carries out still.

When this matter was thus happily terminated, we all three consulted together, how we could induce her husband to enter also into St. Peter's net. Now it so happened that he had fallen sick in London, and his wife on hearing it determined to go and nurse him. We however went up before her, and, travelling more expeditiously, had time to deal with him before she came. I spoke to him of the uncertainty of life, and the certainty of misery, not only in this life but especially in the next, unless we provided against it : and I showed him that we have here no abiding city but must look for one to come. As affliction oftentimes bringeth sense, so it happened in his case ; for we found but little difficulty in gaining his good-will. And as he was a man of solid sense and excellent heart, he laid a firm foundation from the beginning. He prepared himself well for confession after being taught the way ; and when he learnt that I was a priest, he felt no such difficulty in believing it as his wife had done, because he had known similar cases ; but he rather rejoiced at having found a confessor who had experience among persons of his rank of life, and with whom he could deal at all times without danger of its being known that he was dealing with a priest. After his reconciliation he began on his part to be anxious about his wife, and wished to consult with us how best to bring her to the Catholic Religion. We smiled inwardly at this, but said nothing at that time, determining to wait till his wife came up to town, that we might witness how each loving soul would strive to win the other.

Certainly they were a favoured pair. Both gave themselves wholly to God's service, and the husband afterwards sacrificed all his property, his liberty, nay even his life for God's Church, as I shall relate hereafter. For this was that Everard Digby, Knight, of whom later on I should have had to say many things, if so much had not been already written and published about him and his companions. But never in any of these writings has justice been done to the sincerity of his intention, nor the circumstances properly set forth which would put his conduct in its true light.

After this they both came to see me at my residence in the country. But while there he was again taken ill, and that so violently and dangerously that all the Oxford doctors despaired of his life. As therefore in all likelihood he had not long to live, he began to prepare himself earnestly for a good death, and his wife to think of a more perfect way of life. For some days she gave herself to learn the method of meditation, and to find out God's will with regard to her future life, how she might best direct it to His glory. To be brief, she came to this determination, that if her husband should die, she would devote herself entirely to good works, observe perpetual chastity and exact obedience:—that as for her property, which would be very extensive as they were without children, she would spend it all in pious uses according to my direction: she would herself live where and in what style I judged best for the advancement of God's honour and the good of her own soul; and she added that her desire was to wear poor clothing wherever she might be, and observe all the rules of poverty. All this was to be while the persecution might last in England. If however it should cease, and England should become Catholic, then she would give her house (a very large and fine one), and all the property her father left her, for the foundation of a College of the Society; and this would have been amply sufficient for a first-rate foundation.

This was her resolution, but God had otherwise arranged, and for that time happily. For when all the Oxford doctors gave up Sir Everard's case as hopeless, I who loved him much did not lose heart, but without his knowledge I sent for a certain Cambridge doctor, a Catholic, and a man of much learning and experience, whom I had known to cure cases abandoned by other physicians. On his arrival at our house, where Sir Everard Digby then was with his wife, after telling him all about the patient, I got him to examine the sick man himself and learn from him all about his. habit of body and general constitution. Then I asked him if he thought there was any hope. He answered,

"If Sir Everard will venture to put himself entirely in my hands, I have good hopes, with the help of God, of bringing him round."

The patient on hearing this said to me, " Since this doctor is known to your Reverence, and is chosen by you, I give myself willingly into his hands."

By this doctor then he was cured beyond all expectation, and so completely restored to perfect health that there was not a more robust or stalwart man in a thousand. He was a most devoted friend to me, just as if he had been my twin brother. And this name of brother we always used in writing to each other. How greatly he was attached to me may be seen from the following incident :—once when I had gone to a certain house to assist a soul in agony, he got to learn that I was in great danger there ; upon this he at first expressed a terrible distress, and then immediately said to his wife, that if I should be taken, he was resolved to watch the roads by which I should be · carried prisoner to London, and take with him a sufficient number of friends and servants to rescue me by force from those who had me in custody; and if he should miss me on the road, he would accomplish my release one way or another, even though he should spend his whole fortune in the venture. Such then was his attachment to me at that time, and this he retained always in the same—nay rather in an increased—degree, to the end of his life ; as he showed by the way he spoke of me when pleading for his life before the public court. At this time however, as I said, he was restored to health; and he and his wife got together a little domestic church after the pattern of one in our house, and built a chapel with a sacristy, furnishing it with costly and beautiful vestments, and obtained a priest of the Society for their chaplain who remained with them till Sir Everard's death.

CHAPTER XXXIII.

A PROTESTANT DIGNITARY.

WHAT was done by this family was done by others also. For many of the Catholic gentry coming to our house, and seeing the arrangements and manner of life, followed the example themselves, establishing a sort of congregation in each of their houses, providing handsome altar furniture, making convenient arrangements for the residence of priests, and showing especial respect and reverence to them.

Among those who came to this determination was a certain lady resident near Oxford, whose husband was indeed a Catholic, but overmuch devoted to worldly pursuits. She however gave herself to be ruled and directed by me as far as she could, having such a husband. I often visited them, and was always welcomed by both : and there I established one of our Fathers, Edward Walpole, whom I mentioned at an early part of this narrative as having left a large patrimony for the sake of following Christ our Lord, in the first year of my residence in England.

There was another lady also who had a similar wish : she was a relative of my hostess, and she also resided in the county of Oxford.[1] Her husband was a Knight of very large property, who

[1] Father Morris tells us that this lady was Agnes, wife of Sir Richard Wenman, of Thame Park near Oxford.

hoped to be created a Baron, and still hopes for it. This lady came on a visit to our house, and wished to learn the way of meditating, which I taught her; but as her husband was a heretic it was impossible for her to have a priest in her house, as she greatly wished. She took however the resolution of supporting a priest, who should come to her at convenient times. She resolved also to give an hour daily to meditation, and one or two hours daily to spiritual reading, when she had no guests in the house; also to make a general confession every six months, a practice which was followed also by all those of whom I have just spoken, and by many others whom it is impossible for me to mention individually. On her coming to me every six months for her general confession, I found that she had never omitted her hour of meditation, nor her daily examination of conscience, except on one occasion when her husband insisted on her staying with the guests. Yet she had a large and busy household to superintend, and a continual coming and going of guests.

It happened on one occasion when I was in this lady's house, and was sitting with her after dinner, the servants having gone down to get their own dinner, that suddenly a guest was shown up who had just arrived. This was an Oxford Doctor of Divinity, a heretic of some note and a persecutor of Catholics; his name was Dr. Abbott.[1] He had just been made

---

[1] We extract the following from a note of Dr. Oliver's in the Catholic Spectator :—

"Dr. George Abbott was appointed Dean of Winton in 1599; and was successively Bishop of Lichfield and London, and finally Archbishop of Canterbury. He died at Croydon, Aug. 4, 1633. æt. 71."

Dean of Winchester, a post which brought him in a yearly income of eight thousand florins. This man then, as I said, was shown up, and entered the dining-room, dressed in a sort of silk soutane coming down to his knees, as is the manner of their chief ministers. We were in appearance sitting at cards, though when the servants had all left the room we had laid the cards down to attend to better things. Hearing however this gentleman announced, we resumed our game, so that he found us playing, with a good sum of money on the table.

I may here mention, that when I played thus with Catholics, with the view of maintaining among a mixed company the character in which I appeared, I always agreed that each one should have his money back afterwards, but should say an *Ave Maria* for each piece that was returned to him. It was on these terms that I frequently played with my brother Digby and other Catholics, where it appeared necessary, so that the bystanders thought we were playing for money, and were in hot earnest over it.

So also this minister never conceived the slightest suspicion of me, but after the first courtesies began to talk at a pretty pace; for this is the only thing those chattering ministers can do, who possess no solid knowledge, but by the persuasive words of human wisdom lead souls astray, and subvert houses, teaching things which are not convenient. So he, after much frivolous talk, began to tell us the latest news from London; how a certain Puritan had thrown himself down from the steeple of a church, having left it in writing that he knew himself to be secure of his eternal salvation. About this writing however the learned doctor said nothing, but I had heard the particulars myself from another quarter.

" Wretched man ! " said I, " what could induce him thus to destroy body and soul by one and the same act ! "

" Sir," said the doctor, learnedly enough and magisterially, " we must not judge any man."

" True," I replied, " it is just possible that as he was falling he repented of his sin, *inter pontem et fontem*, as they say : but this is extremely improbable, since the last act of the man of which we have any means of judging was a mortal sin and deserving of damnation."

" But," said the doctor, " we cannot know whether this was such a sin."

" Nay," I replied, " this is not left to our judgment ; it is God's own verdict, when He forbids us under pain of hell to kill any one, a prohibition which applies especially to the killing of ourselves, for charity begins from oneself."

The good Doctor being here caught, said no more on this point, but turned the subject, and said smiling,

" Gentlemen must not dispute on theological matters."

" True," said I, " we do not make profession of knowing theology ; but at least we ought to know the law of God, though our profession is to play at cards."

The lady with whom I was playing, hearing him speak to me in this way could scarce keep her countenance, thinking within herself what he would have said if he had known who it was he was answering. The doctor however did not stay much longer. Whether he departed sooner than he at first indended, I know not ; but I know that we much preferred his room to his company.

CHAPTER XXXIV.

THREE FATHERS OF THE SOCIETY.

I MUST now return to London, and relate what happened after John Lilly was taken, and the gentleman imprisoned with whom I rented my London house. This house being now closed to me, I sought out another but on a different plan. I did not now join in partnership with any one, because I was unwilling to be in the house of one known to be a Catholic. I managed that this new house should be hired by a nephew of Master Roger Lee, whom with his wife I had reconciled to the Catholic Church; and as he was not known to be a Catholic, the house was entirely free from all suspicion. I had the use of this house for three years, and during that time it was not once searched; nor, even before the Queen's death, though there were many general searches made, and the prisons were choked with Catholics, did they ever come to this house.

I had a man to keep the house who was a schismatic, but otherwise an honest and upright person. When I was in residence, this man provided me with necessaries; and when I was away, he managed any business for me according to my written directions. In all appearance he was the servant of the gentleman who owned the house, and so he was esteemed and called by the neighbours; and since as a schismatic he frequented their churches, they entertained no suspicion of him, nor of the house.

For myself, when I came to town, I always entered the house after dark, and in summer time scarce went out while I remained there. But my friends would come to visit me by ones and twos on different days, that no special attention might be drawn to the house from the number of visitors. Nor did they ever bring any servants with them, though some were of very high rank, and usually went about with a large number of attendants. By these means I provided better for them and for myself, and was able to continue longer in this way of life.

It was from this house, soon after my taking possession of it, that Master Roger Lee and three others went to the noviceship, all of whom are now priests and labourers in the Society. The only one of them who is not now actually labouring is Father Strange, who is at present suffering imprisonment in the Tower of London, where he has had to undergo many grievous tortures, and a long solitary confinement. This solitude indeed, if we look only to his natural disposition, cannot but be very irksome and oppressive to him; but *he* is not solitary who has God always present with him, consoling him, and supplying in an eminent degree and full abundance all those comforts which we are wont to go begging for from creatures. This Father Strange used to come to me when I was a prisoner in the Clink. He was a Catholic before I knew him; and seeing that he was a youth of quick parts and good disposition, an only son and heir to a fair property, so that he could well associate with gentlmen, I got him to come often to me, and at length to make the Spiritual Exercises. In the course of these he saw good reason to come to the resolution of following Christ our Lord, and entering the Society. Till he could make full arrangements for this, and sell his property, I got him to reside in the same house with Father Garnett, that the good spirit he had imbibed might not evaporate, but be rather increased. He remained with Father Garnett nearly two years before he was able to disentangle himself entirely from his worldly goods : at length cutting the last ties which bound his bark to the English shore, he passed across the channel a free man.

Before he started however, he brought me a friend and companion of his who is now Father Hart. He also is an only son, and his father, a rich man, is I think still alive. I did not give him the Exercises, but I met him from time to time (for I was free now), and instead of the Exercises I taught him the method of daily meditation. I gave him also some pious books to read, among others Father Jerome Platus ; and it was from this last that he acquired the spirit of Religion and of the Society. He is now a very useful labourer in England, and well suited to converse and deal with gentlemen, to whose society he was accustomed before he left the world.

The third was the present Father Thomas Smith, who for these last four years has resided at St. Omer's. He was a Master of Arts of Oxford ; and I found him engaged as tutor to the young Baron, the son of my hostess : so that I had many good opportunities of conversing freely with him. But as he was a schismatic, that is, though a Catholic by conviction yet lingering in heresy from infirmity of will, I found it impossible to move him, or even stir him from his present state of mind. Such people in fact, who can truly say with the Prophet, " My belly cleaveth to the ground," are far more difficult to gain than full heretics, as we find by daily experience. He was often present at my private exhortations, and also at my public sermons, but he slept a heavy and lethargic slumber, so that one might easily recognize the power of the strong man armed keeping his house in peace. However a stronger than he came upon him, and despoiled him, and bound him, and took away his armour in which he trusted. And this stronger one who overcame him was no other than the Child Who was born and given to us. For on the night of our Lord's Nativity, while the whole family were celebrating the Feast, he alone of all remained in bed ; but he could not sleep, and began to feel an overpowering shame, seeing that even the three boys whom he taught had risen and were engaged in praising God, thus teaching their master not by words but by deeds. Roused therefore interiorly by the cradle-cries of the Divine Infant, he began to think with himself how much time he had hitherto lost, and how the very boys and the unlearned were entering into God's Kingdom before him. So, trembling and eager to lose no more time, he rose at once, came to the chapel door and knocked, and asked to speak to me. As I was engaged, I sent him a message, asking him to wait till the morning, when I should be at his service. But he would not listen, and sent back word that he must speak with me at once. I therefore bade him have a little patience, and when I had finished Matins, I came out to him, dressed in my alb as I was. When he saw me he threw himself at my feet, and said, with the tears streaming down his cheeks, "Oh, Father, I beseech you for the love of God to hear my confession."

I wondered at the strangeness of the thing, and bade him be of good heart:—that I would hear him at a proper time, but that he must first prepare himself well for it.

"Oh, Father," he cried, "I have put it off too long already! Do not bid me delay any more."

"It is well," I replied, "that you feel the necessity of instant diligence. But it is not delaying, to take a fair and moderate time for preparation. Nay the confession and absolution would not be good, if preparation and examination are omitted, when they might easily have been made."

"Well, but," urged he, "I may die before the time of confession."

"Then I will answer for you before God," I said: "do you in the meanwhile conceive in your heart a true sorrow for having offended our good Lord."

Upon this he yielded, and retired still weeping; and after one or two days' diligent examination of conscience, he made his confession, and being reconciled celebrated with us the conclusion of the Feast, the beginning of which he had lost.

These three then of whom I have spoken, crossed over into Belgium with Master Lee, and from thence passing on to Rome, made their noviceship at St. Andrew's, all except Father Hart. He was admitted rather later, but was sent in to England earlier than the others on some business, and is a very useful labourer there.

CHAPTER XXXV.

WHEN I was in London, I did not allow every one to come to my house whose desire to converse with me I was willing to gratify ; but I would sometimes, especially after dark in winter time, go myself to their houses. On one occasion I was asked by a certain lady to her house to hear the confession of a young nobleman attached to the court, who was a dear friend of her husband's. Her husband was also a Catholic and well known to me : though quite a young man, he had been one of the principal captains in the Irish War. And the young nobleman just mentioned was a Baron, and son to an Irish Earl, and at this present writing he has himself succeeded to the earldom on his father's death. This young Baron then wished to make his confession to me. As I had not known him before, I put a few questions to him, according to my wont, beforehand. I asked him therefore if he was prepared at once. He answered that he was. I then asked how often in the year he was accustomed to go to the Sacraments. " Twice or thrice in the year," he said.

" It would be better," said I, " to come more frequently and then less preparation would be necessary. As it is I should advise you to take a few days for the exact and diligent examination of your conscience, according to the method that I will show you: then you will come with greater fruit, and with greater satisfaction to yourself and to me. And for the future I would, recommend a more frequent use of the holy Sacraments." And I brought some reasons for my advice.

He listened to me very patiently, and when I had finished, he replied, " I will do in future what you recommend, and I would willingly follow your counsel at present, if it were possible; it is however impossible to put off my present con-fession."

" Why is it impossible? " I asked.

" Because," he replied, " to-morrow I shall be in circumstances of danger, and I desire to prepare myself by confession to-day."

" What danger is this," I asked again, " to which you will be exposed? "

" There is a gentleman at Court," he said, " who has grievously insulted me; so that I was compelled in defence of my honour, to challenge him to single combat; and we meet to-morrow at an appointed spot at some distance from town."

" My Lord," I exclaimed, " to approach the sacrament in such a frame of mind, is not to pre-pare for danger, nor to cleanse your soul (though I doubt not that it was with a good intention you proposed it), but rather to sully your soul more than ever, to affront God still further, and render Him still more your enemy. For to come to confession with a determination of taking vengeance is to put an obstacle to the grace of the sacrament; and moreover this particular action on which you are resolved is not only a sin, but is visited with excommunication. I urge you therefore to give

P

up this intention; you will be able to preserve your honour by some other way. Nay, the honour you think to preserve by this, is not real honour, but merely the estimation of bad men founded on bad principles; men who exalt their own worldly ideas above the law and honour of God."

"It is impossible to withdraw now," he said, "for the thing is known to many, and has been taken even to the Queen, who has expressly forbidden us to pursue the matter any further."

"Well then," said I, "you have the best possible reason for laying aside the quarrel, namely, obedience to the Queen's behest. Moreover you must remember that you are known for the intimate friend of the Earl of Essex, and that if you overcome your adversary, the Queen (if it be only to spite the Earl) will certainly visit you with some heavy punishment for having disregarded her commands: but if you should kill him, unquestionably she will take your life. On the other hand if you should be vanquished, what becomes of the honour you wish to defend, and if you should be slain in that state of soul in which you go to the fight, you go straight to eternal fire and everlasting shame: for while you are defending your body from your adversary's sword, you forget to parry the mortal thrust that the devil is aiming at your soul."

But spite of all I could say, the fear of the world, which is fatally powerful with men of this rank, prevailed, and his reply was;

"I implore you, Father, to pray for me; and to hear my confession, if you possibly can."

"Certainly I cannot hear you," I said, "for that honour, which you worship is not necessary to you, in the sense in which it is to those who are obliged to take their part in a war. Besides, you are the challenger, and you took this unlawful course when it was possible for you to follow some other method of vindicating yourself, and so whatever necessity there is for pursuing the matter has been created by yourself. But this is what I will do; I will give you from my reliquary a particle of the Holy Cross, enclosed with an *Agnus Dei*, and you shall wear it upon you. Perhaps God may have mercy upon you for the sake of this, and afford you time for penance. Understand, however;—I do not give it you in order to encourage you in your bad purpose, but that you may wear it with all reverence and respect, so that should you come into danger (which certainly I do not desire), God may be moved to preserve your life, in the consideration of the good will you have of honouring His Cross."

He took my gift very thankfully and reverentially, and had it sewed inside his shirt over his heart; for it was arranged they should fight in their shirts without cuirass. It happened, God so allowing it, that his adversary made a lunge at his heart and pierced his shirt, but did not touch his skin. He on his side wounded and prostrated his enemy, then gave him his life and came off victorious. He then came to me in high spirits, and told me how he had been preserved by the power of the Holy Cross; then he thanked me very earnestly, and promised to be more on his guard in future. The Queen soon after took a fancy to this young nobleman, and kept him close to her at Court for a time. But tiring soon of this sort of life, at his father's death he married the widow of the Earl of Essex. She was a heretic when he married her, but he soon made her a Catholic; and they both live now as Catholics in Ireland, as I hear.[1]

The Knight moreover, who introduced this young Baron to me, followed my counsel at that time, and after devoting several days to a diligent examination of conscience made a general confession of his whole life, with a view of reforming it for the future. A little later he was desirous of returning to the Irish wars, but as I was in doubt whether this was lawful in conscience, he promised me to resign his appoint-ment and return to England, if the priests there, to whom I referred him as living on the spot and there-fore having a closer knowledge of the circumstances, decided that it was unlawful. Soon after his arrival in Ireland, in a certain fight, while he was bravely mounting a wall and animating his men to follow, he was struck dead by a musket ball. He had however before the fight carefully written me a letter and sent it off, informing me that he had con-sulted the priests in the country, and had received this answer, that it was lawful to fight against the Catholic party, because it was not clear to all why they had taken up arms.

After his death, a remarkable incident occurred which I will relate. His wife, pious 'soul, who never had the least idea of her husband's death, about that time heard every night some one knocking at her chamber door, and that so loudly as to wake her. Her maids heard it too, but on opening the door there was no one to be seen. She therefore got a priest to stay with her and her maids

---

[1] The fact of his marrying the widow of Essex identifies this young nobleman as Richard de Burgh, Baron of Dunkellin. He succeeded his father, as fourth Earl of Clanricarde, in 1601. Later he was created Earl of St. Albans.—M.

till the usual time of the knocking; and when the same noise and knocking at the door were heard, the priest himself went to the door, but found no. one. This knocking went on till such time as news of her husband's death reached her: as if it had been a warning from his Angel to pray for his soul.

CHAPTER XXXVI.

SOME REMARKABLE CONVERSIONS.

WHILE I was in London the opportunity often presented itself of visiting men of rank, confirming them in the faith, directing them, and also of converting some; for every one tried to bring the members of his family and his friends to me. One asked me to mount on horseback and ride to meet a friend of his, whom he would throw in my way at a particular spot two miles out of London. This was a man of wealth and influence, and decidedly the principal man of all the county where he lived. He was of the rank next below that of Baron[1] (for he was not an Earl nor a Baron), and was wholly given up to vanities. I met him, and he, being told who I was (for he was anxious to speak with a priest), saluted me kindly; but at the same time was unwilling to recognize me. I put on the character of a Catholic who wished that all men were Catholics, and said that I had heard that he was a good friend to Catholics but not to himself, because

---

[1] Probably of one of the higher grades of knighthood, as a Knight Banneret. The dignity of Baronet did not exist before 1611.

he was not a Catholic; and so we fell upon the
question whether this was necessary for salvation,
and this I proved in such a manner that he did not
deny it. But I saw that the greatest difficulty lay
in withdrawing his will from the pleasures of the
world, and therefore I directed my attack against
that quarter, and by God's aid I overthrew the
walls, and laid open a way for the entry of good
and sound counsels into his heart; insomuch that
he who had up to that time conversed with me as
with some man of rank, a friend of his friend, at
last said, " You shall certainly be my confessor."
Then we appointed a time and place where this
business might be attended to without inconvenience
or hurry; and after a few days he came to my
friend's house near London, and there he abode
until after fit preparation he made his confession.

The same person also brought to me his brother-
in-law, who was son and brother to an Earl, and
himself heir to the Earldom. I met him also riding
on horseback, and at exactly the same spot, and
before we separated God touched his heart too, and
gave him the grace of conversion. He was fully
satisfied on all points relating both to faith and
morals, and a few days after I received him into
the Church, and I have great confidence that he
will, please God, become one of its chief supports.
I administered the Sacraments to these and others
like them in my own house, and on that account I
kept it from public notice, that it might not be
thought a Catholic house. I thus secured an
asylum in London, where the peril of priests, and
myself in particular, is ever greatest and most
pressing; and men of rank and influence were able
to be there without fear of any sudden and unex-

pected visitation, and so come to visit me with greater confidence. I learned by experience that this care of mine was very pleasing to them, and profitable by the security gained both for them and myself.

Having held this house for three years, I let it to a Catholic friend, and took another house nearer the principal street in London, called the Strand. Since most of my friends lived in that street, they were thus able to visit me more easily, and I them. After my removal I discovered how entirely free from suspicion was the house which I had left, and in which I had dwelt for three years; for the servant who kept my house, sent for a gardener with whom he had been acquainted while living in the other house, (for the garden of the new house needed to be put in order,) and the gardener remarked to him, "Some Papists have come to live in your old house:" as though they who had previously dwelt there had been good Protestants.

This new house was very suitable and convenient, and had private entrances on both sides, and I had contrived in it some most excellent hiding-places ; and there I should long have remained, free from all peril or even suspicion, if some friends of mine, while I was absent from London, had not availed themselves of the house rather rashly. It remained however in the same state up to the time of the great and terrible disturbance of the Powder Plot, as I shall hereafter shortly mention.

Meantime my friends brought me another who was heir to a Barony, and is himself now a peer, and by God's grace I persuaded him to take on his shoulders the yoke of the law of Christ and of the Catholic Faith, and made him a member of the

Church.   Another whom I had previously known in
the world, and had seen to be wholly devoted to
every kind of vanity, fell sick.   He had abounded
with riches and pleasures, and passed his days in
jollity, destined however to fall thence in a moment,
had not God patiently waited and in a suitable time
led him to penance.   He then was lying sick of a
grievous illness, but yet had not begun to think of
death,   I heard that he was sick, and obtained an
entry into his chamber at eleven o'clock at night,
after the departure of his friends.   He recognized   .
me, and was pleased at my visit.   I explained why
I had come, and warned him to think seriously of
the state of his soul, and, instead of a Judge, render
God a Friend and most loving Father, however
much he might have wasted all his substance.   So
then weakness of body opened the ears of his heart,
and in an acceptable time God heard us, and in
the day of salvation helped us ; insomuch that he
offered himself as at once ready to make his con-
fesssion.   I however said that I would return on
the following night, and advised him meantime to
procure that there should be read to him by a
friend, whom I named, Father Lewis of Grenada's
Explanation of the Commandments : that after each
Commandment he should occupy some little time
in reflexion, and call to mind how, and how often,
he had offended against that commandment : that
then he should make an act of sorrow regarding
each, and so go to the next.   He promised that he
would do so, and I promised that I would return on
the following night.   This I did, and heard his confession ; I gave him all the assistance I could, for
the time had been short, especially for a sick man,
to prepare such a confession, but he dared no longer

defer it, although he still seemed tolerably strong. I advised him to use the utmost care in discharging all his debts, which were great, through the extravagant expenditure in which he had indulged : I also exhorted him to redeem his sins by alms. He did both by the will he made the following day, and bequeathed a large sum for pious uses, which as I heard was honestly paid.

I also bade him prepare for the Holy Communion and Extreme Unction against the following night, and to have some pious book read to him meantime. He not only did what I advised, but exhorted all that came to visit him on the following day, to repent at once of their former life, and not defer their amendment as he had done : "Do not," he said, "look for the mercy which I have found, for this is to be presumptuous and to irritate God ; for I have deserved hell a thousand times on this account." And much more to the same effect did he speak, with so much earnestness and freedom, that all marvelled at so sudden a change. They asked him to hide the cross which he had hanging from his neck, (for I had lent him my own cross full of relics for him to kiss, and exercise acts of reverence and love); but he answered, "Hide it ! Nay, I would not hide it, even if the most bitter heretics were here. Too long have I refrained from profession of the Catholic Faith, and now, if God gave me life, I would publicly profess myself a Catholic : " so that all marvelled and were much edified and moved at his words. He spoke thus to all the peers and great men that visited him, His conversion thus became publicly known, and many of the courtiers afterwards spoke of it.. On the third night of my visiting him according to my promise, he

again confessed with great expressions of sorrow,
and begged for the Sacrament of Extreme Unction,
and when he received it, himself arranged for me
more conveniently to reach the different parts of
his body, just as though he had been a Catholic
many years. Seeing him in such good dispositions,
I asked whether he did not put all his trust in
the merits of Christ and in the mercy of God.
" Surely ! " said he ; " did I not not do so, and
did not that mercy give me salvation, I should have
been condemned to the pit of hell : in myself I find
no ground of hope, but rather of trembling. But
I feel great hope in the mercy and goodness of God,
Who has so long waited for me, and now has
called me when I deserved,—aye, and thought of—
anything but this ! " Then he took my hand and
said, " Father, I cannot express how much I am
indebted to you, for you were sent by God to give
me this happiness." I found moreover that he had
no temptation against faith, but most firmly believed
and confessed every point, and I saw most clearly
that God had poured into his soul the habits of
many virtues. Then I erected an altar in his
chamber with the ornaments which I had brought,
and I said Mass, while he assisted with great devotion and comfort. I afterwards gave him the
Viaticum, which he received with the utmost reverence. When I had finished everything, I gave him
some advice that would be useful should he fall
into his agony before my return, and I left him full
of consolation. Now, see the providence of God :
but a few hours after my departure, as he was
persevering in petitions for mercy, and in acts of
thanksgiving for the mercy he had received, he
rendered up his soul to God. But before his death,

he asked the by-standers whether certain purple and red robes could be applied to the use of the altar, which he had received from the King when he was created a Knight of the Order of the Bath. The investiture of this Order takes place only at the Coronation of the King, and the Knights enjoy precedence before all other Knights except those of the most Noble Order of the Garter, almost all of whom are Earls or other Peers. He however was a Knight of the Bath, and he wished that the robes with which he had been invested at the Coronation should be devoted to the use of the altar; for he said that he had derived great comfort from seeing my vestments, which were merely light and portable, but yet handsome, of red silk embroidered with silver lace. So after his death they gave me his suit of the peculiar robes of that Order, and out of them I made sets of vestments of two colours, one of which the College of St. Omer's still possesses. Thus is the pious desire of the deceased fulfilled, in whose conversion I could not fail to see God's great goodness and providence.[2]

[1] In all probability this was Sir William Browne of Walcot who was created Knight of the Bath at the coronation of James I. and died within the year.—M.

CHAPTER XXXVII.

ABOUT the same time I received into the Church the wife of a certain Knight. This lady is at the present day a very good and useful friend of our Fathers. Her husband was at this time a heretic, but his brother had been brought by me, through the Spiritual Exercises, to despise the world and follow the counsels of Christ : he introduced me to his sister, and after one or two interviews she embraced the Catholic Faith, although she was was well assured that she would incur great losses as soon as it should become known to her husband, as in truth it came to pass. For he first tried caresses then threats, and left no means unemployed to shake her resolution, insomuch that for a long time she had nothing to expect or hope but to be separated from her husband, and stripped of all the goods of this world, that so in patience she might possess her soul. When her husband was on her account deprived of the public employment which he held, she bore it with great fortitude, and remained ever constant and even in mind : at length by her virtue and her patience she rendered her husband a friend to Catholics, and afterwards himself a Catholic. He was reconciled by the ministry of Father Walpole, to whom I had recommended her on my leaving England.

There were many other conversions, which I cannot mention separately, for I have already carried to too great length the narrative of these events, which are truly very insignificant if they are compared with the actions of others. But one case I cannot pass over, which gave me especial pleasure for the sake of the person concerned; for I do not know that any one was ever more dear to me.

Sir Everard Digby, of whom I have spoken above, had a friend for whom he felt a peculiar affection; he had often recommended him to me, and was anxious to give me an opportunity of making his acquaintance and gaining him over, if it possibly might be: but because he held an office in the Court, requiring daily attendance about the King's person, so that he could not be absent for long together, our desire was long delayed.[2]

At last Sir Everard met his friend, while we were both together in London; and he took an opportunity of asking him to come at a certain time to his chamber, to play at cards, for these are the books gentlemen in London study both night and day. He promised to come, and on his arrival he did not find a party at play, but only us two sitting and conversing very seriously; so Sir Everard asked him to sit down a little, until the rest should arrive. Then in an interval of silence Sir Everard said,

"We two were engaged in a very serious conversation, in fact concerning religion. You know,"

[2] The account here given enables us to identify this friend of Sir Everard's as Sir Oliver Manners, youngest son of the Earl of Rutland. He was knighted by James I. in 1603, and made Clerk of the Council.—M.

he said, addressing the visitor, "that I am friendly
to Catholics, and to the Catholic faith; I was
nevertheless disputing with this gentleman, who is
a friend of mine, against the Catholic faith, in
order to see what defence he could make; for he is
an earnest Catholic, as I do not hesitate to tell
you." (Then turning to me he begged me not to
be vexed that he betrayed me to a stranger.) "And
I must say," he continued, "he so well defended
the Catholic faith that I could not answer him, and
I am glad that you have come to help me."

The visitor was young and confident, and trusting
in his own great abilities, expected to carry everything before him, so good was his cause and so
lightly did he esteem me, as he afterwards confessed.
So he began to allege many objections to the arguments before used. I waited with patience until
he ceased speaking, and then answered in few
words. He urged his points, and so we argued one
against the other for a short hour's space. Afterwards I began to explain my view more fully, and
to confirm it with texts of Holy Scripture and
passages from the Fathers, and with such reasons
as came to my mind. And I felt, as I often did,
God supplying me words as I spoke on His behalf
in great might, not for the sake of me that spoke,
nor for any desert of mine, but just as He gives
milk to a mother when she has an infant who needs
to be fed with milk. My young friend was of a
docile nature, and could no way bear to speak
against the truth when he saw it, so that he listened
in silence, and God was meantime speaking to his
heart with a voice far more powerful and efficacious.
God, too, gave him ears to hear, so that the word
fell not upon stony ground, nor among thorns, but

into good soil, yea, very good, that yielded by God's grace a hundredfold in its season. So before he left he was fully resolved to become a Catholic, and took with him a book to assist him in preparing for a good confession, which he made before a week had passed. And from that time it was not enough for him to walk in the ordinary path of God's commandments, but God prepared him for higher things; and whatever counsels I gave him he received with eagerness, and retained not only in a faithful memory, but in a most ready will. He began to use the daily examination of conscience, and even learned the method of meditation, and made a meditation every day. He was forced to rise very early to do this before he went to the King, which in summer was at break of day, for the King went hunting every day, and he, by duty of his office, was necessarily present at the royal breakfast. He would moreover so with his whole soul devour pious books, that he always had one in his pocket; and in the King's Court and in the Presence Chamber, while courtiers and ladies were standing around, you might see him turn himself to a window, and there read a chapter of Thomas à Kempis' "Imitation of Christ," a book with which he was most intimate; and after he had read it, you might see him turn in body but not in mind towards the others, for there he would stand rapt in thought, while the rest perhaps were supposing that he was admiring the beauty of some lady, or thinking over the means to climb to great honours. In truth, he had no need to take particular pains about this, for in the first place he was son and brother to an Earl, and moreover the place and office which he filled were very honourable, giving him the ear of the King every day. His wit could not fail to distinguish favourable opportunities for gaining his requests, and in fact the King had given him an office which he afterwards sold, but which, had he kept it, would have brought him in more than ten thousand florins a year. In short, such was his position that he would undoubtedly have soon risen to great honours; for he made himself acceptable to all, and was not a little beloved, insomuch that after he had left the Court and given up all hope of worldly honour, I heard it said by some persons of the greatest eminence and experience in the ways of the Court, that they had never in forty years' space known any one so highly valued and beloved in every quarter.

But, what is far more important, he was beloved in the Court of the King of Kings, and inspired to desire and seek after greater and more abiding blessings. So he conceived the wish of trying the Spiritual Exercises, in the course of which he determined to desert the Court, and devote himself to those pursuits which would render him most pleasing to God and most profitable to his neighbour: so with as little delay as possible he made such a disposition of his goods as would enable him freely to make his escape from England. He then, to the surprise of all, asked and obtained the King's leave to go to Italy, where he still resides, and he is so well known to our Fathers that there is no need to write anything more concerning him; but this I can say, that wherever I have known him to have been, he has left men filled with great esteem for him, and expectation of yet greater things.

Besides Sir Everard Digby, he had another friend, a man of much influence and heir to a large estate, and of great talents, but wholly devoted to the world. He brought his friend to me, and by my agency caused him to become a Catholic. I knew also two young ladies of rank, who were so deeply attached to him that I doubt not they would have preferred him to the greatest lord in England. One was attached to the Court, and had an honourable post about the Queen's person; the other, who dwelt in the country, was of a noble Catholic family. He himself introduced the first to me, and by my ministry rendered her a Catholic. He then begged her to set her love on a higher object, on God, to Whom the chief love of all was due, and he added, that he had resolved never to love any woman in this world except with the love of charity, and that he would never enter into wedlock. The second he persuaded to become a nun: she is still in religion, and making good progress. I feel confident that he has been chosen and reserved to be the instrument of bringing many souls to follow the counsels of Christ by word and example.

¹ Sir Oliver Manners was ordained priest at Rome in 1611 (after the above account was written) by Cardinal Bellarmine, and returned to England, where he died soon after.—M.

CHAPTER XXXVIII.

A CONVERSION IN THE COUNTRY.

THE conversions which took place in the country were not few, and some were cases of heads of families ; but I have already gone to great length, and I will here recount one only, the beginning and end of which I saw to be good.

There was a lady, a kinswoman of my hostess, whose husband had now many years been a Catholic, yet neither her husband, nor any of her friends, nor my hostess herself, who loved her as a sister, could ever lead her to become a Catholic. She did not object to listen to Catholics, even to priests, and was fond of earnest argument with them ; but she would believe no one but herself, and indeed her talents were greater than I have often met with in a woman. My hostess often mourned over this lady, and grieved that no remedy could be found ; she wished that I should once see her. She spoke highly in praise of her talents and amiable disposition, and of her life and behaviour in all respects, with the one solitary exception of her being an obstinate heretic. I asked my hostess therefore to invite her to pay us a visit, although she lived in a distant county. She came according to the invitation, and we took care that she should find me showing myself in public, and dressed as though I had been a guest just arrived from London.

On the two first days we did but little, for we knew that we should have plenty of time afterwards, and I wished to remove all timidity from her; for though she had been accustomed to meet priests at that house, yet they had kept mostly to their chambers. But as soon as I judged her to be convinced that I was a Catholic but not a priest, I began slowly to turn my conversation with her often upon religion. At first I spoke little, but to such purpose that she could not answer me; and so I left her, not urging her, but rather leaving her with a desire to hear more. At length after a few days I judged her thoroughly prepared, and I arranged that my hostess should begin to talk seriously upon these topics, and that when she saw me enter into the conversation and carry it on, she should leave us in company with one or two of the lady's daughters, for she had brought three with her. This having been done, we began the combat with, as it seemed to her, various success, for one or two hours; and then she listened to me as I spoke without interruption for two or three hours more. She spoke little in answer, and did not like on the spot to acknowledge herself vanquished, but she thanked me heartily, and went away quite red and flushed in the face. She was truly moved, or rather changed interiorly, and straightway ran to my hostess and said, "Oh, cousin, what have you done?"

"What have I done?" replied the other.

"Oh, who is it," she rejoined, "that you introduced me to? At any rate he is . . . ." and she spoke in much higher terms of my learning and language than I deserved, and she added that she could not resist what I urged, nor answer it.

On the following day God confirmed what He
had wrought in her, and she surrendered at discretion, and accepted a book to help her to prepare for
confession. Meantime with the mother's consent
and assistance I instructed her three daughters,
and when they had learned the catechism, I heard
their confessions. The mother, however, during
the time of her preparation, began to be filled with
trouble and sorrow, not on account of leaving her
heresy, but through fear of confession. I, on the
contrary encouraged her to persevere, and adduced
arguments against her timidity, but I could not rid
her of it, and so seeing that she was ready as far
as examination was concerned, but nevertheless
put the matter off from day to day, and begged a
little more time to prepare, I would not consent.
I told her that this came from the enemy, who
grieved to leave his habitation, and at length she
saw and acknowledged this. For as soon as out
of obedience she had made her confession, she felt
relieved of a great burden and filled with consolation; and she told me that now she was glad not
to have delayed longer.

I have often found this, that some souls experience great trouble when first they make confession on being reconciled to the Church of God.
Some persons even fall sick and faint, so as to be
forced to cease speaking for a time and sit down,
until they have recovered a little and are able to
continue; and this has happened even when at
their first coming they were in sound health, and
ready to confess. And then when they recom-
menced, they again fell ill, and this happened two
or three times in the course of their first confession.
But when the confession was finished they not only

felt no sickness, but having received absolution they went away full of joy and consolation. Some in fact have remarked to me that did men but know what consolation is gained in confession, they would refuse to be deprived of so great a happiness.

Among these was to be reckoned this lady, who came forth from confession full of consolation, and gave most hearty thanks to her cousin, for that by her means she had been admitted to share in so great a happiness. So great was God's mercy towards her, that thenceforth she gave herself wholly up to devotion. On her return home she devoted herself to making handsome vestments, and whenever she was able she procured the company of priests. And not content with this, she was anxious to return wholly to our house, and to dwell with us, in order to have more frequent access to the Sacraments, and the opportunity of hearing the public and private exhortations that we had every Sunday and festival day. She stayed with us about two years, and all that time she gave herself up to devotion and to the constant reading of pious books. She was clearly led to this course of life by the special mercy and providence of God; for at the end of the period I have mentioned, although she seemed stout and strong, she was suddenly attacked with disease, by which within a few days she was so weakened, that no skill of the physicians could restore her strength. She was warned to prepare for the life to come, and she repeated a good and careful confession of her whole life.

At length finding herself in her last agony, she wished to write a letter to her brother, who was a heretic, and almost the greatest enemy the Catholics had in the county where he dwelt. To him then she wished to send a letter, written by her daughter's hand but subscribed with her own, to the following effect :—That he knew that she had long been a strenuous upholder of this new religion, so that he might be the more convinced that she would not have changed it without good grounds, and that she had certain and unanswerable authorities for the faith which she had adopted : wherefore she protested to him that ever since the time when she embraced the faith, she had lived in peace of conscience, and that never before that time had she enjoyed true internal consolation : finally she begged him to have a care for his soul, and proceeded thus ; " I, your sister, now at the point of death, by these my last words, beg and beseech you to embrace the Catholic and ancient faith ; and I protest that there is no other in which you can be saved." These were her sentiments when almost come into her last agony ; from which I perceived that she was wholly converted from heresy, and full of charity towards her neighbour ; so having asked her a few questions, and found that she was not troubled with any temptations of presumption or of despair, I gave her as much help as I could in forming and uttering acts of the opposite virtues. After which when she was on the point of death, I offered her a picture of the Passion of Christ, and she embraced and kissed it with the greatest affection. I put also a blessed medal into her hands, and reminded her to invoke the Name of JESUS in her heart at least, in order to gain the indulgences, although she could not speak. I then asked her to give some sign to show that she did thus from her heart, whereupon she caught hold of the medal and kissed it, repeating this action several times. Observing

she made answer to me by signs, I bade her conceive a great sorrow for having ever offended God,
Who was so good in Himself, and had shown so
great mercy to her, and to give a sign of it by
raising her hand: she did so with great earnestness: then to conceive sorrow that she had ever
been in heresy, and had resisted God and the
Church, of which also she gave a sign: then to
conceive the wish that all heretics might be converted, and that she willingly offered her life for
their conversion, and she again made the signal
with great earnestness, and also took my hand
within her own, which were already chill, and held
it firmly, repeating the signs that she was pleased
with the suggestions I made to her. And I continued up to her last gasp, encouraging her, and
exhorting her to praise God in her heart, to desire
that all creatures should praise Him, and to offer
her life for this end. And she gave me answer to
everything, now raising, now lowering her hand,
just as I asked her to do in assent to what I suggested. All the by-standers, who were numerous,
and a priest also who was among them, were in
great admiration, and declared that they never
witnessed such a death as this. For she continued,
as I have said, responding to my suggestions up
to the very last breath, raising her hand slightly
when she could no longer raise it much. In these
interior acts she gave up her soul, without any
trouble of mind or convulsion of body, but like one
going off to sleep, she went to rest in peace.

Her youngest daughter had already died holily
in our house before her mother. The second
daughter married a rich man, and brought him to
me from a considerable distance to be made a

Catholic. The eldest still lives in the same house, to be espoused not to man but to God, for she has a vocation to the religious state. In the meantime she lives there religiously, and devotes herself to the service of religious, as the lady of the house always did, and does still.

CHAPTER XXXIX.

THE TROUBLES OF THE POWDER PLOT.

IT is now high time that I bring this narrative to a close, for I have far exceeded the limits which I first proposed to myself; what remains therefore I will state briefly.

I gave the Spiritual Exercises in this house to many others, as well to those who formed part of the family as to others; and in each case the fruit which I hoped for was produced. There were two persons who made only the Exercises of the first week, with the view of leading a good and holy life. One of these, now the father of a family, practises many acts of charity, and is no small friend of Ours. The other came to me, unasked and unexpected, to make the Exercises, and when I asked him whence he got this idea and intention (for he was a very young man, the grandson of an Earl, and the heir of a large property), he replied,

"I read in a book put forth against the Society by one of its enemies, that by means of these Exercises you have induced many to embrace a religious life, and have robbed them of their property. Among other names mine was mentioned as that of one who had made the Exercises under you, and it was said that though you did not succeed in making me a religious, yet you wheedled me out of a large sum of money. Now, I know," he continued, " that my wife is much devoted to you because you made her a Catholic ; but I know too, that neither from her nor from me have you ever received a penny. Since therefore they have done you so great a wrong, I have come to make good what they have falsely stated."

So he made the Exercises, and with no slight profit ; and he afterwards sent me word, begging me to provide him a priest who could join in society publicly, and without suspicion. I therefore provided one, and was about to send him, when suddenly all things were upset for a time, and all good hindered by the Powder Plot, as it is called. And if proof were wanting that I knew nothing of this affair, this alone would be sufficient, that at that very time I had sent several from England across the sea into these parts. One was a lady, who was going to be a nun in the Benedictine Convent at Brussels, whither I had sent two others not long before, who are now in high authority there. Another had been an heretical minister, whom I had brought to the Faith and instructed. He was the last that I received into the Church before these disturbances. When these persons with certain others were on the point of crossing the Channel, orders were sent to allow no ships to leave; they were consequently all taken and thrown into prison, from which they were released two years ago. He who had been a minister is at present studying in the Roman College ; and the lady of whom I spoke is now professed in the

Convent whither she was going when she was taken. Only one other minister, besides the one just mentioned, did I convert in England, and he is now a priest and is working in that vineyard. I also sent over many youths to the Seminaries while I was in this last residence of mine, who will, by God's help, give their fruit in due season.

But if we have received good things from God's hands, why should we not also bear with evil things ?—if those things can be truly called evil which are sent from Him, and sent that He may draw good from them, for those who receive them well, and humbly recognize and adore His providence both when He gives and when He takes away. He had indeed given me many and great consolations in this residence ; interior consolations chiefly, from conversions and from the signal progress in virtue of many souls ; but exterior consolations also were not wanting. For in external matters everything was well and abundantly supplied me. I had several excellent horses for my missionary journeys and all that I could wish for to carry on the work I had in hand. Then, in the house itself, the arrangements were made in the best way both for our health and our convenience. And for companion I had Father Strange, who is now in the Tower, (for Sir E. Digby had obtained Father Percy from the Superior,) and another priest who resided a long time with us. We had moreover good store of useful books, which were kept in a library without any concealment, because they had the appearance of belonging to the young Baron, and of having been left him by his uncle, who was a very learned and studious nobleman, and was well known for his piety. He had in fact resigned the right and title of the Barony to his younger brother, the father of the present lord, in order that he might more entirely and securely devote himself to God and his studies. If he had lived a little longer, he would assuredly have been a member of our Society, for on his death-bed this was the only thing that caused him regret, viz., that he could not then be admitted into the Society, a thing that he desired most earnestly.

Our vestments and altar furniture were both plentiful and costly. We had two sets for each colour which the Church uses; one for ordinary use, the other for feast days: some of these latter were embroidered with gold and pearls, and figured by well skilled hands. We had six massive silver candlesticks on the altar, besides those at the sides for the elevation: the cruets were of silver also, as were the basin for the lavabo, the bell, and the censer. There were moreover lamps hanging from silver chains, and a silver crucifix on the altar. For greater festivals however I had a crucifix of gold, a foot in height, on the top of which was represented a pelican, while on the right arm of the cross was an eagle with expanded wings carrying on its back its young ones, who were also attempting to fly; on the left arm a phœnix expiring in flames that it might leave an offspring after it; and at the foot was a hen with her chickens, gathering them under her wings. All this was made of wrought gold by a celebrated artist.

These ornaments are still kept there in trust for the Society: and in the meantime serve for the use of that domestic church and the residence of our Fathers. But I who was not sufficiently grateful to God for these benefits which I have mentioned and many others, was compelled to leave them to others who could use them better and to greater advantage.

For since it was my chief friends who were involved in that disaster of the Powder Plot, the Council on this account believed me to be privy to it, and from the first sought for me with great persistence and severity. They sent certain magistrates to search our house most exactly, with orders, if they found me not, to stay in the house till recalled, to post guards all round the house every night, and to have men on the watch both day and night at a distance of three miles from the house on every side, who were to apprehend all whom they did not know and bring them before the said magistrates. All this was done to the letter. But immediately the news reached us of such a plot having been discovered, and we learnt that certain of our friends had been killed and others taken, expecting that in such a season we too should have something to suffer, we had made all snug before they came, so that they found nothing. They continued searching however for many days, till at last my hostess discovered to the justice in chief command one of the hiding-places in which a few books had been stowed away, thinking that he would then desist from searching any further under the impression that if a priest had been in the house he would have been hidden there, yet they continued in the house for full nine days; and I meanwhile remained shut up in a hiding-hole where I could sit, but not stand upright. This time however I did not suffer from hunger, for every night food was brought to me secretly: nay after four or five days, when the rigour of the search was somewhat relaxed, my friends even took me out at night and warmed me at a fire; for it was wintry weather, just before Christmas-tide. And when nine days had passed the searching party withdrew, believing it impossible I could be there so long without being discovered.

In the meantime they had taken a priest who, knowing nothing of the watch set about the place, was coming to our house for safety. This good priest (by name Thomas Laithwaite,[1] who is now of our Society, and is labouring in England) had left us a few days before at my request, when we heard of the plot, in order to communicate with Father Garnet, and obtain from him for me instructions how to act in the present crisis. Even on his way thither he was taken, but escaped again for that time in the following manner. His captors took him to an inn, intending to bring him up for examination and committal the next day. On entering the inn, he took off his cloak and sword and laid them on a bench; then on pretence of looking after his horse and getting him taken to water, he went to the stable, and as there was a stream near the house, he bade the boy lead the horse thither at once, and himself went along also. When they had come to the stream and the horse was drinking, "Go," said he to the lad, "get ready the hay, and the straw for his bed, and I will bring him back when he has drunk." The boy returned to the stable without further thought, and he mounting his horse spurred him into the stream, and swam him to the opposite bank. Those in the inn, seeing his cloak and sword still lying there,

[1] Father Thomas Laithwaite died in England in 1655, in his seventy-eighth year, forty-nine years after his admission into the Society, having spent thirty on the English Mission.—M.

had for some time no suspicion of his stratagem; but hearing from the stable-boy what had happened, they saw they had been outwitted, and immediately set off in pursuit. They were however too late, for the fugitive, knowing the way well, got to the house of a Catholic before night, and lay hid there for a few days. Then, finding that he could not get to Father Garnet, and thinking all danger had passed in our direction, he tried to return to me. But while avoiding Charybdis he fell into the clutches of Scylla; for, as I said above, he was taken on his way to our house, and dragged to London. They were not able however to prove him a priest, and his brother was allowed to buy him his freedom for a sum of money.

Two other priests who were resident with me in that house (one of whom, as I said before, was Father Strange) at the beginning of their troubles wished to go to Father Garnet and remain with him. Both of them however were taken prisoners on their way; one was thrown into Bridewell, and was afterwards banished together with other priests; while Father Strange, the other, was sent to the Tower, where he suffered much, as has been before mentioned.

CHAPTER XL.

FATHERS GARNET AND OLDCORNE.

THE history of this plot, its causes and consequences, is but too well known; since it has been
written by both friends and enemies, though perhaps
by neither exactly as it ought to be. I myself when
I came from England to Rome, was ordered to put
in writing an account of the whole affair, and did
so as well as I could. There is no need therefore
to repeat here, what I wrote at length on that occasion,—in what state England then was;—how the
persecution not only was not relaxed on the accession of the King [James I.], but was even em-
bittered, and carried on more grievously than ever.
All the Catholics therefore expected, and some
knew for certain, that new laws would be made
against them in Parliament, more severe and cruel
than the former ones; that not only would nothing
be relaxed of the tyranny of the Queen [Elizabeth],
but that the yoke which they had so long borne
with weary necks would be made yet heavier to
bear. Hereupon some of the younger and more
impatient sort, seeing that they were scourged now
not only with whips but with scorpions,—that no
human hope was left them except from such aid as
they could give themselves, since peace was now
concluded between His Catholic Majesty and the
King of England, from which peace the Catholics

were excluded (though it was they who had a right
to peace and not the wicked),—these persons, I say,
seeing this, and forgetting at last that patience in
which we ought to possess our souls, and not
enduring any longer to see holy things trodden
under foot, and the faithful robbed of their goods
and loaded with innumerable evils, to the daily
lamentable ruin of weak souls, determined to raise
the people of God from this disastrous state, and to
wage war in strictest secrecy against the enemies
of their own souls and bodies and of the Catholic
cause. I say, in secrecy; because it must be
acknowledged that any open opposition was no
longer possible, since the Catholics were broken in
strength, and ground down to the earth, and all
their arms had been taken from them. Thus it was
that these persons I speak of, wishing to deliver
themselves and others from this terrible slavery of
soul and body, devised this plot, which they thought
the only possible way of accomplishing what they
wished, viz., by taking off at a single blow all the
chief enemies of the Catholic cause.

On all these points I have written at full in the
treatise I mentioned. I have also detailed there
the way in which they had determined to proceed,
and how one of them[1] disclosed the matter in confession to one of our Fathers when it was already
ripe for execution, who refused to hear him any
further unless he was allowed to inform his Superior:
—and how the 'Superior [Father Garnet], upon
hearing so bloody a scheme, at once commanded
the Father to deter and prevent his penitent as
much as he could from prosecuting it, and imme-

---

[1] This was Catesby, the prime mover of the whole plot.

diately wrote to the Pope, entreating His Holiness
to forbid the Catholics to take any measures of
external violence. I have also there set down how
the Superior himself and Father Oldcorne were at
last taken at the residence of the latter, after
remaining pent up for twelve days in a hiding-hole :
—how with them were also taken two serving-men,
or as I have heard since and fully believe, two Lay-
brothers of our Society, both of whom suffered
martyrdom. One of these, Rodolph by name,
suffered with Father Oldcorne, whose companion
and attendant he had been, and whose feet he kissed
as the Father was ascending the ladder to his execution, giving him thanks aloud for the charity and
benevolence he had experienced from him, and
praising God for having allowed him to die in the
company of so holy a priest. The other was Little
John, who for nearly twenty years had been Father
Garnet's companion, and of whom I have made
frequent mention in the course of this Narrative.
He was well known to the persecutors as the chief
deviser and maker of hiding-places all over England, and consequently as one who could discover
more priests, and do more harm to Catholics, if he
could be brought to make disclosures, than any
other man. They therefore tortured him so long
and so cruelly, that at last he died [2] under their
hands ; but they were never able to shake the constancy of his soul.

[2] After thus wringing his life from him by torture, his gaolers
gave out that he had committed suicide in prison, to escape
further question : thus adding calumny to murder. And this
statement is found in most of the larger histories of England.
The holy brother was never brought into any court, nor allowed
the least chance of communication with any friends ; nor could
anything be learnt of him after his capture, but what his gaolers

R

I have related also ·in that treatise how Fathers
Garnet and Oldcorne were brought up to London,
and frequently examined, especially Father Garnet;
how both of them were tortured, but Father Oldcorne [8] most : how this latter was then taken back
to Worcester, and there, though nothing but his
priesthood was proved against him, condemned and
executed by hanging and quartering, and so died a
martyr : how Father Garnet was brought to trial
in London, and gave so clear and eloquent defence
of himself, that all were struck with admiration;
but after a time was so interrupted and brow-beaten
by Cecil and others, that the gentle Father could
not proceed with his defence as he had begun [4]:
and how when brought to the place of execution,
by the firmness and modesty of his whole demeanour,
and by the heroic calmness with which he received
or rather embraced his death, he touched the hard
hearts of his cruel enemies, and rendered them well-
affected towards him.

All these details, which I have here barely enu-
merated, in my other narratiye I have described at
full.   I will however add here something on the

chose to tell. That he was tortured barbarously they acknowledged, by saying that he committed suicide to escape their
cruelty ; that he never revealed anything was also acknowledged.
It must be remembered that those who were killed in prison were
always given out by the authorities as suicides. But who can
believe that a man who would suffer the extremity of torture
rather than offend God by revealing what would injure his neighbour, would not also suffer the same extremity rather than offend
God by self-murder ?   The Day of Judgment will refute this
calumny as well as others.

[8] He was hung up by the hands, in the way Father Gerard has
described of himself, for five hours at a time, and that for five
successive days.

[4] James himself said that "the Jesuit had not had fair play."

way in which the straw was obtained, on which
appeared the miraculous likeness of Father Garnet; for I was afterwards present at the death-bed
of him who found the straw, or rather to whom
God granted it. This person [John Wilkinson]
then narrated to me a little before his death, that
on the morning of the holy martyr's execution he
had felt himself moved by an unusual fervour, and
by a desire of being present at his martyrdom,
mainly with the view of obtaining some portion of
his relics. He had therefore, he said, pushed
forward close to where the executioner was hacking
his body in pieces, but durst not touch anything for
fear of the officers standing round; just then, the
executioner having severed the venerable head from
the body threw it into a basket full of straw, upon
which an ear of straw leapt out into his hand, or
so close to it that he could remove it without
attracting any notice. This ear of straw he found
was stained with blood,[5] so that he kept it with
great reverence and joy; and he protested to me
that for some days he found himself more inclined
to spiritual things and to follow the counsels of
Christ than he had ever been before; so that. he
felt no peace till he gave up all he had, and made
arrangements for coming hither across the water,
to make his studies for the priesthood. He had
also a strong desire of entering the Society; and in
these pious sentiments he continued to his death,
which took place at St. Omer's, and in which he

---

[5] This was the celebrated " Garnet's Straw," splashed with the
martyr's blood, on one ear of which a spot of blood had dried in
such a way as to delineate a human face, said to resemble Father
Garnet. It was certainly a sacred relic, and was thought to be
miraculous.

gave such edification to all about him, that no one there remembers a holier death than his.

I will also add here a further testimony regarding an incident of Father Oldcorne's martyrdom. I mentioned in that other narrative of mine, that I had had information by letter from England, that this holy martyr's intestines, being thrown into the fire according to sentence, burned for sixteen days, exactly the number of years during which he had kindled in that country the fire of divine love and maintained it by his word and example. Now quite lately I had a conversation on this subject with a pious priest, who at present goes by the name of Father North at St. Omer's. He tells me that he was himself a prisoner at Worcester at the time, and that he heard then from many persons, not only that the fire lasted all that time notwithstanding a great deal of rain that fell, but that it broke out into high flames, and that multitudes went to see it, who on their return acknowledged the truth of the report; so that at last, on the sixteenth or seventeenth day they were obliged to extinguish the fire, or at least cover it up by heaping earth upon it. This same Father also declared that he subsequently saw in the courtyard of the house where these two Fathers were taken the form of a crown traced out by grass that had grown there. He said that this grass was different both in kind and colour from any other about; that it grew taller also, and traced clearly out the shape of an imperial crown. He added moreover that the beasts that got into the court-yard through the broken gates (for the house from the time of the capture had been neglected and abandoned), browsed there for many months, yet never during the whole time touched this crown or trod upon it. He looked on it as a symbol of the innocence of these Fathers and of their eternal reward.

CHAPTER XLI.

THE REST OF MY PERSONAL HISTORY.

I WILL now add a few words about myself before closing this narrative. I have stated in the other treatise, of which I spoke, that a proclamation was issued against three Jesuit Fathers, of whom I was one; and, though the most unworthy, I was named first in the proclamation, whereas I was the subject of one, and far inferior in all respects to the other. All this however I solemnly protest was utterly groundless; for I knew absolutely nothing of the Plot from any one whatsoever, not even under the seal of confession as the other two did; nor had I the slightest notion that any such scheme was entertained by any Catholic gentleman, until by public rumour news was brought us of its discovery, as it was to all others dwelling in that part of the country.

When I saw by that long search of nine days that I was sought after and aimed at in particular, I wrote a public letter, as if to some friend, in which by many arguments, and by protestations beyond all cavil, I maintained my entire innocence of the charges brought against me. Of this letter I caused many copies to be taken, and to be dropped about the London streets very early in the morning. These were found and read by many persons, and a copy was shown to the King by one of the Lords

of Council, who was no enemy either of mine or of
my cause. The King, as I heard, was personally
satisfied by this. Afterwards, however, when information was given them of Father Garnet's
hiding-place, and they conceived hopes of catching
him, and of turning the whole charge on the Society,
they thought it necessary to publish the names of
some of Ours as the principal contrivers of the
Plot. So they put my name down, as well as those
of the other two Fathers, of whom they had heard
from a certain servant of Master Catesby. This
man however before his death, repenting of this
injury he had done them, confessed that he had
been induced to say what he did of them against
his conscience, by the fear of death on the one hand,
and by the hope of pardon, and by the persuasions
and suggestions of Secretary Cecil on the other.
And it is possible that some persons at that time
had a real suspicion that I was privy to the thing,
because they knew that many of the gentlemen who
had been taken were friends of mine, and were in
the habit of visiting me at my London house. This
indeed was acknowledged by one of them in his
examination, though at the same time he affirmed
that I knew nothing of their scheme. Nor did they
ever get a single word against me from any of
their examinations. Sir Everard Digby indeed,
who was known to be most intimate with me, and
for that reason was most strictly examined about
me, publicly protested in open court that he never
dare mention a syllable of it to me, because I
should never have permitted him to go on with it.
When I had heard of all this, and besides had learnt
several particulars concerning Father Garnet, which
proved that any knowledge he had was under seal

of confession; and imparted to him by the only priest of the Society who knew it, and that also only in confession; it seemed to me that I was sufficiently cleared of the charge, and in order to bring this fact into notice, I prepared three letters to three Lords of the Council, a little before the death of the condemned conspirators, in which I showed more at full that I was completely ignorant of the whole matter, and pointed out how they might satisfy themselves of the same while those gentlemen were yet alive. Whether they did so or not, I do not know: but this much I know, that in the whole process of Father Garnet's trial, in which after the receipt of these letters they tried their utmost to defame the whole Society, and in particular to charge this Plot on the English mission, they never once mentioned me. They spoke indeed of three Fathers as guilty, but they named those two who had heard of it in confession, and Father Oldcorne, not as privy to the Plot beforehand, but as an accomplice *post factum*.

Nevertheless I took the greatest precaution to remain hidden; and I lay at a place in London known to no one. So by the protection of God I continued safe, and if it had seemed good, I could have remained so still longer. I did not therefore leave England to avoid being taken, but as in that great disturbance it was no time for labouring, but rather for keeping quiet, I took a favourable opportunity that presented itself of passing over into these parts,[1] and reposing a little, that after so long a period of distracting work in all kinds of company, I might renew my spirit, and recover strength for

---

[1] This was written in Belgium.

future labours. Why, even at that very time when I was keeping so close, and when nearly all my friends were either in prison, or so upset that they could scarcely help themselves, much less me, though I had lost the house I had in London, through the fault of one who disclosed it as I have said, and though strict watch was kept everywhere, and danger beset one on all sides ; yet, before I had settled to leave England, I managed to hire another house in London very fit for my purpose, perhaps more so than the former. I managed also to furnish it with everything necessary, and made some good hiding-places in it ; and there I remained in safety the whole of Lent before my departure. Besides this house I also hired another, finer and larger than this, which I intended should be in common between Father Antony Hoskins and me. This house after my departure was used by the Superior of the mission for a considerable time.

The first of these last-mentioned houses I brought into some little danger, about the end of Lent, in order to rescue one of our Fathers from imminent danger. The thing happened in this wise. The good Father, by name Thomas Everett, had gone to a gentleman's house in London, where there were some false brethren, or else some talkative ones ; for the fact reached the ears of the Council. And as he is something of my height, and has black hair, Cecil thought it was I of whom notice was given him, and said to a private friend of his, " Now we shall have him," meaning me. However, he had neither the one nor the other. For I, learning that the Father had gone to this place, where he could not possibly remain hidden, asked my friend, in whose house I had myself been con-

cealed before I had procured and furnished my new
abode, to fetch him and keep him close in his house
for a time, which he did. Here he remained while
the house he had just left was undergoing a strict
search. Now it so happened that, after a few days,
a search was also made in the very place to which
he had been brought, on account of some books of
Father Garnet's which had been seen, and which
this gentleman used to keep for him. After rifling
the place well and finding no one, for Father
Everett had betaken himself to a hiding-place, they
carried off the Master and mistress of the house,
and threw them into prison. Now when I heard
this, and knew there was no Catholic left in the
house, fearing lest the Father should either perish
with hunger, or come forth and be taken, I sent
persons from my own house, to whom I described
the position of his hiding-place. They went thither,
and called to him, and knocked at the place, for
him to open it : he however would neither open nor
answer, though they said that I had sent them for
him. For, as he did not know their voices, he was
afraid that this was a trick of the searchers, who
sometimes pretend to depart, and then after a time
return, and assuming a friendly tone go about the
rooms, asking any who are hidden to come out, for
that the searchers are all gone. The good Father
suspected that this was the case now, and therefore
made no answer. My messengers remained a long
time trying to reassure him, and at last were obliged
to return, but so late that they fell into the hands
of the watch. They were detained in custody that
night, and got off with some difficulty the next day.
One of them however was recognized as having
formerly lived with a Catholic, and was therefore

believed to be a Catholic himself, and as it was now known where he lived (viz., in the house I had hired), this brought that house into suspicion, though it had been ostensibly hired by a schismatic, who was under no suspicion at all. The consequence was that some four days later the chief magistrate of London, who is called the Mayor, came with a *posse* of constables to search the house.

In the mean time hearing that Father Thomas would not answer, and knowing well that he was there, to prevent his perishing from starvation, I sent another party with the man who had made the hiding-place and knew how to open it. The place was thus opened and the good Father rescued from his perilous position. They brought him to my house, and there he remained. I myself however, before he arrived, had gone to a friend's house, a very secure place, with the purpose of staying there a little, as I had some fears that the apprehension of my servants a day or two back might bring the searchers to my house. My fears were well founded: for on Holy Thursday while Father Everett was saying Mass, and had just finished the Oblation, there was a great tumult and noise at the garden-gate; and the Mayor used such violence, and made such quick work of it, as to have entered the garden and the house, and to be now actually mounting the stairs, just as the Father, all vested as he was and with all the altar-furniture bundled up had entered his hiding-place. So near a matter was it, that the Mayor and his company smelt the smoke of the extinguished candles, so that they made sure a priest had been there, and were the more eager in their search. But of the three hiding-places in the house they did not find one. So they departed, taking with them those men whom they found in the house, and who acknowledged them-selves to be Catholics, and the schismatic also who passed for the householder. After this, having again released Father Everett from his hiding-hole and advised him to leave London, I determined not to use that house again for some time. And seeing that the times were such as called us rather to remain quiet, than to gird ourselves for work, I took the first opportunity of crossing the sea and coming into these parts.

I recommended my friends to different Fathers, asking them to have special care of them during my absence. As for my hostess [Lady Vaux], she was brought to London after that long search for me, and strictly examined about me by the Lords of the Council; but she answered to everything so discreetly as to escape all blame. At last they produced a letter of hers to a certain relative, asking for the release of Father Strange and another, of whom I spoke before. This relative of hers was the chief man in the county, in which they had been taken, and she thought she could by her intercession with him prevail for their release. But the treacherous man, who had often enough, as far as words went, offered to serve her in any way, proved the truth of our Lord's prophecy, " A man's enemies shall be those of his own household;" for he immediately sent up her letter to the Council. They showed her therefore her own letter, and said to her,

" You see now that you are entirely at the King's mercy for life or death; so if you consent to tell us where Father Gerard is, you shall have your life."

"I do not know where he is," she answered, "and if I did know, I would not tell you."

Then rose one of the Lords, who had been a former friend of hers, to accompany her to the door, out of courtesy, and on the way said to her persuasively,

"Have pity on yourself and on your children, and say what is required of you :—for otherwise you must certainly die."

To which she answered with a loud voice, "Then, my Lord, I will die."

This was said when the door had been opened, so that her servants who were waititg for her heard what she said, and all burst into weeping. But the Council only said this to terrify her, for they did not commit her to prison, but sent her to the house of a certain gentleman in the city, and after being held here in custody for a time she was released, but on condition of remaining in London. And one of the principal Lords of the Council acknowledged to a friend that he had nothing against her, except that she was a stout Papist, going ahead of others and as it were a leader in evil.

Immediately she was released from custody, knowing that I was then in London, quite forgetful of herself, she set about taking care of me, and provided all the furniture and other things necessary for my new house. Moreover she sent me letters daily, recounting everything that occurred ; and when she knew that I wished to cross the sea for a time, she bid me not spare expense, so that I secured a safe passage, for that she would pay everything, though it should cost five thousand florins : and in fact she sent me at once a thousand florins for my journey. I left her in the care of Father Percy, who had already as my companion lived a long time at her house. There he still remains, and does much good. I went straight to Rome, and being sent back thence to these parts, was fixed at Louvain. What happened to me there may be read, together with the labours of others, in the Annual Letters.

I have received two signal benefits on the 3rd of May, through the intercession, as I think, of Father Garnet, who went to Heaven on that day. The first was as follows :—When I had come to the port where according to agreement I was to embark with certain high personages in order to pass unchallenged out of England, they, out of fear, excused themselves from performing their promise. And in this mind they continued till within an hour of the time for embarking. Now just at that time Father Garnet's martyrdom was consummated at London, and he being received into Heaven remembered me upon earth ; for the minds of those Lords were so changed, that the ambassador himself came to fetch me, and with his own hands helped to dress me in his livery, so that I might be taken for one of his attendants, and so pass free. All went well, and I do not doubt that I owed it to Father Garnet's prayers.

The other and greater benefit is that three years later, on the same 3rd of May, I was admitted into the body of the Society by the four vows, though most unworthy. This I look upon as the greatest and most signal favour I have ever received, and it seems to me that God wished to show me that I owed this also to the prayers of Father Garnet, from an exact similarity in the circumstance of time

between my profession and his martyrdom. For
the day originally fixed for both had been the first
day of May, the feast of the Holy Apostles SS.
Philip and James, and in both cases unforeseen
delays postponed the event till the 3rd of May.

God grant that I may truly love and worthily
carry the Cross of Christ, so that I may walk
worthy of the vocation whereto I am called. This
one thing I have asked of our Lord, and this will
I continue to ask, that I may dwell in the house
of God all my days, until I prove myself grateful
for so great a favour, and though hitherto unfruitful,
yet by the fertility of the olive tree in which I have
been grafted, I may at length begin to bear some
fruit !

PRAISE BE TO GOD, TO THE MOST BLESSED
VIRGIN, TO BLESSED FATHER IGNATIUS, AND TO
MY ANGEL GUARDIAN. AMEN.

DEATH OF BROTHER NICHOLAS OWEN,
OR LITTLE JOHN (*p.* 257).

FATHER MORE[1] has a few words on the death of
Brother Nicholas Owen, *alias* Little John, which
throw a little more light on the subject than we
were able to in the course of Father Gerard's
narrative. It will be remarked that he calls him
John Owen, a name in itself more likely to be
correct than Nicholas, as it would sufficiently account for the affectionate sobriquet by which he
seems to have been known. We have hitherto
called him *Nicholas,* because we find the name so
given by Dr. Oliver in his *Collectanea.* Father More
says,

" John Owen (called Little John from his diminu-
tive stature), was taken with Father Garnet, and
racked in the Tower. He had long suffered from
rupture, and the second racking was too much for
the invalid : it caused a new and aggravated rupture,
and he died shortly after being carried from the
rack to his bed. The report was industriously
spread that he had committed suicide : this however was subsequently denied by the executioner,
who moreover asserted that he had scarcely ever
witnessed greater firmness under torture. In con-
firmation of his testimony comes the fact that he
was buried in the Tower, not like a suicide in the
open country, or in the King's highway, with a
stake through his body."

[1] *Hist. Prov. Angl. Lib. VII. c.* 27.